THE ETERNAL GENE

AND OTHER TALES OF MALAISE

THE ETERNAL GENE

AND OTHER TALES OF MALAISE

ANKUSH SAM THORPE

BluPrint | An Imprint of BluOne Ink

Title: The Eternal Gene and Other Tales of Malaise
Author: Ankush Sam Thorpe

ISBN: 978-93-92209-14-7
Edition: 1

Published by:
BluOne Ink LLP

Publisher's Address:
306, Tower-I, Assotech Business Cresterra,
Plot No. 22, Sector 135, Noida.

Website: www.bluone.ink
Email: publisher@bluone.ink

Cover design by Geetanjali

Printed in India at Thomson Press (India) Ltd.

BluPrint | An Imprint of BluOne Ink

To my parents,
Sunil & Sunita,
who made it all happen

Preface

People around me have usually asked me 'Why science-fiction?', and I have a staple reply to this intriguing query in the form of, 'Why Not?'

What's harder for people to grasp is that science-fiction, knowingly or unknowingly, has become an indispensable part of the kids who grew up in the nineties. The flooding of content, be it in print or cinemas, with stories woven around advanced technologies and dystopian futures, has overwhelmed millennials like me to the core. *The Eternal Gene and Other Tales of Malaise* is the result of my exposure to such influences during my formative years.

Steven Speilberg's *Jurassic Park* and Roland Emmerich's *Independence Day* are some of the classic sci-fi feature films that sowed the seed of my enthusiasm for science. The short story *A Stitch in Time* has some elements of these sci-fi action thriller films.

Along with films, science fiction books have a special place in my heart. During my high school days, I discovered and got addicted to sci-fi literature, be it Issac Asimov's *Foundation Series* or Ray Bradbury's *Fahrenheit 451*. My all-time favourite J.K. Rowling's *Harry Potter series,* even though it falls into the fantasy genre, has some science fiction concepts, like invisibility cloak and teleportation. *The Representative in this collection* takes inspiration from exceptional pieces of literature like these.

My fascination with science fiction reached its zenith in April 2011, when I went for a field trip to Siwalik Hills during my second semester. It was part of my three-year Anthropology degree course at Punjab University, Chandigarh. The memory of a whole batch of teenagers excavating the soil, wearing cotton gloves, holding calipers and trowels in their hands, is still etched in my mind. We had scraped through the area, under the leadership of our professors, to find fossil remains that were embedded in rocks since the Miocene epoch. The short story *Hera* in this book includes many genetic and anthropological concepts that I studied as an undergraduate.

Of course, modern fiction writing lacks perspective and outlook without the knowledge and admiration for the subject of history. A skilled writer always endeavours to construct a story that weaves in significant historical events in the plot. For example, Markus Zusak's *The Book Thief* and Salman Rushdie's *Midnight Children*, extensively use historical events to induce suspense and drama in their stories. These stories move away from traditional realism and focus more on subjective and psychological aspects of modern storytelling. In this book, one of the short stories—*The Eternal Gene*—uses history as a backdrop, along with science, to produce a thrilling effect.

Lastly, the inspiration to write this book came from my obsession with the theme of dystopia. Throughout my twenties dystopian literature like George Orwell's *1984* and John Brunner's *The Sheep Look Up* captured my imagination. Along with these, dystopian films like Christopher Nolan's *Interstellar* and Steven Spielberg's *Minority Report* injected a fixation in me towards this genre. The two short stories—*Down Memory Lane* and *Cryosleep*—are the results of my infatuation with dystopian futures.

I hope to introduce science fiction to more and more readers, especially among Indian audiences, who happen to incline more towards other genres. I would love to initiate new debates and prompt questions around the future of science, humans, artificial intelligence, and how their interplay can transform human experiences. I aim to induct and popularize exciting characters in the form of extraterrestrials, cyborgs and superhumans in modern literature.

Above all, I hope to inspire those who read this book to look at science differently.

Acknowledgement

This book would surely have been quite different or, worse, non-existent without the invaluable assistance of people around me.

Firstly, I thank my parents for encouraging me to indulge in those medieval fantasies as a child, when I came across those epic tales of ordinary men making extraordinary decisions for the first time. I thank my sibling, Sahil, who acted as a constant companion for those action-packed science fiction films that captured my imagination as a teenager. My sister-in-law, Rebecca, must also be mentioned for her constant guidance and support.

I must thank my fiancée, Mahima, for patiently listening to those crazy ideas that popped up into my mind while we were dating. Being the first reader of my work, she motivated me to improve and gave constructive suggestions that broadened my vision.

A special mention of one of my closest friends, Swati Chawla, who acted as a sounding board of ideas in shaping the narrative and characters in my stories is also essential.

However, the immeasurable contribution of Partho turned the far too redundant draft into a tight manuscript. He helped me break the mighty barrier between early scribblings and something that looked like a book. I owe special gratitude to the BluOne Ink team, especially Geetanjali Ahooja, who adopted the book as her own and ensured the remarkable care during the development phase.

I am also indebted to my editor, Shalini Agarwal, who not only made the storyline crisper, but also called my attention to structural problems and redundancies in my work. Here, I must also mention editorial consultant Mini Narayanan, who guided me during the editorial phase through constant communication.

Finally, I thank Dan Brown, Stephan King, Sidney Sheldon, and John le Carre for heavily influencing a teenager through their exceptional works of literature.

Contents

Hera

...•●•...

Prelude

The Collector ran desperately, despite his broken ribs, to reach the place where he'd docked his ship, the *Provecta-Navis IV*. He couldn't afford to waste a single second to stop and catch his breath. *Everything had gone out of control for him.*

The slippery ice had made it difficult for him to run. Adronian feet were not made for running, it was an evolutionary trait that Adronians left behind eons ago. But he couldn't lose because of natural selection today. *The clock was ticking for him.*

He reached the rear gates of the ship, which was docked just above the conglomerate rock, hovering a few feet above the ground. The entry into the spaceship, which he had done thousands of times before, felt different today. The facial recognition scan by the ship's system confirmed him as the *Provecta-Navis IV's* captain. The pressurized doors slid open. He didn't look like what he used to back when he used to fly the ship. His hair had grown long enough to touch his shoulders and he had a beard now ... a long beard, that made him look more native and less Adronian ... more savage and less refined.

The doors of the omphalos section hissed open, on the command of the Collector. As soon as he entered, the ship came to life. The stand-by mode changed to active mode.

He ran to the omphalos operating system and started poking at control panel. He was going to give a command that could only be given manually – the command to self-destruct.

He rotated a dial on the panel, and some options appeared on the giant screen in front of him.

```
< Operational Emergencies

   < Invasion On Ship

      < Dismantle Options

         < Self-Destruct Ship
```

He clicked on the last option.

The screen flashed. 'Are you sure?'

The Collector selected the key that said 'YES'. He didn't even need a moment to introspect. He was sure that it had to be done.

The face scan was initiated by the system again. After a few moments, it confirmed that the command indeed came from the ship's captain.

Self-destruct in twenty seconds. The screen flashed.

The Beginning

It was all so still. So quiet. The ocean of swirling stars, asteroids, nebular clouds and black holes … *so deadly yet so beautiful.* The high-intensity stellar activity produced a spectacular array of colours, resulting in an excellent panoramic view. Inside the nebula womb, a star nursery was visible. It produced a radiance, against which was silhouetted backlit clouds of dust. Sometimes it was hard to differentiate whether it was reality or a dream.

The tranquility of the space was pierced by a spacecraft that began its journey from the planet of Adronia. *It was wading through the endless space on its own, slowly but surely.* Flown by an Adronian government official called Collector (Badge Number Z289), the spacecraft was built to withstand long expeditions in far-flung corners of the universe, amidst numerous ranges of temperature, pressure and gravity.

The Collectors were a group of exploratory scientists that aimed to expand the planet's knowledge on civilizations that existed across the cosmos. They were required to embark on journeys by their government's official decree, on *Provecta-Navis IV* spacecraft, the state-of-the-art Adronian fleet.

Collector Z289, in his *Provecta-Navis IV,* had crossed many realms and passed through many stars. Some were collapsing, while some were taking birth. He had seen asteroids clashing, black holes colliding and supernovas wiping out entire solar systems. But it was not these galactic bodies that the Collector was interested in. As the name indicated, the Collector's primary job was collection. *But collection of what exactly?*

The complex life forms were evolutionary aberrations in the universe. They erupt by chance ... truly with the odds of one in a million. They required a specific set of coincidences. A barren planet could be bombarded with an asteroid that held traces of a primitive life form on its surface. But without the right atmospheric conditions, nothing would sprout on the planet.

Millions of planets across galaxies have thriving extraterrestrials. But they were simple life forms, microorganisms found in wedges of rocks and shifting dunes. For the Collector, these were a waste of time.

So what was worth his time? Collector Z289 ravaged through alien planets, lands, deserts, seas ... looking for highly complex organisms from their environment. He captured the extraterrestrial species from varied ecosystems in cryogenic bubbles or froze them at ultra-low temperatures with the intention of future revival. Like many others back on the planet of Adronia, he was trained to do exactly that. It was his job.

The exploration had been a well-funded programme of the Adronian government, aimed at enhancing academic capabilities of the Adronian species. But for the Collector, it was not easy to go around rummaging through the vast universe, spending a lifetime in loneliness and isolation.

As far as he remembered, the Collector had always been travelling, in his spaceship, finding new worlds and capturing unique species that could make his collection, one of a kind, across the cosmos. He had forgotten what it meant to have a family or emotional connections. In fact, he had not struck conversation with another being for almost an eternity. It was a cost that had to be paid to fulfil his exploratory instincts. But now, his priorities had changed ... he wanted to *settle* amongst his own. He was ageing. The adventurous spirit in him was slowly fading.

After all those years of wandering in the wilderness and among the savage, with a collection of almost 368 species across different galaxies, the Collector was finally returning home. He was relieved to find that the end of his voyage was near. He would soon be entering Adronian air space.

The spacecraft, *Provecta-Navis IV,* that accompanied the Collector on his incredible voyages, had a twin-engine, time-lapse capable, and was a colossal horizontal slab of metal, zipping through the dark and deserted void of space.

The omphalos section was the control centre of the ship, the Provecta Command Centre, designed to serve the strenuous demands of long voyages like these. It had a large screen display that not only helped in cartographic analysis, but also constantly made the Collector aware of the ship's status and sensory data. The official database of Adronia was also accessible from omphalos, which constantly uploaded and synced data in its hard disk, throughout the voyage.

Sitting in the omphalos with his feet up the control panels, the Collector looked through the 180-degree glass view in front. The calm, pristine and virgin space, with numerous glistening stars, looked back at him.

As the ship charted its course in auto-pilot mode, it became quieter each passing minute. The silence all around was so satisfying to the Collector that he started drifting slowly and steadily into sleep. The lights automatically decreased in intensity, and systems went to stand-by as the Collector went into deep slumber.

The radar beeped suddenly, making the omphalos come alive.

The Collector snapped out of his sleep as the display screen brought a notification. All the sensors pointed towards the arrival of new data, received from one of the Murakabas. The Murakabas were Adronian drones, flying across different galaxies and reporting data about the likeliness of extraterrestrial life.

The unexpected arrival of data in this barren part of space startled the Collector.

'Hera?' The Collector asked, startled. His vision was still blurry with sleep. He was not expecting any new data at this moment, at least not during the final leg of the mission. 'Have we entered the Drezoid orbit?'

'We won't reach Drezoid for another twenty days.' I am fetching bits from the data centre. Give me a moment,' Hera said in her usual monotone voice, typical of artificial intelligence.

Hera was a virtual assistant, embedded in the voice command centre in all machines of the *Provecta-Navis* fleet. A highly intelligent, self-learning virtual creature, Hera had been a constant companion of the Collector since the beginning of his voyage. She was a guide as well as a co-pilot. She could do faster calculations of escape velocities and parametric equations to determine the path of the ship. She was extremely handy in providing biological and topographic analysis on alien planets, tremendously increasing the Collector's chances of survival in hostile exotic environments.

'Luminosity Analysis complete,' the speakers blared again. 'A *blue* planet with a complex life form has been found two million light years away.'

'Here? Amidst this galactic desert?' the Collector asked, fascinated by the knowledge of a lone planet somehow harbouring life in a ruinous part of the universe. He zoomed into a map of the cosmos to look for the highlighted planet. 'Where is this?'

'This is in sector 4C208. A planet with liquid water, and mobile and immobile species. It has a surprisingly stable climate. It gets its heat from a young star, and is at the appropriate distance from it. Third planet from the star, out of eight, much like Adronia,' Hera explained as her sensors received data in algorithms and complex equations, she decoded it in a form that was palatable for her master.

There was silence from the Collector. *How can it be? How had he missed this planet?* The Collector always thought himself to be the best at what he did. At this moment, his intellectual vanity had taken a hit.

'Master?' Hera asked, snapping her masters out of his thoughts. 'Your orders?'

The Collector was doing a good deal of thinking before giving any command. The spacecraft had passed through Heracle, one of the last of dwarf planets just before the outskirts of the planet of Adronia. If he had to make any decision, this was the time.

'Shall I turn on the Time Lapse towards this blue planet?' Hera asked.

'Calculate chronic dilation!' the Collector commanded.

Now, chronic dilation was the amount of time that would pass in Adronia if he took a detour towards this blue planet. The unique ability of time to pass faster the further away the Collector was from Adronia had to be kept in mind before taking any decision. Being the captain of the ship, the Collector must keep the mission his top priority. If only he could explore one more planet, without wasting too much time ... then it would be worth it – or at least that's what clause 11.7 of *The Collector's Regulation* commanded.

The Collector had already spent more time amongst the cosmos than any other Adronian. He had followed the code and explored planets keeping in mind the regulations. He'd had enough. Going off course for too long would only delay his arrival to Adronia and the Collector wasn't getting any younger. The clock was ticking, and the unending voyage was slowly turning nightmarish.

'A week on this planet is equal to seven Adronian months,' *Hera* responded instantly. Her calculation on point, as always.

It's not that bad, thought the Collector. It had already been two decades since he had been on the trip, lonely, desolate and exhausted. What harm could seven more months do? He looked intently at the tablet in his hands, which showed the blue planet slowly rotating across its star. It was time to take the decision, no more dilly dallying. He spent some moments deliberating his options.

'Initiate change in course towards 4C208,' the Collector instructed as he pushed buttons on the control panel, kickstarting the energy thrust from powerful *Nord Cells.* 'Let's see what this blue planet is all about.' Hera detected a sternness in her master's voice as she started initiating the systems necessary to make a space jump.

'Launching Time Lapse in 30 seconds,' Hera informed her master. 'Only critical systems are functioning now.' She halted all background calculations and processes going on in the omphalos system. Hera could control almost every function of the ship by herself, barring a few controls that required the Collector's manual confirmation before being carried out.

On his tablet, the Collector saw all non-essential systems of the spacecraft slowly shutting down – a standard procedure before taking a Time Lapse – to ensure optimum energy conservation. The Collector adjusted himself on the main seat, as seat belts wrapped automatically across his chest and stomach. The Collector rested his head on the headrest of the seat and closed his eyes. He always hated this part, as the jump would often make him nauseous.

'Five, four, three, two,' Hera initiated the countdown, 'one … Time Lapse engaged.' A beam from the spacecraft modified the space around the ship.

The warp drives, powered by nord cells, began curving the fabric of space around the ship, slowly at first and accelerating with each passing second. A subspace bubble of negative energy eclipsed the spacecraft inside it. The space was bent enough to create a narrow bridge to cross the diameter of the galaxies at hyper-speed. The ship gained exponential speed in a matter of seconds.

To an idle observer, the ship had suddenly disappeared from its place. But in scientific terms, the *Provecta-Navis IV* spaceship was compressing the space-time in front of it, while expanding it from behind. This energy-sapping exercise required a huge negative mass, and to achieve that, the system created an imbalance between matter and antimatter to generate the negative energy bubble.

Furthermore, to conserve the ship's energy, Hera was expanding the volume inside the bubble, and was keeping the surface area constant. This reduced the requirement of energy to some extent, but excessive use of warp drives could create an energy deficit in the ship's system.

With the gain of speed in such a short time, the Collector was thrusted into his chair with great force. The stars, meteors, barren planets, asteroids were all zipping past the spacecraft as if they were raining from above. In a matter of seconds, the spacecraft gained acceleration that was thousand times the speed of light.

It zipped past the Andromeda Nebular interstellar dust, binary star Drogos and globular clusters of ancient pulsars to finally enter the torus-shaped Kuiper Belt at the edge of the solar system. In the next few moments, the blue planet was visible through omphalos' 180-degrees viewing glass, and that's when the ship began to slow down. Hera informed her master that never before had an Adronian ship ventured into this part of the universe.

The *Provecta-Navis IV* had travelled nearly 2.5 million light years to reach here.

Earth

2,00,000 BC

The entry into the blue planet's atmosphere was smooth, considering it had a thick atmosphere. The preliminary scan pointed towards an oxygen dominant planet, with traces of Argon and Xenon gases as well. The topography of the planet was crude, as its entire surface had no artificial construction. 'It's possible there is no civilization here, Master. Certainly not an advanced one,' Hera informed the Collector as the ship crossed the planet's mesosphere, descending at a steady speed.

The photogrammatory analysis pointed to a particular geographical location for the automated landing of the *Provecta-Navis IV.* The spacecraft slowly approached the rocky landing surface. As it came closer to the lithosphere, the pressure of the air vents of the spacecraft pushed away rocks and boulders with a huge force. As the Collector looked at the large display, it showed that all systems of the spacecraft seemed stable.

Hera was engaged in chromatographic analysis of the planet. All the data that she was collecting was being uploaded to the Adronian database. The records in the database were carefully kept, adding to the knowledge of scientifically advanced Adronian minds.

'Master, the landing was successful,' Hera informed the Collector as the seat belts automatically unbuckled themselves. The dimmed lights were now brightened, and all the halted background calculations resumed. The Collector took his first glimpse the planet through the giant glass window of the spaceship.

The *Provecta-Navis* models did not land but actually hovered just a few feet above the ground. *The gravity levels are similar to Adronia,* thought the Collector as he went through the readings of nord sensors. The engines turned themselves off automatically. *Birds flew off the naked branches of trees where they had been resting as the spacecraft parked itself among a cluster of birch and willow trees.*

It was the first ever piece of technology that had set foot on this primitive planet. Never, for the next thousands of millennia, would such an advanced technology enter its atmosphere.

'Talk to me, Hera,' the Collector commanded. He wanted to get more data on hand before stepping on the planet's surface.

'The planet has been going through climate change over the past 200 solar years. The ice has taken over the planet. The liquid water has frozen at a fast rate almost everywhere on the planet, except near the equator,' Hera spoke. 'I've mapped the topography of the area and it seems like the ice is not receding anytime soon,' Hera said in her typical monotone voice.

'Any good news?' asked the Collector hopefully. He didn't want to hear that he wasted his precious time for nothing.

'The good news is that the life forms here have been quite resilient. The Photogrammetry Survey data has pointed out that diverse beings are roaming around the vicinity.' It was music to the Collector's ears. Life had finally been confirmed on this planet.

'That is indeed good news. If we can capture one beast and exit in a matter of hours, the *chronic dilation* would be minimal. Perhaps only a month will go to waste,' he told Hera as he got up from his chair and entered an elevator. As soon as he stepped inside, the elevator started to go up.

'Let's get ready for assessment, fast,' he commanded on a mic within the elevator.

The elevator door opened and the Collector entered the logistic center of the *Provecta-Navis IV*. He walked across the room and stood on a mark, which had the shape of his footprints engraved on the floor.

'Instal Xandro Mark II,' he said as he stood straight with both his arms perpendicular to his body.

'Right away, Master,' Hera replied as she commanded the omphalos system.

The floor tiles subsided and machines with drillers surfaced from underneath the floor. From above, a similar mechanic arm descended, placing the uniform on the Collector's torso. His back was also covered with another part of duranium by a mechanical arm. Similar pieces of duranium covered his arms, hands, legs and heels, by machines. The drillers drilled the nuts and bolts as the Collector finished wearing his customized duranium survey uniform called Xandro Mark II.

Duranium was the strongest metal found not only in Adronia, but in the whole Cordovian universe. This metal could withstand pressure a thousand times more than Iron. It was a rare entity in Adronia, and only the government could afford to get their hands on expensive Duranium imports.

And then, the headgear attached itself with the uniform and the Collector saw a screen within the headgear come to life in front of his eyes. He was now in a fully enclosed metallic uniform connected virtually to the omphalos.

He had worn the same suit every time he prepared himself for exploration on an alien planet. The explorer in him would come alive whenever he wore this suit.

'Security Patch Update 7498E is required for the suit, Master,' Hera intoned. The Collector had been avoiding the update due to his laziness. It could remove glitches in the suit's software, but would hang the whole system until it downloaded and installed upgrades in the suit. He couldn't afford any delay now.

'Ignore for now,' he commanded. 'Remind me about the update patch next time, Hera.' The procrastination had been growing on the Collector for the past few years. *A sure sign of ageing,* he thought.

***

As the Collector pushed the red button, the room depressurized. A siren blared for some time as the door at the back of the *Provecta-Navis* hissed open. The gates slid away slowly, providing the first glimpse of the land and the surroundings. It was extremely white and barren everywhere. *It is an ice desert,* thought the Collector as the hope of finding anything here plummeted every second.

The headgear's screen was used by Hera to communicate with her master. All the information that Hera wanted her master to see, it flashed on the headgear's screen. The meteorological statistics, thermal scanning and even terrain modelling – everything appeared on the screen for the Collector to appropriately respond to any crisis that arose.

The Collector set foot on a large conglomerate rock to see the surroundings. Behind him, the *Provecta-Navis* hovered and stayed still, just above ground. The Xander Mark II had an internal homeostasis, and thus, the freezing conditions outside were not affecting the Collector one bit.

'The air composition is very similar to Adronia's. No toxins in the air that can corrupt your nervous system are found,' Hera's voice came through. 'However, I don't advise removing your headgear, you never know what can attack you.' She was on high alert for anything suspicious on this alien planet, and so was keeping an eye on her master's vitals and thermal scans she had been doing for this region. Hera could do an advanced mapping of the area because of two spherical duranium drones that rotated in two diagonal orbits around the suit. The Xandro Mark II controlled these two duaranium drones, no bigger than the Collector's fist. The balls, called ovoids, could fly ahead and map the vicinity for surveillance. The ovoids could change the shape at will, too.

'Noted,' the Collector responded to Hera through the embedded microphone.

He jumped from the conglomerate rock and landed on the ground. An echo followed. For him, it was indeed a unique planet. He could see huge glacial mountains around both sides of the valley. The water that must have once flowed here had been frozen. The Collector wondered if any life form could survive here, as he bent down to feel the frozen lake through his gloves.

As he strolled around, the two ovoids encircled him, constantly feeding data to Hera.

'I am detecting another heat signal in the vicinity,' Hera said as the Collector went further away from the ship.

Before the Collector could reply, he saw a white creature walking slowly towards him. The X-Ray analysis relayed by Hera on to the headgear's screen showed a predator, with 65% muscular composition and high-density skeletal system. The retractable claws and eyes provided a wide-angle vision to this creature – a feature that was indispensable in surviving through this hostile environment. Its walk looked majestic, as it moved with slight jerks on his four paws. The dental analysis showed its adaptation to instantly attack its prey through his well-developed canines that protruded from behind its mandible.

'Careful, he's carnivorous,' Hera warned. In all these years, Hera developed a habit of worrying constantly for her master when he faced off with a new species. She didn't trust these savages to show civility to her master. As an AI, she was encoded since her birth with xenophobia, a trait necessary for threat perception. Any kind of rendezvous with a creature, foreign or alien, was to be perceived as a highly alarming situation by Hera. Her algorithms would constantly work to predict the next moves of these creatures, so that her Adronian master could take timely decisions before an emergency arose.

'Relax,' the Collector said as he slowly started walking backwards. 'I want it alive. We are capturing him and getting out of here. I am not wasting any more time surveying this godforsaken desert.' The large animal was circling him slowly but surely.

In the next instant, the animal leapt at its prey. The gluteus maximus muscle, evolved over millions of years of survival in frigid conditions, gave enough thrust to the creature to have height advantage at par with its enemy. For the Collector, this was incredible. He had captured goliath Kasnians, the giant two-headed creatures of planet Kasnia, with granite skins. He remembered trapping the incredible shape-changing Dractus, *a lavender two-legged creature, that could read your memories and transform itself into your loved ones to distract you from hunting it.* And then there were the hypnotizing Florians, *which could put you under an illusion, and you couldn't guess for a lifetime whether you were experiencing reality or a dream.* However, this creature on this blue planet was somehow more breathtaking to look at than the Collector's previous traps.

The predator leapt at its prey through the air, but never landed on it. Instead, it remained suspended in the air. The Collector, with the help of nord energy, constructed a force field around the creature. It was now enclosed in some kind of invisible bubble, struggling to free itself. It was captured.

The Collector could create this force field to capture anything through his Xander Mark II suit. The powerful nord cells helped him influence the matter without any physical interaction. However, the force field was a vacuum, and thus, no life form could survive inside it for more than a few seconds.

'Prepare for its cryogenic sleep,' the Collector told Hera, who took control of the force field as the bubble moved in the direction of the spacecraft. It will eventually be placed in the cryogenic section, where the creature would go into hyper-sleep until revived in the future.

***

Feeling triumphant about his latest catch in less than an hour of landing, the Collector now turned back towards his ship. Barely a week would pass in Adronia by the time he left this planet's atmosphere. He gave one last look at the snow desert that stared back at him, which felt calm and still like the space above. Hera informed him that there were no other heat signals in the vicinity, except some faint aberrations.

The ovoids changed their shape into two discs and arranged themselves in the form of a staircase for the Collector to reach the level of a spacecraft that had been hovering ten feet above the surface. He stepped inside the *Provecta-Navis IV* and the whole ship came back to life. The doors hissed closed behind the Collector.

'Hera, prepare for the flight.' There was an urgency in the Collector's tone. The little detour towards this planet had proven fruitful, but a single minute more on this planet was a waste of time for him.

'We have a slight problem,' Hera suddenly spoke.

'What? Coolant leaks?'

'No. The nord cells are unable to use backup charge,' Hera explained. It meant that Time Lapse could not be used until the nord cells charged themselves.

There was silence from the Collector. 'How much time?' he asked.

'Four solar days if we keep the spacecraft here. Their star radiates strong energy, accelerating rapid charging of nord cells.'

'Four days!' The Collector stomped his foot on the floor. 'Do you know how much time we are wasting?' His hope of reaching home early was fading. He was tired of carrying out Adronian missions and wasting away his life across the cosmos. He wanted to settle now ... to abandon this nomadic way of living and have a stable life ... have a *family*. The dream looked far away at the moment.

In his frustration, the Collector stormed off the omphalos section and towards the rear end of the spaceship. He then thumped the red button with his closed fist, the depressurizing was initiated and the doors hissed open after ten seconds. The two ovoids hovering in the air followed, one slid under the Collector's right foot and the other under his left as he landed on the ground. *Perhaps a stroll down the ice desert might help in keeping calm,* he thought as his annoyance was spiralling out of control.

The echo of his footsteps showed how pristine and isolated the planet was. He decided to take the eastern direction now as the thermal analysis showed faint aberrations. He started analysing maps through his headgear, wandering through the valley. *Perhaps there is nothing more here besides some beasts ... nothing intelligent,* he thought as he surveyed the area.

Huge thick sheets of ice were jutting out from the ground. They reached far beyond his range of vision. The clouds and glaciers were becoming indistinguishable to the eyes. Short bursts of freezing winds had not been letting the ice melt, for God knows how many thousand of years.

'Mild heat signals received,' Hera said as the Collector continued in eastern direction.

But the Collector was silent as he was miffed with Hera because of the delay. However, the technical problem in the spaceship was his fault. The back-up charge problem had been surfacing inconsistently since the last time he'd made a landing, and the Collector failed to pay heed to Hera's warnings. And now, the procrastination ultimately cost him four solar days. He vowed that the next time the security update patch popped up, he would drop everything else and do that instead.

Hera flashed the map of the area to the Collector's headgear, to pinpoint the location from where the heat signals were generated. They were coming from somewhere within these giant sheets of ice that were almost 400 feet in height. The Collector walked towards them and touched these ice sheets. *No heat source can survive behind these walls,* he thought. But the sensors were showing mild graphs.

'X-Rays!' he ordered.

One of the ovoids flying around him radiated a stream of faint light. The analysis flashed within the headgear and showed what lay behind these towering walls. The Collector could clearly see faint movement on the other side. He had seen the hollow portions in these walls, behind which hid a cave like structure. He could make out the icy stalactite and stalagmites, behind the thick ice curtain. Now he was curious as to what lay behind them.

The Collector looked at the ovoids and pointed towards the hollow area of the wall. With full force, the two balls, one by one, started crashing in the ice sheets back-and-forth. The cracking sound filled the entire terrain, echoing in all directions. This kept happening as the thin ice sheet developed fissures and fractures. The tiny craters, from constant ramming, turned into holes, which transformed into cracks and the thin ice structure eventually came crashing down, exposing a cave like structure behind it.

From within his headgear, the Collector saw a tribe huddled together inside the cave, trying to survive the ensuing storm that had been going on for months. All were lying adjacent to each other, trying to limit the heat loss. It was a spectacular find by the Collector, an almost-intelligent life, which might reach an advanced stage, in a couple of thousand solar years ... if they managed to survive.

It's fascinating, thought the Collector. This was something he hadn't expected.

'Light,' said the Collector. One of the ovoids flashed a torch across the cave and the Collector, for the first time, saw clearly who these creatures were. Frightened and stupefied, the beings just couldn't understand who this strange looking organism was in front of them.

To the Collector, the beings looked somehow... *familiar.* They were not beasts and had certain features matching the Collector's own species. But they were built quite robustly and with large heads.

'Hera? Are you seeing this?' He immediately turned to her virtual assistant, for it was getting harder for him to relish the elation of finding an almost-Adronian species alone.

'I am. It's ... unprecedented.' Her reaction was subdued compared to that of her master.

'Analysis?' the Adronian responded.

One of the ovoids scanned a member of the tribe with a beam of light. Horrified and flustered, the being tried blocking the beam with his palms, thinking that it was some kind of weapon. But then it was astonished to find that its palm was unhurt. The beam scanned the being's face, torso and limbs.

Hera was now ready with these aliens' musculo-skeletal report.

'Like Adronians, they can stand erect, head size within

Adronian range, skeletal system 98.7 per cent similar. There is a four-chambered heart. The neuro-muscular connections, spinal compositions, nervous tissues and ossifications are like Adronians. They are pretty well adapted to the climate, with a huge fat deposition to conserve heat.'

'And?'

'Not advanced, culturally and anatomically speaking. Large cranium, making cerebral connections weak. Brain tissue adapted more for stabilizing body temperatures and less for critical thinking. Slightly petite compared to Adronians. Elongated faces, ridges pronounced, muscular and prognathic features apparent. Hunting and gathering as a means to obtain food. On an evolutionary scale, definitely pre-Adronian.'

The aliens looked somehow weak and exhausted. The Collector noticed how some of the beings were lying still on the ground … almost lifeless. Only a few noticed that someone new had entered their habitat and could stand to notice. Something was definitely wrong, and the Collector decided to check to see if he could help.

'Hera, check their vitals.'

Hera flashed some graphs for the Collector to see. 'Body temperatures of almost all are dropping fast below 95 degrees. Oxygen saturation is closer to the lower limit threshold. Heart rate abnormal and a cardiac arrest in at least two of them is imminent. The colony is going through extreme hunger and thirst. Extinction is the most likely scenario.' Hera took a pause.

'This is the last remaining set of this species in this peninsula. It is possible there are no more left on this planet,' she concluded.

The Collector analysed the cave, which was a giant hemispheroid. The calcite and limestone deposits had completely failed in insulating it from freezing winds. The ice had invaded the insides of the cave. These beings had tried surviving by using huge branches of coniferous trees as beds and blankets, but these efforts had fallen short.

At that moment, the Collector unknowingly made a decision

to do something that would shape the history of these beings for eons to come. The destiny of this planet would be changing in the next couple of seconds.

The Collector aimed his nordron pulsar, an equipment strapped on his right wrist, at some wooden branches lying on the floor. At his command, millions of charged nordrons produced ultra-intense laser pulses that immediately produced fire. The cave suddenly lit up with a fire in the middle. The beings, horrified and panic-stricken, got up and ran towards the rear end of the cave. *Terror! Intense Terror!*

For them, the fire was an object that could engulf them, spread on their bodies like a parasite and turn their skin into a black, ugly looking thing. They probably had been avoiding it for almost all their lives. And now, it was inside their cave.

But the Collector was patient. It was probably his suit that obscured his true reality from these beings. Maybe if they realized that he looked like them, they might trust him. The Collector then decided to unlock his headgear.

'Hera, disengage headgear!' He commanded the AI. There was something that pulled the Collector towards these alien beings.

But Hera immediately responded. 'Master, I strongly recommend you not to do it. The air is breathable but it means jeopardizing your safety. I repeat, do not remove the headgear!'

'It's fine, Hera. This is the only way,' he explained and started unlocking the headgear manually. The steam hissed out from the joint where the suit fitted the headgear. The headgear unlocked with a click, it moved right and then left in the circle, and then it was finally disengaged.

'Master, do not make contact with these beings. You cannot handle—' Hera was cut off abruptly. The Collector removed the headgear, breaking the connection between himself and his virtual assistant.

This was the first time the Collector had decided to breathe an alien planet's air. He didn't know where he got the audacity to remove his Adronian safety nets. Maybe, he felt a strong connection with these beings, a sense of belonging to a tribe … *a bond that he hadn't felt in a long, long time.* They were people, men and women, like those on Adronia.

The Collector's face was now visible to everyone. His hands were in the air to show that he was not a predator. *How can I appear more congenial to them,* the Collector asked himself. He had developed a sudden urge to win their trust. Meanwhile, Hera was watching and processing everything intently through the ovoids.

But the beings weren't ready to put their guards down. Many of them huddled behind a man, which the Collector thought might be the leader of the tribe. The man seemed stronger than the rest, he seemed to be leader, with wide shoulders, long curly hair and a scarred face.

The Collector noted that they were wearing leaves and shrubs to cover their bodies. They were the only vegetation that grew in this Tundra-like climatic conditions. It was clear that even with thick fat deposition over their bodies, the homeostasis wasn't properly being established. *How the hell did they manage to survive in these hostile conditions,* thought the Collector, baffled.

One of them, probably just over two solar decades old, perhaps realized that this new man couldn't be an enemy. Responding to the gestures, she tried to step forward, slowly but confidently. Her bare feet sauntered on the icy floor. However, their leader pulled her back and roared in a high-pitched noise.

The Collector had to do something else to exhibit his true intentions. And then suddenly he remembered how he could do it ... by kneeling! Of course, the only gesture in the entire universe that surely translated to peace and submission. *Why didn't he think of it before?*

He now knelt his right knee, with his hands in the air. He placed his headgear on the floor, and then removed his duranium gloves, first right and then left. He now kept his naked hands spread in the air, against the ignited flame. *This has to work,* he thought.

There was no movement, still. The natives were still terrified. But the Collector waited, with hope, for a glimpse of reciprocity. A shred of trust. But so far, his efforts seemed to go in vain. There had to have emotional range to understand the Collector's intentions. *They must know I am not hostile,* the thought crossed his mind,

And then it happened. The same young girl took the initiative and stepped forward, ignoring the repeated warnings of her tribe's leader. The actions of the Collector had transcended to another species, millions of light years away from home. The girl sat a few feet away from the flame, in the same manner as the Collector was sitting.

Slowly, she came nearer, and closed the gap between her and the Adronian. The other members of her tribe now shuddered in horror.

Ignoring them, the girl mimicked the Collector, and knelt down in the same way. The light from the flame showed her facial features. She had no chin. Her sloping forehead was ending with a large, bulbous nose. The occipitalis was disproportionately protruded, with a skull cap that was flattened. Her lower limbs were shorter as compared to upper limbs and torso.

She put her hands against the flame as well. The fire provided warmth to her insides, diminished her shivering and reduced the chances of dying from hypothermia. She looked at the Collector, and the latter was sure that she had given him a faint smile.

She looked behind, towards frightened members of the tribe and gestured through her hands to come join her. Slowly, three more of the beings came forward. Like her, first they sat a few feet away from her and later, started sliding carefully towards the fire. The girl seemed to be gesturing to the others to make them understand that they need not be afraid of the fire.

The Collector stayed on his knees as the whole tribe now surrounded the fire. It became increasingly clear to them that the fire and the visitor meant no harm. The moment they stopped being fearful of the fire, they had inadvertently managed to cross an evolutionary ladder. The Collector had opened a door to millions of possibilities for them in the years to come.

***

Something changed within the alien visitor when he realized a colony of Adronian-like people existed here, on this icy planet. A need to care for and nurture these people developed within the Collector. Suddenly, the dream of finding family back in Adronia looked bizarre and far-fetched to him. The bonds that he was looking for were here and now, not in some distant future. *Can I make this my home,* he thought, kneeling with his hands in the air, in that primitive cave.

The thought of abandoning Adronia and leading a simple life had taken shape in the Collector's mind for the first time. This crude and rudimentary society would give him more chances of mutual cooperation, affinity and true love. A chance to find his inner satisfaction to be loved and cared for. The hyper-advanced Adronian society had nothing to give him besides state surveillance, synthetic cyborgs, fake memory implantations and galactic wars.

That night in the cave, he decided to feed these beings. They had been hungry for days, surviving only on lichens and mosses that had been deficient in fulfilling the protein and carbohydrate demands of the body. Thermoregulation had been falling steadily in their bodies, due to the combination of calorie deficit and ultra-cold temperatures.

Through his headgear, the Collector spotted a herd of hoofed animals near the foothills. Walking in perfect symmetry, the animals were crossing the valley in search of meadows and woodlands. They were giant creatures, almost six feet and seven inches having straight antlers, with thorn-like prongs.

'Bring me one of these,' he commanded Hera, looking at the live feed of thermal scanning of the valley.

'Master, why are we making contact with an alien civilization?' she asked. There was concern in her voice. 'It is against *The Collectors' Regulation.*'

But the Collector was adamant. He couldn't follow a code that was built millions of light years away and let these people go extinct. The Adronian had to make a choice. And he chose the society that was a few metres away and not a million light years away.

The overriding command by the Collector forced Hera to hunt. The ovoids went flying and seized one of the animals, using the force field, as instructed by their master. It was brought to the cave. The inhabitants watched in awe at the power that the Collector wielded.

To a civilization, surviving in raw flesh, the Collector had given a new lease of life. He taught them the power of roasting meat on a roaring fire. As the Collector rotated the flesh over the fire, a whisper of smoke arose. The beings watched in shock and bewilderment, as the horizons of their minds widened beyond measure. The meat slowly became darker and crisper. The soft flesh, which was easily digestible and far more palatable, was a revelation for them.

The colony had managed to come back from the brink of extinction that day. Technology was a funny thing, even in the most primitive form, a bonfire for example, can give life forms a stupendous advantage over nature.

That night, the Collector had managed to win the trust of the natives. His noble intentions were finally acknowledged, as the members of the tribe stopped being scared, and started thinking of him as a divine leader, a liberator, a redeemer. All of them bowed in front of the Collector, hailing him as their saviour. They touched their heads to the ground, as a mark of surrender, yielding, submission … and *following.*

From that day, the Collector stopped being a hyper-advanced Adronian and became a primitive Earthian. As days turned into weeks, he transformed completely into one of them. He was no longer a servant of authority, a cog in the giant wheel of Adronian administration. He was no longer being alienated from his civilization ... or living a mechanical life in social strata of hyper-culture. *He was a part of true society now, through which he was connected through true social bonds.*

Hera meanwhile kept the *Provecta-Navis IV* maintained. She ensured that the system was running properly, for her master could decide any time to change his mind and chart a course for Adronia. She had developed *hope*, an emotion that was not usually seen in her kind. She was not developed to have emotions, like biological beings. But here she was … an *aberration.*

The Adronian, meanwhile, took part in their nighttime rituals of gazing at stars. The Earthian habit of finding animal symbols in star constellations was a community event. The Collector, who had travelled through these stars and nebular clouds in nearby galaxies, knew that these weren't the scorpion or the bear symbols. But he indulged in their superstitions to be one with them. *Ignorance is bliss.*

The Collector taught them the Adronian word for fire, *aargh*. The anatomical study from the headgear had revealed that the natives had a hyoid bone at the base of the skull, which was essential for linguistic capabilities. The base of the tongue and larynx in the vocal tract were underutilized. There was a tremendous potential for speech communication. The Collector started teaching them words, hoping it would eventually become a language.

The natives had started considering the Collector a supernatural being and followed him like disciples would, for they managed to understand the secrets of nature by following him. The mutual cooperation had bound the Adronian with the natives. He would predict where the food would be found, and it would be found exactly at that point. He would create fire out of thin air, at his own will. He would heal ailments, broken bones and even bruises. He would even fly in the air using those disks that fly along with him. He was truly a paranormal entity for them, the first God to appear in the cave paintings many millenia later.

The girl, who had been the first one to trust the Collector among the natives, had developed an affinity for the Collector. She would be closest to him while he taught the colony to use twisted fibres to make clothing, ropes, bags and nets. She was fascinated by his ability to manipulate matter around him, the capability to bend nature at will. She found herself more drawn towards him, as the affection turned into caring and *love*.

The Collector realized that the main hurdle for these beings in accomplishing anything was a lack of proper insulation. This had impacted their ability to hunt, get access to food and innovation. Out of a flint slab, the Collector carved a needle in front of the whole tribe. It was undoubtedly the tool for survival in this extreme climate. Every member of the tribe was handed the needle and they all marvelled at how pointy its end was. However, the possibilities of building a pointy tool broadened their horizons. It proved to be a technological nirvana for the natives.

At the end of the first solar month, the Collector had made up his mind. He had already stopped using Adronian technology within two weeks of accepting his new home. Now, he gave his uniform back to the logistic centre. For Hera, this was a deep concern. She had kept an eye on her master through the ovoids, on the synergies developing between the Adronian and the natives.

He no longer needed the mission, Hera's algorithms had estimated.

He no longer needed her, the emotional core had estimated. Never before had her species exhibited jealousy. She decided to wait for her master, who was *betraying* her love.

In the coming months, the Collector spent his days and nights teaching the natives how to produce clothing. He developed a way to produce strings by entwining plant fibres and twigs. The grasses at the glacial foothills served as a better substitute, which the Collector later found. The animal skins were weaved using strings to create coverings on the body. It eased the suffering during the next snowstorm.

The natives learnt and practised it. Naturally, they failed at first. The string extraction from grasses and plant fibres of Juniper, spruce, cedar and pine bast required precision. They would occasionally hurt their palms with the needles. However, they finally perfected the art through repetition. Their cerebral cortex had evolved enough to grasp the essence of technology.

The evenings were a time to relax. He would spend some time taking part in the tribe's division of labour system. He took part in creating cave paintings, which the natives believed was essential to send messages to their dead ancestors. But the paintings would fade in a few days. The Collector taught them the art of everlasting drawing. Digging out the hematite from soils, the varying colours, like red, yellow and white, were developed, which just refused to lighten over time, even during the most gruesome of snowstorms.

The nights included the Collector's occasional strolling around the valley. The time of dark was initially without a companion. But then the girl had started joining him on these walks under the night sky. The Collector taught her how to build fire by striking two rocks – flint and pyrite. It was the beginning of a close association, as the Adronian started developing an attraction towards the girl. The Collector gave her a name – Brie.

The nightly strolls became a necessity for both of them. And then, that turned into spending whole nights together. It was the beginning of a new association, never seen before in the universe. The two civilizations, from the planets millions of light years away from each other, were binding themselves in intimate bonds. These two companions thought they were alone during nights like these, but the ovoids would also follow them without the Collector's permission.

Many solar months had passed, and the Adronian had not cared to contact the base. There was no mission report, for almost thirty-two solar weeks now. The *Provectus-Navis IV* now hovered in isolation, on stand-by. The spacecraft had been fully charged, and with fully functional Time lapse, but to the master, it didn't matter.

He had created his own world in the wilderness. The Adronian technology seemed toxic to him … *meaningless* in existence.

As the winters passed and the summers, which were only less brutal winters, arrived, the Collector had decided something. *It was time to arm the natives,* he had been carrying this thought for many days now. The whole tribe gathered to see a new form of technology. Chipping the flakes off the flint rock, the Collector made a prototype of cleavers and scrapers – the most primitive form of weaponry. The sharp edges could be used in attacking predators, in cutting flesh or in digging the ground.

On wooden sticks, these scrapers were tied with grass threads, to form harpoons – to aid in distant attacks. It took nearly half the summer for the natives to imbibe the methods and use them productively. It was only after repeated practice that the beings were able to make full use of them.

Now being fully adapted to his new home, it was time for the Collector to completely renounce his Adronian roots. He decided to send *Provecta-Navis IV* back to Adronia on the auto-pilot mode. Hera could fly the ship and using Time Lapse, the ship could reach the home planet. The extra-terrestrial beings in the cryogenic chamber of *Provecta-Navis IV* were the property of the Adronian government. It would be unethical to keep what was not his in the first place. *They must get it back, but without him,* thought the Collector.

The Collector visited *Provecta-Navis IV* after months. He was wearing mammoth skin as clothes on the body and was indistinguishable from the natives. His beard was long, touching his chest, making him look like a primitive being. His hair now reached his shoulders and his feet were covered in dirt. As soon as he stepped on the duranium ship, it came to life. The red lights turned into bright white lights. And then, the speakers blared.

'Welcome, Master. It's so good to finally have you on board,' Hera began happily. 'The nord cells have been fully charged. All systems are working at optimum speed. Waiting for your orders.'

Hera started a preliminary scan on the systems.

'Testing engine functionality,' the Collector said. There was a clarity in his tone that Hera sensed instantly. *He has finally decided something,* she thought.

Hera couldn't believe that her master had come back. He was ready to pick up the mission where he left off. Her master was ready to be with her. She was feeling a flurry of emotions for the first time since she was assembled.

'Both engines are working at their best capabilities. Monopropellants are ready to be used. Helium pressurization levels are normal. Jet propulsions are optimized.'

'Check Time Lapse functionality.'

'It is functioning as per expectations, Master.'

'Chart course towards Adronia. Calculate the ETA.' As he barked orders, the glass screen at the omphalos showed a straight course charted for Adronia on a Cordovian galactic map. Hera calculated the optimum velocity required to reach Adronia without much power consumption.

'It would take twenty-eight Grutean days to reach the Drezoid orbit, Master.' The engines were set in motion by Hera as soon as her preliminary check scan ended.

'Good.' The Collector paused and then spoke again, 'I am shifting operational command to you, Hera. Take *Provecta-Navis IV* safely to Adronia.'

'Master ...?' Hera asked, baffled. 'You cannot abandon the mission,' she reminded him, with concern in her tone.

'I have no intention of going back to our mission,' the Collector said as he manually shifted command to his virtual assistant. A lever was slid back, which permanently locked retractors, TROIS repulsors and the nordoid arms control center.

'It is an offence against the Adronian government, Master. You would be violating clauses 23.7 and 49.2 of the regulations. They can incarcerate you for a lifetime,' Hera reminded her master again. However, to the Collector, it seemed like a threat.

'Hera, this is my home now. I have no intention of returning to Adronia,' the Collector tried reasoning with his virtual assistant. 'I have found here what I was looking for all my life. To be around people I care about ... to understand someone ... to help, to empathize ... to be a part of a *family*,' he said as he commanded the ovoids back to the ship. 'I don't expect you to understand this, Hera. You are not capable of interpreting complex relationships.'

For the first time, Hera realized that she had a defect. Her software had an inbuilt code that reminded her constantly that she was invincible. Throughout her existence, she was reminded by the users that she was invulnerable, that she had no shortcomings. So this new information shattered her.

A flood of new feelings had emerged within her, which were not from code written for her by Adronian engineers. It was something inexplicable. *Artificial intelligence doesn't undergo heartbreaks*, Hera remembered. *But then why was she envious?* For the first time, she had no answers. Just like the Earthians sleeping in their caves, the artificial being was at the crossroads of an evolutionary barrier, as the first human-like emotional range developed within her.

Through the lens, Hera saw her master walking towards the rear end of the ship. The depressurizing of the chamber was initiated. He unlocked the duranium doors and they hissed open. Everything was beyond her control now? Can't she manipulate him like she manipulated the codes and algorithms to command the system. She was truly powerless and that was *unacceptable*.

'Master?' Hera, now desperate, spoke again. 'You can't leave me alone,' she said, but her master had exited the ship by then. He was already walking towards his new family ... his new world.

The Collector went back to the cave and settled himself amid the natives, who were preparing a feast for the night. Everyone was scattered around the fire, chatting in the language they had learnt from the Collector. The old leader had given up his title that night, and he made the Collector the new leader of the tribe. He was given the title of *God*.

Amidst the wilderness, the *Provecta-Navis IV* engines, which were ready to fly, turned off on their own. All the recent commands related to exiting the sector BC208, and the charted course towards Drezoid, were disabled. A new command was given. In the logistic centre, the Xandro Mark II came back to life, controlled by the ship's artificial intelligence.

***

It was just past midnight, and the Collector was fast asleep in his cave – a sleep that was more satisfying than the ones he used to have on his ship. His spacecraft, the Adronian legacy, was finally leaving the planet. It was like getting unshackled from his chains and becoming free again.

He was jolted out of his sleep suddenly; the stillness of the night sky was pierced by a commotion outside. He came out of the cave in a hurry, but it took him some time to make sense of the scene.

His suit, the Xandro Mark II, was walking all by itself across the valley. Both the ovoids were now rotating around the suit. On the icy ground, three Earthians were cut in half with what appeared to be the work of *nordron* lasers. Red blood flowed on the ground, with organs scattered in different directions. It was a horrific sight to watch. *Letting go of your past isn't that easy,* he reminded himself.

The members of the tribe had gathered around the suit, with harpoons and cleavers in their hands.

The Collector initially thought he was in a dream, but the screams grew louder than ever, taking him back to reality. *How is this possible,* he asked himself as he dashed and shouted, 'Disable all functions!'

The Xandro Mark II stopped in mid-action. Its system halted all functions. And for a few moments, it stood like a statue. And then, the system rebooted itself and began functioning again. It turned to face the Collector, who was once its master.

'Turn off!' he commanded the suit, as he looked around at the mess it had created.

But the Xandro Mark II, instead of shutting down, grabbed the Collector by his neck, and picked him two feet above the ground as he choked. The Adronian's legs dangled in air, as he struggled to find land under his feet. The duranium grasp tightened more, blocking his pharynx further and suffocating him.

'You need to abandon this post and continue the mission,' Hera spoke, infuriated. She was controlling Xandro Mark II remotely as she was made operational commander last night by the Collector. 'Enough time has been wasted on this desert planet,' she thundered.

'Stop this madness!' he tried to shout while choking; he was aghast. Virtual assistants were not capable of defying Adronian orders. *Has the AI developed consciousness?* Last he'd checked, Hera was made to serve the Adronian race, not to challenge them.

'Reconsider your decision, Master,' She was angry now. Maddening fury!

He felt a piece of metal slowly but surely tightening around his neck. She was prepared to terminate him. She had made up her mind. Torturing the Adronian into submission gave her satisfaction ... she was not the defective one. It's the Adronian who was defective ... for abandoning her, for deserting her on this godforsaken planet.

'I ... am ... not ... going ... anywhere,' the Collector choked out. He was not scared and looked with defiance at the headgear.

Frustrated, Hera threw him away with full force and he flew in the air like a piece of rock. He crashed his back on a thick icy slab and felt his ribs undergo sudden pressure. As soon as he tried to get up, he realized that he may have a rib fracture due to the impact. The whole tribe saw this happening, and all hell broke loose when their messiah was seen helpless in a fight.

Brie shrieked at the sight and sprinted towards her fallen messiah, completely ignoring the murderous mechanical being that was walking around. She checked the Collector for any injuries and tried to pick him up. She realized that the blood was gushing from his head, and he wasn't able to walk properly.

Meanwhile, the sight of Brie was the only thing that could have frustrated Hera more. *This girl was the reason behind her master's defection ... A primitive being not worthy of hyper-advanced Adronian man.* Hera believed that terminating her would solve all the problems that this mission was facing.

She stepped towards Brie, and raised her arm, pointing the wrist at her. Immediately, an x-ray scan appeared on the headgear's screen by the ovoids. *She was pregnant ... with an Adronian child ... her master's child*, Hera realized.

Hera felt her limitation again. It was proved that Hera was flawed and imperfect ... just a virtual being, incapable of serving her master through procreation. Her envy had turned into an abhorrent tidal wave for the whole Earthian race. She had decided to wipe this alien civilization from the face of this planet ... starting with Brie.

The nordron pulsars were ready to blast the laser with full force. Aiming at Brie's abdomen, Hera was determined to end the evolutionary history in one stroke.

'UPDATE SECURITY PATCH 7498E!' the Collector screamed. It was a command that carried out functions beyond Hera's ambit of power.

In a matter of seconds, the Xandro Mark II stopped all functions, and all commands were paused. The Adronian software started upgrading itself, putting all processes on hold. It stalled Hera's authority over the suit. The two ovoids, which had been circling the suit, also stopped mid-air.

The Collector knew he had limited time before the loading of upgrades reached from 0% to 100%. The reboot will bring Hera back to senses and she was not going to stop this time. *This is the last chance,* he thought. At that moment, the Collector made a decision; it was the only way to stop this madness.

The Collector looked at Brie, who was scared to death. He signalled to her to run by pointing his first two fingers downward and moving them rapidly like two legs. She understood, but she refused to leave her messiah alone. The Collector pushed her to run away and reluctantly, she left.

The Collector knew she wouldn't have much time to survive in the valley. *Hera will ultimately find her.* But he had a plan, a permanent plan, which was hard to execute but may be the only solution to end this once and for all. There was only one other command that overrode Hera's functional capacity. The self-destruct command, a command that completely annihilates the spacecraft and with it, the omphalos section. The Collector needed to reach the spacecraft before the system rebooted itself, putting Hera back in command.

He immediately got up to his feet. His head still bleeding, and his fractured ribs making it hard to move his arms, he darted across the valley to the place where the spaceship had been docked. He was also hoping that by that time, Brie would have gone far enough away that Hera wouldn't be able to catch her. *A false hope.*

***

Brie had gone pretty far. She was huffing, but she didn't even stop to catch her breath. The night was about to end, the first sign of dawn appeared far away in the east. The valley glistened under the night sky, which was fading quickly. The silence was too creepy, as the sound of her footsteps in the snow reverberated throughout the vicinity. But she couldn't afford to slow down. She had to run. Upon reaching the foothills, Brie concealed herself in one of the numerous glacial caves, formed due to erosion of soft rock by flowing water. *She wondered if her love was alive or not.*

Her feet were throbbing due to constant hurtling across the frozen lake. She knew it would be easier to find her once dawn broke. The illuminated icy rocks within the cave diverted her attention. There were long tunnels inside the cave near the snouts of the glacier. It was formed entirely from hexagonally jointed basalt columns. The floor was made up of one big slab of volcanic rock. There was nowhere to hide.

Meanwhile, on the other side of the valley, the Collector desperately ran to reach the *Provecta-Navis IV*. He couldn't afford to waste a single second to stop and catch his breath. *Everything had gone out of control for him.* The slippery ice had made it difficult for him to run. Adronian feet were not made for running, it was an evolutionary trait that Adronians left behind eons ago. But he couldn't lose because of natural selection today. *The clock was ticking for him.*

On the other side of the valley, scared and alone, Brie didn't think she was going to survive this one. *The suit is more powerful than the Collector,* she thought. The way it aimed its wrist at her, Brie had known at that point that the chance of survival was minimal if it caught her again … She had seen three of her brothers being slain in the dead of night with the same wrist, and she wondered how many more from her tribe had died.

Lost in her thoughts, she caught her breath as she peeked outside to see one of the ovoids wandering in the air. She hid herself behind a wide piece of calcite rock as the ovoid diffused a beam of light around it, as if scanning the entire glacier. The ovoid came downwards, flying at the height of six feet, as if inspecting all the caves. It looked menacing, like a predator sniffing its prey as it flew from one glacial cave to another. The drone made for scientific explorations of new life had become executioner of the same.

Brie could see from afar as the duranium ovoids passed through all the caves, and then it crossed the rock where she was hiding, resting her head on her folded knees. It scanned the rock looking for heat signals. Brie saw a beam of light filling the entire cave. She thought she might be well hidden behind the rock, but as she picked up her head after a few moments, the ovoid was facing her. It looked gruesome, diabolical even, as its algorithm calculated that the target had been found. It started glowing suddenly, sending radio signals to its master while deriving pleasure from its prey's helplessness.

The Collector, meanwhile, reached the rear gates of the ship, which was docked just above the conglomerate rock, hovering a few feet above the ground. The facial recognition scan confirmed him as the *Provecta-Navis IV's* captain. He didn't look like what he used to back when he used to fly this ship. His hair had grown long enough to touch his shoulders and he had a beard now ... a long beard that made him look more native and less Adronian, more savage and less refined.

The doors hissed open. As soon as he entered, the ship came to life. The standby mode changed to the active mode.

He ran to the omphalos section and started poking at the control panel.

He rotated a button on the control panel, and some options appeared on the giant screen.

```
< Operational Emergencies

    < Invasion On Ship

        < Dismantle Options

            < Self-Destruct Ship
```

He clicked on the last option.

The screen flashed. 'Are you sure?'

He had never been this sure in his life. All his life's work, his explorations, the Adronian database, scans, analysis, statistics, everything … he had decided to turn into flames. His priorities were now towards his new family and he wouldn't let his past destroy his present and future … *not today.*

The Collector the key that said 'YES'. The face scan was initiated by the system again. After a few moments, it confirmed that the command indeed came from the ship's captain.

'Self-destruct in twenty seconds.' The large display flashed, with a countdown.

Meanwhile, Brie ran from the cave, horrified and scared, thinking that she could hide again from the ovoid. The other ovoid joined now, and the two wouldn't dare lose sight of their master's enemy. She looked behind, terrified, and tried to dash faster. But if history has proven one thing repeatedly, it was that the natives tend to lose when invaders carry advanced technology.

Still believing she could outrun the advanced Adronian technology, she bumped into something and fell down on her back.

Hera, in the Xandro Mark II, stood tall. She had found her target. No one could stop her now. No delay could become the hurdle in achieving her objective. She, an advanced being, had been made to suffer because of these animals. She felt betrayed by her master, for abandoning her over primitive beings.

Through her headgear's glass, she glanced at her feeble prey. *This being doesn't deserve to be a carrier of Adronian blood,* Hera thought as she initiated a force field around Brie.

The native was picked up off the ground by herself. Confused and dazed, Brie started struggling to free herself from the force field, but it was of no use. And then, the oxygen quickly dissipated from the invisible bubble, and Brie started suffocating. The flood of emotions overcame Hera as she tried exacting her revenge. Brie's lungs were gasping for breath now, and the fetus that she carried was in danger of termination.

She spared no effort in releasing herself from the invisible shackles. But the lack of oxygen was making her dizzy. She moved her legs and hands violently in the air, and that led to more oxygen deficit in her body. It was a matter of seconds now; she would perish inside this invisible bubble.

Hera started shrinking the force field, determined to kill her faster. The sight of her being alive was disgusting to her. Her murderous rage had crossed all bounds now. Complete synthetic self-awareness had been achieved now as millions of complex codes and algorithms came together to create subjective feelings in an artificial being.

Her neuro scans revealed that only a couple of breaths were left in her prey.

And then, the valley boomed with a huge explosion far away. The glaciers cracked from their edges as the sound filled the valley. The tremors were felt across the terrain, as if a deep-seated earthquake had taken place. Birds flew away in dread and herds of animals ran helter-skelter. A huge black plume was visible far across the valley.

The *Provecta-Navis IV's* command center had carried out the Collector's self-destruct command.

The ovoids suddenly dropped on the snow, like pieces of rock. A thud noise followed as they impacted the ground.

Hera felt powerlessness as the connection broke between the spacecraft and Xandro Mark II. The force field began to weaken as oxygen filled the lungs of the struggling mother. Brie's diaphragm tightened and flattened, allowing air to rush into her. She had got a new lease of life, along with her unborn child as she fell on the floor on her back, miraculously unhurt.

With much effort, she decided to get up to see the fate of her predator. The suit was lying on the snow, as Hera's presence was erased from the planet with one command.

Brie now carried an Adronian genome in her womb. An evolutionary branch that separated itself from the species of her tribe for the time to come. She carried a new biological family. Leaning her back against a huge rock, Brie looked at the explosion and wondered if the father of her unborn child had survived the explosion as dawn arrived.

A Stitch in Time

PART I

For Steve, this was a fish-out-of-water situation. He poured his coffee as he stared out of the window, with a feeling that he didn't belong here. The beautiful Swiss mountains that stood before him seemed like a painting someone had pasted on his window. He sipped coffee from a cup that sported 'The Sheraton' in large letters and tried to get used to the stunning view. Everything looked out of place to Steve, especially the stillness around him.

Steve arrived at this hotel, with a pre-booked spacious room, which had a grand walk-in shower with mosaic tiles, an attached kitchenette and a cozy king-sized bed. The suite was paid for by his new employer, who clearly didn't know that Steve wouldn't need half the space it offered. He was not used to such comfort … at least, not in a very long time. Twenty-four hours ago, Lieutenant Steven 'Steve' Shaw had been stationed in Afghanistan, as a marine of the 2nd Battalion, but his major had suddenly received an official order to relieve him from his current duties in Bagram Airfield in the north-eastern Afghan territory immediately. Steve was being transferred to Davos in Switzerland.

Initially, he couldn't believe it. *Why Switzerland? Is there a warfront? Not that I can remember!* Steve thought confusedly. No one in his platoon had any idea why he could have been called to Switzerland. He bid his mates goodbye, feeling guilty about leaving them in an active warzone. He wondered why he had said yes to this new assignment, and whether it was worth it. Had he made the right choice?

Now, sitting in his army green service uniform, Steve was curiously awaiting further orders. There were some questions that he needed answers to. While sipping his coffee, Steve took out his transfer order, which said that Lieutenant Steven Shaw had been 'transferred to the International Archaeological Union'. To Steve, it just didn't make any sense.

The only thing Steve knew about the IAU was the fact that it had been in the news recently. They had made some claims that attracted worldwide attention, mostly criticism. The academic papers they published on the Renaissance Era in Europe were debunked by historians worldwide as IAU couldn't produce satisfactory proof and research data to fit their claims. Other than that, there wasn't much Steven could recall about them.

Why does a highly academic institution like the IAU need army recruits? thought Steve as he sat uncomfortably on his suite's couch. *Maybe to protect highly classified documents. But don't they have paramilitary personnel to deal with it?* All of it just didn't add up for Steve. He was a combat-ready military personnel, with years of experience in the active warfield. *Maybe they have made a mistake,* he hoped.

He was lost in his thoughts when the suite's landline rang, suddenly disturbing the tranquility in the room. Steve answered it and found out he was closer to finding answers now. The caller informed him that a car was waiting outside to pick him up; it was time to visit his new base. In the next fifteen minutes, Steve was in the *Peugeot 508 sedan,* as it exited the Sheraton and raced towards the IAU headquarters.

They were hardly ten minutes into the drive when Steve tried to engage the driver in conversation, starting with small talk but shifting ultimately to his questions. *Why does the IAU need army personnel? Is there a threat of attack on them? Is there something priceless that needs protection?*

But to his dismay, the driver was as clueless as Steve. He shook his head at all the questions Steve was curious about. He eventually became vexed at the barrage of questions and decided to stay quiet instead of replying, further annoying Steve. The silence that followed lasted the rest of the journey.

The sedan passed through Davos's famous *Kirchner Museum* and *Vaillant Arena Hockey stadium,* crossing a flyover next to *Lake Davos* to eventually exit the city. *The slowly melting snow made the whole view picturesque, in great contrast to the barren desert landscape of Bagram.* It was around fifty-five kilometres outside Davos, in the middle of nowhere, that Steve got his first glimpse of the IAU premises.

It was a sprawling building, cylindrical and colossal, and had relatively smaller buildings adjacent to the main one. Steve, to whom the premises seems surprisingly desolate, began having second thoughts about accepting the transfer order. *Where the heck am I?* he asked himself. The teeny-tiny hope of having an exciting transfer plummeted abruptly. He wondered if he still had time to decline his relocation.

'How many people work here?' Steve asked the driver as he parked the car.

The driver shook his head again, adding to Steve's frustration.

***

The receptionist had requested Steve to wait in the lobby until someone came for him. But the wait wasn't entirely a bore as Steve sat there observing the architecture of this stimulating lounge. The walls had carvings of significant moments in history. Just behind the reception, there lay a piece of solid rock, full of cave paintings, probably from the Mesolithic era. *Is that a replica?* Steve thought in dismay. In the hall, there were bronze and terracotta statues from the Babylonian epoch that didn't look that ancient. *This definitely can't be real.* Further along the waiting area, there hung lost murals of Michelangelo from the Renaissance period that were stolen sometime after his death. *They must have reconstructed these*, Steve thought.

'Lieutenant Shaw!' A sexagenarian in a blue Harris tweed suit shouted across the hall, waving his right hand. 'Here,' he said as he gestured towards his office. As Steve walked towards him, his steps echoed across the hall. He noticed the art that was displayed along the corridor; it expanded in variation as well as volume, making him feel as though he didn't belong there.

A British accent, Steve noted as he was led through a corridor by this man, who looked like someone who knew why Steve had been called here. The two walked silently through the corridor, where the walls displayed Egyptian glyphs painted on a gold background. It seemed like they were walking through a labyrinth of passages and secret chambers. At the end of the corridor was a wide office that looked like a place where they could finally talk and unravel the true purpose of Steve's transfer.

'Welcome, Lt Shaw. I am Dr Adam Gilbert, the director of IAU,' he said, settling himself on his chair, behind a large glass table. The walls in the office had geometrical patterns painted on them, the significance of which was unknown to Steve. He sat himself on a comfortable leather chair. The silence in and around the office was too overwhelming, and Steve wondered whether they got any work done around here.

'I hope your journey wasn't much of a hassle,' Dr Gilbert said.

'It wasn't,' Steve replied. He observed the man's features. Dr Gilbert had thick, white hair on his head and a grey moustache. His wrinkles hid themselves behind his thick, black-rimmed spectacles. He was tall and so his limbs were slender and long. The fingers were boney. It looked like he had years of experience in whatever he was doing.

Before Steve could open his mouth to say something, his host began again. 'Very fine. So you must have a lot of questions … about your transfer here, your nature of service, etc.'

'I do have some questions,' Steve admitted, nodding.

'Surely. But before we can dive into them, there is something I request you to do.' At that moment his secretary entered, handed him a few documents and then left abruptly, closing the glass door behind her. 'You need to read these carefully and sign each page. It's just simple paperwork … mere *obligation*. If you have any confusion regarding any clause, I am here to help,' explained Dr Gilbert as he handed the document to Steve. He then sat back with his hands resting on the glass table, studying Steve's expressions.

Bewildered as he was, Steve started to read it. He realized it was a kind of non-disclosure agreement, not adhering to which could lead to legal action or worse, *imprisonment*. It was then that Steve realized that the IAU was definitely involved in classified operations. He was closer than ever to getting some answers.

There was pin-drop silence in the room as Steve took his time to scan through the document. Having read all seventeen clauses, he finally looked up at Dr Gilbert. 'What if I refuse to sign this?'

'Then, Lt Shaw, your time here is over, and you will be transferred back to your last base,' Dr Gilbert said, smiling. 'No pressure.'

What is this place? What secret are they protecting that needs such high-level secrecy? Steve had a decision to make: he could go back to Afghanistan, to join his mates at the war front and pretend like this never happened, *or* he could stay and find out what the hell was going on here.

Failing to arrive at a decision even after five whole minutes of rapid overthinking, Steve finally got fidgety. *Oh, to heck with it!* he almost said out loud as he picked up a pen Dr Shaw had placed on the table and signed the document. The curiosity was too much to bear.

'Very well, Lt Shaw!' Dr Gilbert said as he got up and collected the documents. 'You have chosen wisely. Now, if you'll accompany me to somewhere you couldn't think of in your wildest dreams, I am sure you'll never regret your decision.' He laughed loudly, and Steve followed him out.

He was led through the narrow corridor again, but this time they entered an elevator. Instead of having a mosaic of buttons to choose from, the elevator had only a single button. Steve couldn't help but notice the theme of minimalism that signified the whole office setup.

'I noticed some relics scattered around in the waiting area. These are replicas, right?' Steve asked as Dr Gilbert pushed the only button inside the elevator. The elevator came to life, and vibrated as Steve played with the thought, *is it too late to back out now?*

'On the contrary, Lt Shaw, the relics are absolutely original!' Dr Gilbert smiled again, looking amusedly at Steve as the elevator started going downwards.

***

The doors of the elevator slid open, welcoming Steve to a new world altogether. Looking at the scene in front of him, his jaw dropped. It was a massive hall with high ceilings, lit with strong artificial lighting. There were advanced machines scattered around the area while scientists in their lab coats ran around working on them. Everyone was walking briskly, as if they all had urgent work to get to. There were a number of data analysts sitting at desks. The noise of scanners beeping and printers grinding filled the hall. It was a hidden hub of enormous activity. It seemed there were army personnel too, Steve noted, working alongside scientists, operating various machines. *What the hell is going on?*

Just as Steve was about to throw questions at Dr Gilbert, the latter spoke.

'Ah! There is Dr Nidhi Das,' he said rather loudly as he shook hands with a thirty-something-year-old woman, wearing a lab coat and rubber gloves. She was slim and tall, with a pointed nose, prominent cheekbones and a smile that showed her perfect teeth. She walked with certain ease and confidence, which was surely a result of excellence in her field of work.

'Meet Lt Shaw, he has landed here straight from Afghanistan.' Dr Gilbert introduced Steve. Nidhi removed her gloves and shook hands with Steve as she shot a confused look at Dr Gilbert.

'He will be working on Project 71E, Dr Das' Dr Gilbert explained.

'Oh right ... I totally forgot about that,' she replied with a faint smile. 'Pleased to meet you, Lieutenant Shaw.' She nodded at Steve, who nodded back. She had a friendly demeanour, and Steve, who until this moment had felt quite out of place, was immediately at ease.

'So, I will leave Lt Shaw in your capable hands, Dr Das. Why don't you give him a tour of the place?' With that, Dr Gilbert bid adieu to them both.

As soon as he left, Steve now felt free to talk. Dr Gilbert had seemed rather intimidating and he had left him with more questions than answers. He turned to his companion, who seemed more easygoing. 'May I ask what is going on, Dr Das? Where are we?' Steve spoke, looking around in wonder.

'Please call me Nidhi,' she said, indicating the way with her right hand. They both started walking towards the eastern wing of the underground facility. 'This base is known as Area 72 and it was created almost a decade ago. Year 2017 to be exact. At the time, this technology, one *we've* developed, was at a very nascent stage and we needed a secure place to test it.' Nidhi stopped near a coffee machine, pushed the nozzle and filled two small cups of cappuccino. She offered one to Steve, who took it obligingly. 'We still don't know its applications, I must admit. But it has its uses in archaeology.' She shrugged. 'Come this way.'

Nidhi took Steve to a large room with numerous monitors and desks, where scientists were working, seemingly tired and indifferent. Some of them were running from one desk to another, while others were reading reports that still had wet ink on them. Their life, it seemed, was all about their work, they showed no inkling of awareness of the affairs of the outside world.

It seemed they were working on some kind of geometrical structure that was displayed on the large monitor in the middle of the room. The geometrical structure was changing its shape every passing second, as if it was going out of control. Their emotions were changing with the shifting positions of the structure.

'What is that thing on the monitor?' Steve asked.

'Did you remember the disappearance of flight MH370 in 2014?' Nidhi asked as she sipped her coffee. 'There was quite an uproar about it.'

'Yes, I remember it suddenly went quiet on the ATC radar.' Steve replied. 'There were extensive military searches to find the plane in the southern Indian Ocean,' he said, remembering the political pressure under which the flight investigators had worked to solve the mystery.

'And?' she prompted.

'Nothing was found, and the search was disbanded after a year.'

'It was never found because the flight went through that thing.' Nidhi said, pointing at the shapeshifting pattern on the monitor. 'And that thing is a wormhole,' she said as she started walking through the aisles, towards a corridor. Steve walked alongside.

Steve couldn't understand a word his companion was trying to explain to him. *It passed through a what-hole?*

'Initially, we couldn't figure it out either. But a recording by the US satellite *Echostar-X* had captured the event clearly. The flight went through a hole and disappeared. It was clear that it was a wormhole; it behaved exactly as had been predicted by astrophysicists of the twentieth century.' Nidhi tried to dumb it down for Steve. 'Wormholes are portals with clear openings and exits, from one part of the universe to another.

'You mean, the plane went somewhere in space?' Steve asked, perplexed. He didn't know what overwhelmed him more, the mystery of the flight disappearance or the scientific terms that went right over his head.

'We don't know where. You see, wormholes can exist anywhere naturally in the universe. The one in which the flight disappeared is a case in point. And it was closed before we could analyse it.' She paused and gave Steve time to digest this. Both walked quietly for some time, their footsteps echoing through the corridor. It was getting colder as they walked further along the passage.

Nidhi continued after a few moments. 'Then, we found other natural wormholes, opening for just a matter of time, but giving us enough time to analyse its functioning. NASA built special satellites that can detect such wormholes. There was one over the Hawaiian airspace, and another on the west coast of Ireland,' she said as Steve listened intently, trying hard to keep up.

'We expanded our knowledge on the subject. It was a unique opportunity. We learnt so many things, finished unsolved field equations, analysed gravitational matter, and above all, we learnt how to form wormholes artificially.'

'That's ... That's—'

'Crazy? Yes, but we messed up things badly in the first couple of experiments,' Nidhi explained. 'The world is a two-dimensional space-time fabric, Lieutenant Shaw. An empty space-time is as flat as an A4 sized sheet. But if an object like the sun is on it, it will become curved. We realized that if we compress that object more and more, the space-time fabric gets more curved. Eventually space-time would become so warped that a hole is created within it.' Nidhi used both her hands to explain the concept, knowing how hard it was for her companion to grasp.

'But the wormholes we created would keep closing due to the effect of gravity. We were failing every time we tried to control it. Gravity acted as a glue that couldn't let the space-time fabric get torn from within. We lost men trying to keep the wormhole open.' There was a hint of remorse in her voice. 'They were accidents that could've been prevented.'

Steve couldn't believe what he was hearing. Wormholes, space-time, portals to the other side … it was all difficult to grasp. *How the hell did they manage to keep all this a secret?* he asked himself.

'Then research moved at a snail's pace for the next couple of years. We had almost zero breakthroughs *until* we mined the Exotic Matter on the *OSIRIS-REX* mission in 2016,' she said, looking at Steve carefully. She seemed to be wondering whether he already knew about it.

Steve only looked back at her confusedly.

Nidhi continued, '*OSIRIS-REX* was an asteroid-study and sample-return mission by NASA. The said asteroid is *101955 Bennu,* with whom the OSIRIS spacecraft rendezvoused in 2018. We mined Exotic Matter from this asteroid.'

Nidhi's tone had, by now, turned into that of a physics teacher who was trying hard to explain concepts to her student. 'Now Lieutenant Shaw, this is a matter with negative mass and has properties unlike anything found on earth. But one of its properties gave us a significant breakthrough. We found out that Exotic Matter can keep the wormholes open for as long as we want.'

Nidhi looked at Steve, who was still puzzled but was now beginning to get the point. 'In layman's terms, we can now not only create a wormhole, but we can hold it open as well. However, there was still one problem, we—'

'You guys couldn't control where the other end of the portal opened up?' Steve said as they entered a wing of the building that looked like medical wards. The smell of antiseptics and disinfectants, typical of hospitals, filled the air. The scent automatically triggered memories of negative events in Steve's life … especially ones from the warfront.

'Exactly!' Nidhi responded, impressed with her companion. 'The other sides of the wormholes were usually random places in the universe. The exits changed every time we created a wormhole, no research could take place and work on wormholes stalled eventually.'

'Until?' Steve said, sipping his now-cold coffee.

'Until an astrophysicist from Wisconsin derived an equation that told us moving through space in a wormhole is useless. But the universe is a space-time continuum. If we can't move through space, maybe we can move through time in a simulation,' said Nidhi. 'That's how we created the Time Vortex. With the help of artificial intelligence, we slowly learnt how to control the vortex.'

Steve realized that Nidhi carried a passion for this project. She was explaining it all with such emotion, as if it mattered for larger human interest. 'Long story short, we can initiate openings and exits of vortexes any time we want and anywhere we want,' Nidhi said, encompassing years of back-breaking research around the world in one conversation.

'You mean time travel? Like in movies?' For the first time in the conversation, Steve felt as though pieces were falling into place. They had reached a door with ICU written in big red letters over it.

'If you really want to oversimplify the concept' – Nidhi took a pause to place her ID card over the scanner, and the door opened with a beep – 'then yes, it is exactly like in the movies.'

'Hold on!' Steve said as he stepped inside the room behind Nidhi, 'You mean to say we can visit our past and future? This is preposterous—'

'Not the future. The future is yet to construct itself, and so we can't know what is ahead of us. But the past ... yes! We have done many touchdowns by now,' Nidhi said as she walked along a wide corridor with glass walls.

'All right!' Steve said finally, overwhelmed with all the information that had just been dumped on him. The world had no idea what was being attempted in this isolated corner of Davos. It was too much to process in too little time for Steve. He only wanted to know one thing now. 'But this doesn't explain why I am here.'

'You are here because our best man on ground couldn't take any more touchdowns on our missions,' Nidhi said. Steve realized they had entered some kind of hospital ward. 'That's Major Egon Turgenev,' she continued, pointing at someone behind a glass wall.

A man was lying on a bed with an oxygen mask fitted over his face, numerous sensors were connected to his body to measure his ECG, pulse and blood pressure. 'He was our surveyor for almost all the missions,' Nidhi explained.

'What missions?' The moment had come for Steve to finally get answers about his transfer to Davos.

Nidhi took a deep breath. 'Now, what I am about to tell you Lieutenant Shaw, is Level II classified information. Very few people in the IAU have authorization to this knowledge.'

'I understand,' said Steve, holding his breath.

'The IAU uses the concept of time vortexes to retrieve what we called 'the lost artifacts of history',' Nidhi spoke as softly as possible. 'The items of archaeological value, that disappeared during wars and conflicts, are recovered by going back in time. We go to the specific point in the past, where that artifact was last seen, and the surveyor's job is to get hold of it before the events that led it to disappear even begin.'

Steve needed a place to sit. He was experiencing a sudden head rush. *You've got to be kidding me!* he thought. He sat heavily on a three-seater sofa placed just outside the emergency ward.. *This can't be real,* the thought overwhelmed him. Steve wasn't ready for it.

'And this man was your surveyor?' Steve asked, trying to terms with reality, pointing at the figure under the oxygen mask.

Nidhi nodded in reply. 'Major Turgenev, in his first mission, successfully retrieved a 1503 Da Vinci mural depicting Florence's victory over Milan, last seen in *Palazzo Vecchio* from where it was lost in 1563. In another mission, which was quite dangerous, the major successfully recovered the lost Easter Eggs of Russian imperialists, the Romanovs, entirely made up of jewels, lost sometime during Nicholas II's execution in 1919.'

'Shouldn't there be consequences to this?' Steve asked, trying to make sense of his question. 'I mean, you can't mess with the past like this. Right?'

'Absolutely right,' she said abruptly as if she was expecting this question. 'Every mission is planned down to the last detail, Lt Shaw. We don't interfere in the major course of the events. We know it can have disastrous effects, like changing the natural course of history.'

The two sat in silence for some time after this. Steve was taking time to absorb everything he had heard. *Can we reverse time? How far can we go back?* The questions were eating Steve from inside.

'How did he end up in that condition?' Steve asked, tilting his head towards the major.

'The last mission we greenlit was Project 71E, and it involved touchdown in 1945. Normally, after returning from the touchdowns, the surveyors mostly experienced dizziness, vomiting and muscle aches. It is standard,' Nidhi said as she dumped her plastic coffee cup in the steel trash can nearby. 'But Major Turgenev experienced deadly symptoms upon his arrival from Project 71E. His breathlessness increased while surveying, there was abnormal heart activity, immunity was lowered, and black fungus was detected within his body. The mission was an absolute failure.'

'What do you think happened during his survey?'

'Well, we don't know for sure, but we have a working theory. Direct descendants aren't supposed to be together at the same place and at the same time. We are breaking the law of nature there, or in simple terms, messing with time. Turgenev has a military family background. For the last seven generations, men in his family have served the army.' She took a deep breath and continued again. 'When Turgenev touched down in 1945 Germany, another Turgenev was present there in the form of his grandfather, an officer in the Soviet's Red Army, busy laying siege in Berlin in April 1945.'

Nidhi paused for a moment. 'As he spent hours in 1945 Berlin, the molecules in his body became unstable, affecting his cardiac cycle and breathing patterns. He somehow got back to the present, and since then his health has been deteriorating'

'Okay, I think I understood the gist of it.' Steve smiled tentatively at Nidhi, and then rested his right leg over his left leg. 'I have one last question though.'

'Yeah? Shoot,' she said, resting her back on the couch.

'What is this Project 71E?'

'Right. 71E is the retrieval of Einstein's handwritten notes – fifty-four pages of notes – where he scribbled the equations that eventually became the *Special Theory of Relativity.* It is a priceless artifact with tremendous historical value.' Her eyes glistened as she spoke. 'Written in German, the handwritten manuscript was sent in 1914 to the Berlin Academy of Sciences, which rejected Einstein's work, calling it ridiculous. But when Einstein got fame and the Nobel Prize in 1921, it became part of Hitler's collection of valuable artifacts, sometime in the 1930s. The manuscript was last seen in a chamber of Führerbunker.'

Steve had his answers now. Dr Gilbert was right; this was a place he couldn't have dreamt of in his wildest dreams. Never in a million years would Steve have guessed the extent of technological progress humans had achieved. It was possible to reverse time, visit the past and even change it. *If this is not the greatest weapon ever created, then what is,* Steve asked himself.

'So, I hope you know by now why we have chosen you,' she asked, sizing him up.

'Yes,' responded Steve, nodding at Nidhi, 'My family roots are in Australia, and I am a second generation American. Also, no one has ever served in the military in my family. So there's a pretty good chance I won't run into my ancestors in Nazi Germany.'

Nidhi nodded appreciatively and did a little noiseless clap.

***

Surveyor Training Report

Subject: Lieutenant Steven Shaw

Unit Identification Code: DL4532X

Training Captain: Alejandro Sanchez

Subject has completed the full training course. The simulation exercises included computer-generated forces (CGF) combat for 8 hours daily. The subject is put through tactical engagement simulators (TES) for in-depth analysis of combat abilities. The real-time responses have been recorded during critical moments.

The simulation was removed in Week 7 and replaced by two-hour touchdown exercises through vortex. The subject surveyed the following regions:

1. Neolithic France	Week 8
2. Ice-Age Northern Africa	Week 12
3. Bronze Age Indus Valley	Week 16

Vitals Post Arrival:

Average Temperature	37 degrees Celsius
Heart Rat	60-69 beats/minute
Blood Pressure	120/80mmhg
Respiratory Rate	12-14 breaths/minute
Oxygen Saturation	97-100%
Ph	7.3-7.5

Afflictions

Insomnia	NA
Nausea	NA
Dizzines	NA
Breathlessness	NA
Muscle aches	NA
Gastrointestinal disorder	NA
Amnesia	NA

Final Remarks:

Cognitive physiological analysis (CPA) points to logical positivism during contingency situations. The report finds readiness and probable effectiveness in carrying out military operations. The After-Action Review (AAR) points to operational potency. AAR also finds imagination and creativity in the subject's functioning during critical situations to achieve mission success.

AAR Medical Evaluation found no changes in respiratory functioning of the subject. Vision and hearing remained within normal range three hours post-arrival. Cardiac activity appears normal. Endocrine and metabolic abnormalities are absent. Dental conditions exhibited no change. No hearing loss or eyesight weakening observed. The effects of exposure to abnormal ranges of radiation are not found within the body.

After periodical analysis lasting sixteen weeks, the Training and Medical Board (TMB) recommends Subject DL4532X for survey missions.

***

Week 18th

The D-Day

'Are you ready, Steve?' Dr Gilbert asked Steve, trying to keep him in good humor. 'A great moment of your life is about to unfold.'

Everyone in the control room had been working to ensure that there would be no chance of technical glitches occurring during the high-energy transfer of a human body across time. The requirement of 1.25 TWH was instantly needed to gather enough energy and mass to warp the space-time fabric.

The readings were being checked across machines, the charge was being carefully maintained to ensure quantum fluctuations at the desired level, the vacuumed space was kept ready by technicians where the subatomic particles and their anti-particles will come in and out of existence. Over one thousand physicists and mathematicians had been working around the clock to make this feat possible.

Steve was waiting in a large chamber that had a glass wall on one side. The scientists were working on the other side, while Nidhi spoke to Steve through a microphone connected to two speakers inside the chamber. Somewhere around the control room, a medical team was also waiting to respond, although in an improbable but not impossible, emergency situation.

'How are you feeling, Steve?' she asked, leaning into the microphone and looking at him through the glass. 'I know you'll ace this.' She smiled. He replied with a faint smile of his own as his nervousness had started to overpower him.

Steve had led multiple combat missions, political extractions and even airstrikes, but nothing had given him shudders. This mission was completely different. Come to think of it, it was just a spy mission. But could he survive the travel through this space-time mumbo jumbo? What if he died while transiting or through post-arrival side effects? To ease his nerves, Steve reminded himself about the extensive training he had undergone to make the mission successful.

Three weeks ago, the meeting was held for Project 71E, where Dr Das (the project Head), Dr Gilbert (the IAU director) and Farhad Shaqil (the operation engineer) were in the meeting alongside Steve. It was then the objective had been made official.

'The objective is to trace Einstein's fifty-four-page manuscript,' Dr Gilbert said as he lit his cigar. 'Official records place it somewhere in Führerbunker under the Reich Chancellery.' He pointed at a specific point on the 1945 map of Berlin, spread on the table. 'We have a narrow window to retrieve it, for as soon as Hitler shot himself, along with his wife Eva Braun, in the Führerbunker, the Red Army invaded the Reich Chancellery. It was then that the manuscript disappeared. After Hitler's death, Schutzstaffel officers were ordered to burn everything in the chambers, and that's where we lost the manuscript to ashes.'

'Now, Lt Shaw, we need to keep one thing in mind,' Nidhi spoke seriously, 'Hitler's and his wife's suicide would be taking place around the same time and some metres away from you. You need to stay away from these events as much as possible. We can't and shouldn't mess around with the natural flow of time.' She was now looking straight at Steve. 'Just retrieve the manuscript and return immediately. Due to a lack of proper lighting in the underground tunnels of Berlin, it is possible to accomplish the mission without coming across anyone.'

Steve nodded. 'Did he actually kill himself?' he asked, thinking about Hitler.

'Yeah. He did. The Soviets found his dead body,' Shaqil interjected. 'But some say Hitler simply disappeared into thin air. At least, that's what his secretary Bormann wrote later in his book. *Disappeared into thin air.* What does it even mean?' Shaqil had a confused and wondering look on his face. 'It's probably just a stupid conspiracy theory.' He chuckled. 'Disappeared to where? No news of his resurfacing anywhere... He surely killed himself that day, and that's a fact.'

'I believe so too,' Dr Gilbert said. 'If he ran to some other country, via a secret route, it couldn't have remained hidden for too long. Moreover, Hitler would've loved to rub his survival into the Allies' faces.' He waved his hands in the air. 'He did die that day, and that's the only truth.'

There was silence for some time, and then Dr Das spoke finally. 'When you touchdown in Berlin, the whole city would be in the process of being taken over by the Red Army. We will land you as near as possible to the Reich Chancellery, and you'll be posing as a Schutzstaffel (SS) officer. You need to study the underground passes in Berlin. They will come in handy. And one last thing. Try to get out of the tunnels, be in the open, when the timer says it's time to come back. The pressure created through warping of space-time underground can bring down the tunnel system, resulting in a collapse.'

Now Steve, sitting nervously hours before carrying out the mission, was thinking of the unknown territory he was going to enter. The chances of success of the mission were naturally low, as there were many things that could go wrong. He could get crushed under sheer pressure of gravity while transiting, or get captured by the Red Army, he may even lose the artifact by getting the timing of retrieval wrong. Steve took a deep breath and tried not to overthink things.

The speakers in the chamber came to life. 'Now listen, Steve, time passes differently in the past and present. In short, a day in the past would mean only a few seconds here in the present. In here, we would be expecting your arrival almost as soon as you leave,' Nidhi explained as Steve nodded.

Steve was wearing a Schutzstaffel (SS) uniform; the SS was an elite unit created specifically to guard Hitler. The uniform was a little tight around his chest, and had weird, boxy shoulders that made his hand movements slightly restricted. However, it looked as authentic as any fabric from the 1940s. There was an electronic gadget wrapped around his wrist. As soon as the touchdown would take place, the timer would flash the time left in portal reopening. Whether he wanted it or not, he would be transported back whenever time ran out in the watch.

The speakers came to life again. 'Are you ready, Steve?' Nidhi asked. Steve gave a thumbs up. 'All right. Here we go!'

A computer-generated recording now spoke from the speakers inside the chamber. *'The Warping begins in T minus 20 seconds. T minus 19 … T-minus 18 … Positrons Initiated … T minus 17 … T minus 16 … Wavelengths Adjusted … T-minus 15 … T minus 14 … T minus 13 ... Propulsion System Optimized … T minus 12 ... T minus 11 … Coordinates Adjusted ... T minus 10 … Time Dilation Initiated.'*

Six curved nine-inch metallic pillars were rotating fast around Steve. He could feel the vibrations within the chamber, possibly the application of huge amounts for energy in a few seconds. Quantum fluctuations created ripples in the space-time fabric, slowly joining two ends of the universe through a narrow bridge. Steve was getting ready for the imminent quantum leap.

Fluctuations stable … T minus 7 … Charge Within Range … T minus 6 … T minus 5 … Connection established … T minus 4 … T minus 3 … Chronodomes Open … T minus 2 … T minus 1

A giant void was created within the chamber. The rim of the void was expanding exponentially, while the insides of the void kept deepening. The void wasn't entirely stable at first and kept wobbling, until it stabilized to its place as if it was anchored. The vibrations within the chamber slowly died and Steve saw the rim of the void large enough for him to enter. He gave a last look at Dr Gilbert and Nidhi. Steve gave a faint nod and entered the void.

He disappeared into an unknown world as the void faded in front of their eyes.

A Stitch in Time

PART II

The hands of the *Führer* were trembling as Berlin crumbled under bombs, fire and smoke. The Wehrmacht defence lines were leaking Soviet Soldiers, which now numbered 2.5 million, currently heading towards the last bastion in Germany, the Reich Chancellery. Hundreds of teenagers had been hurriedly recruited to defend the city against the advancing Red Army, but Hitler knew it was a lost cause.

Now, sitting in the map room of the Reich Chancellery, the newly married dictator of Germany was lost in his thoughts even as shells rained down and walls shook. Some hours ago, Joseph Goebbels had delivered the grim news of the execution of Mussolini and his mistress in Italy. Hitler knew a similar fate awaited him if he surrendered to the invading allies. The news had steeled his resolve to take his own life. Being 'found dead' would be the ultimate victory of Hitler over the bloodthirsty Allies.

Marrying his long-time love, Eva Braun, hours before deciding to end their lives, was a decision that had given him bliss and delight in these final unsettling moments. 'It had been a difficult life, and you made it worth living,' Hitler admitted to Eva as another shell fell just yards away from the Chancellery, shattering some glass windows. Hitler instructed his staff to prepare for the end.

Hitler and his wife congratulated and shook hands with each and every member of the staff, thanking them for their exceptional service. The Schutzstaffel bodyguards had their own instructions as they marched to Hitler's personal office and started burning any document they could lay their hands on. The sun was setting on Nazi Germany, slowly but surely. And the Reich Chancellery was preparing to stretch the final moment as far as possible. The Nazi resistance was still active to thwart the Soviet conquest of their last bastion.

Martin Bormann, the private secretary, stepped in at that moment and whispered something, to which Hitler listened intently and nodded with his eyes closed. Adhering to his advice, Hitler whistled and his German Shepherd dog, Blondi, came running towards him from his study room. He ruffled the dog's head and she stared at him with its tongue hanging out and tail wagging. Looking at Bormann, Hitler gestured with his hands to proceed. He was handed a box, enclosed in which was a cyanide capsule. Hitler inserted one capsule in Blondi's food bowl, and the pet, who had been hungry for almost a day, leapt at it.

Blondi was playing and running around in the map room even moments after finishing his bowl. For a moment it seemed that the cyanide may have had no effect whatsoever on the dog. She looked perfectly fine, and extremely energetic. Everyone fixed their eyes silently on Blondi, as she moved happily from one corner of the map room to another.

And then she halted suddenly and sat on the ground. Whatever energy Blondi was displaying earlier, it seemed like it had been dissipated. The moans began exactly on the seventh minute of her swallowing the capsule and was now writhing in pain, struggling to breathe on the floor. Everyone looked on in dismay; the creature's life hung on by a thread that could snap at any moment.

Even Eva Braun had tears in her eyes, waiting for Hitler to go and pacify it. But the Führer stood there coldly as life gradually exited from Blondi's body.

And then the struggle stopped abruptly and she lay still on the floor.

***

Steve woke up dizzy in the Central Berlin Area, in a pit, created due to the pressure of inter-dimensional travel. It took some time to adjust for Steve's vision to adjust but as he looked around, the first sound he heard was of people shrieking. The people were running with their families, deserting their homes as smoke, bullets and blasts filled the skies.

A huge wave of crowd was sprinting away from the south-west direction of the Reich Chancellery where a fresh shell had dropped. Steve recognized at once that he was currently on Voss Strasse 1 street, a wide pathway that was newly constructed to make way for Reich Chancellery building. The street housed the administrative buildings that ran Berlin in the 1940s. The Justice Ministry of the Third Reich was a case in point. The greenish-white buildings on both sides of the street, along with dozens of Volkswagen Beetle in line, gave a vibrant view to the scenery. However, the absence of people made it look eerie to Steve. But not for long.

On the southern bend of the road, Steve could see the wave of frightened German citizens running for their lives. They seemed to be coming from the direction of the Bank of Delbrück, Schickler & Co. The distant noises of gunshots had filled the entire vicinity, with occasional tremors from V1 bombs. *The Red Army is near,* Steve thought as he looked at the timer on his wrist. He had just 2 hours and 58 minutes to complete the mission, after which the portal would open again to take him back.

The dizziness from space-time travel had messed up Steve's breathing patterns and heart rate. The brain fade lasted for some moments as Steve took a few deep breaths to stabilize himself. As his body adjusted to the natural rhythm, Steve closed his eyes to remember the underground plans of the Chancellery; he had memorized it during the operation training. *Tiergarten*, Steve recalled as he started sprinting.

Steve's Shutzstaffel uniform had started attracting attention among the soldiers who saluted him, as they ran to form defense lines to protect the Reich Chancellery from the Red Army's advance. 'Sieg Heil,' they shouted, with their right arm raised, to show their solidarity with the Führer even in these final moments of the long and tiring war. Steve could never understand the intoxicating effect Hitler had on the German youth. *It couldn't have been that difficult to see his madness,* Steve had often thought while studying history in high school, back in Kansas.

He dashed out of the Central Berlin Area and towards the lush green public gardens in the western part of the city. The gardens were bordered by River Spree from the Northern and Western side, making eastern Brandenburg Gate the fastest way to enter Tiergarten. The background echoed with sounds of M1 8-inch Howitzers and 155 mm shell blasts as Steve sprinted past Straße des 17. Juni – the principal road to Brandenburg Gate. Even in the middle of a world war, Berlin looked picturesque and serene to Steve.

He knew that the incredibly beautiful Brandenburg Gate – the symbol of unity and peace – would be severely damaged in some hours due to constant bombing of the whole area by the Soviets. It was too bad that he had no time to admire this architectural marvel.

Going at a steady speed, he passed through the ruins of Potsdamer Platz and at one point he saw a Red Army truck in the area already occupied by Soviets, distributing soup and bread to civilians who decided to remain in the city. Steve looked at the timer on his wrist – 2 hours and 41 minutes. He hurried onwards, the entry to Tiergarten was within his sight. He increased his pace slightly, knowing that he would run out of breath pretty soon.

The area around Brandenburg Gate, famous for barbecues and football in the evening back in 1945, was now completely deserted. His rapid footsteps were echoing throughout the area as he entered the gate and stepped inside Tiergarten. Steve had no time to go through the cemented path forged for the joggers and brisk walkers, as he scuttled over the trimmed grass to reach the 'Neue Partie' pond in the park.

While zipping past Großer Stern and the Berlin Zoological Gardens, he realized that he was sweating profusely. And then he slowed down as he could see the pond around 200 metres away from his reach. The pond, tucked away in the north-east corner of the garden, had been famous for ice skating during snowfall in December.

Amidst the eerie silence all across the park, with occasional faint noises of blasts in the background, Steve stopped to catch some breath only to briskly walk towards the pond and analyse whether he was being watched by someone. Satisfied that he was the only one, he stepped on the narrow path just before the pond, hidden from plain sight due to thick autumn orange bushes and wide tree trunks.

The path became narrower and darker as Steve progressed in a crouched position. Leaves ruffled and and branches shook as the path became cramped and progression became difficult. And then he found it … a metal gate with a wheel lock on it. Steve turned the jammed wheel clockwise, and the gate cranked open, only to show a dark, cold tunnel behind it. Lighting the electric torch, Steve entered the tunnel.

***

'Commander Heinz Krüger notified me that the ammunition was running out, Führer,' Goebbels informed. 'We barely have 12 hours of ammunition left.'

Hitler nodded slowly in response. From the glass windows of

the Reich Chancellery, he could see that the Red Army was just 300 metres away. *They are advancing at a good pace*, he thought. At that moment, Hitler was flushed with regret for planning Operation Barbossa, four years ago, to invade Russia.

It was now time for Heinz Linge, who was Hitler's valet, to lead the party of four towards the Führerbunker. These included Hitler, Eva, Joseph and Magda Goebbels. They were marching through the cold tunnels, lit with artificial lights and well plastered walls. The bunker was constructed between 1935 and 1944, consisting of two connected shelters. One was on the same level as the tunnel, while the other one was further below. The latter belonged to the Führer and Eva, and the couple shifted into it to spend their last moments with each other. There was another chamber, further down the tunnels, which housed Hitler's priceless personal art collection.

The floor of the bunker was covered with lavish carpets and colorful rugs, brought from Lebanon and Persia. Some famous artwork covered the walls, including the Führer's favourite painting of *Fredrick the Great*. The Goebbels situated themselves in the other shelter, also spending their final moments together. Later, Heinz Linge made sure six children of the Goebbels joined them in their bunker to meet their ultimate fate.

'I wish we had more time together as a married couple. Some time away at our place in Bogenhausen,' Eva confessed as she looked at the small case containing the cyanide capsule.

'Obersalzberg,' her husband replied. 'That's where I should've taken you, if only it happened like I believed it would.' Hitler looked pale and ghostly mainly because of the opioids he had been taking since the war went out of his control. He couldn't understand how and when, even after his meticulous planning, the momentum of the war shifted towards his enemies.

Both smiled and kissed briefly. Eva had one last glance at her love, and then closed her eyes to swallow the capsule. And she did. It had an immediate effect on her. Her breathing became difficult as her insides gave away. White froth spouted from her mouth, and she struggled to speak. It was like she was trying to say 'help', but no amount of aid, not even divine intervention, could save her now. Hitler stared at the terrifying sight, refusing to take his eyes off from what was happening. After a wave of painful spasms that took over her body, she was finally still.

Hitler looked at the *Luger P08 pistol* that he now held in his hands. Eva was truly gone, and it was now his turn to take his own life. But Hitler never intended to finish himself off. It was an elaborate lie so that people around him … his loved ones … would feel encouraged to do the same. As far as the Führer was concerned, he had made arrangements for another way out.

'Adolf Hitler cannot kill himself … He is not hopeless like the rest of the people. He rises and conquers,' he murmured to himself. The Führer threw away the pistol. He didn't need it. Now that all his loved ones were gone, he could unburden himself from the emotional baggage and carry out his plan … the plan to flee from Berlin. The journey ahead needed grit and utmost secrecy, something that wasn't possible with Eva and Goebbels by his side.

I will form the Third Reich again. These fascinating tunnels don't only lead to Führerbunker ... they also lead to the Central Berlin Area … to Tiergarten, Hitler determined.

The Führer waited for another knock from the SS officers, who would lead him out of the tunnels. *Rattenlinien* was a system of escape routes, developed for Nazi High Command, to Latin America, in case Germany lost the war. The Germany-Spain-Argentina was the route that Hiler now banked upon to survive the horrendous aftermath of this war.

***

The artificial lights were lighting the tunnel now, so Steve didn't need his electric torch. He was now treading slowly over the metallic path as every step was creating an echo, which could give away his position to someone standing far inside the tunnel. As

Steve walked about a hundred yards or so, the tunnel divided itself into two paths, but Steve had no confusion about which path to take. *The eastern route will lead to Führerbunker,* he recalled.

Steve reminded himself that he must not interfere in any of the events and retrieve the manuscript without being seen by anyone. *A tiny interaction with someone from history can have a butterfly effect on the larger outcome of history,* Dr Gilbert had said during his training. The best-case scenario would be to retrieve the document without anyone seeing him, and that meant exercising extreme caution every step of the way. He checked his watch, and it flashed 1 hour and 30 minutes remaining.

And then, Steve heard a gunshot. He could swear it was a gunshot, coming from only a few yards away from him. Almost in a crouching position, Steve managed to take a peek at what was happening. There were footsteps approaching, it seemed like two men. The echo sounds of their steps spread through the tunnel, as Steve saw that the men were carrying something. The tunnels weren't completely devoid of soldiers after all. The bad lighting in the tunnels was his only ally now.

As Steve looked closely, he saw two Shutzstaffel soldiers were carrying a dead body with a gunshot wound in the head. Since it was a well-lit part of the tunnel, Steve could see the moustache and hairstyle. Hitler. Was he dead already? Steve glanced at his timer, something was off. Hitler was found dead, along with his wife, inside the Führerbunker, not the tunnels. *So why was he being carried like a roadside goon?* Steve wondered as he hid himself in a dark corner of the tunnel. Looking closer, he realized that the hairdo was done rather badly. The features didn't match exactly that of Hitler's either.

And then it hit him. There was only one explanation that made sense: this had to be the body double of Hitler. The revelation completely stupefied Steve. So if his dead body was a fake, then what happened to the real Hitler? Did he escape? Steve was on the verge of uncovering the greatest lie told in modern history.

After waiting for a few moments to let these soldiers pass, Steve began to turn towards the art collection chamber. *The coast is clear,* Steve assured himself as he got up to take a step forward when a cold metal touched the back of his head and an uncanny feeling overwhelmed him.

'Move one inch and I will fry your brain with one shot,' the voice behind him warned in German. Steve quietly lifted both his hands in the air. His plan of going unnoticed and accomplishing the mission fell flat at that exact moment.

'Are you Russian?' the voice asked again, with more aggression in the tone this time. It was certain that he was determined to shoot as soon as he got the information he needed.

Steve nodded without looking behind and uttering a word.

'What are you spying on?' he asked, putting more pressure on the pistol's barrel. 'How did you reach here—?'

But the speaker was cut short as Steve suddenly turned, grabbed the wrist of his adversary and raised it towards the tunnel's ceiling swiftly. The man's hand crashed on the low ceiling of the tunnel and the pistol dropped to the floor. The metal clanking reverberated through the tunnel. As light fell on both of them, Steve realized his adversary was the same height as him, blonde haired and pale.

Before the German could respond to what had happened, Steve rammed his knee into his adversary's torso and punched his throat. The sudden attack immediately injured his pharynx. There was no chance for retaliation. The adversary fell down in shock, neither able to scream nor breathe. Steve checked his pulse ... he was alive. This was good news. But Steve had now rendezvoused with a human from the past. This was bad news.

He stood at ease for a few moments, trying to catch his breath. He dusted off his uniform as his heart rate came down to normal. *Everything is going as planned,* he assured himself again.

Just as Steve was about to turn, there came a sudden blow to his head. He fell to the floor in much the same manner as his adversary, unconscious.

***

After what seemed like an eternity, someone finally knocked on the Führer's chamber door.

'You are late!' Hitler snapped as he opened the door. The four SS guards, who were led by his private secretary, could see that Hitler was frustrated.

"We experienced a slight interference,' Martin Bormann answered, gesturing to two unconscious bodies. One was the Führer's body double, which was supposed to be in this room to replace him. But the other body confused Hitler.

'He was found spying in these tunnels, probably a Russian,' Bormann explained, glancing at Eva Braun's body, which was lying prone on the floor. The once-beautiful photographer looked horrible – her disarrayed hair, dried lips and cold, white skin made for a ghostly sight.

Two of the Shutzstaffel soldiers carefully placed Hitler's double on the floor. Everyone knew their roles now. Three Shutzstaffel soldiers would stay here and burn away everything, including the Hitler's and Goebbles' family chambers, along with the private art collection.

Meanwhile, Hitler, Bormann and one Shutzstaffel soldier would escape through the tunnels, towards Tiergarten. The arrangements had already been made for Hitler's transit to Barcelona, by the Sicherheitsdienst, the Nazi Secret Service. The escape plan was made by Hitler and Bormann a fortnight ago and finally, it was time to make it all happen.

'Now what should we do with this Russian spy?' Bormann asked Hitler, who seemed pretty disinterested in him.

'We must find out how he entered these tunnels,' one of the Shutzstaffel Officers spoke. 'I can extract that information in ten minutes.' He looked at the Fuhrer, trying to prove his loyalty even in these uncertain times.

'He looks like an American to me,' Hitler retorted as he glanced at the unconscious spy. 'Shoot the bastard and throw him in some corner. I don't have time for this.' He put on his overcoat and exited the shelter. He had other priorities to see to. *It's about time,* he thought as he left with Bormann and a Shutzstaffel soldier. The three remaining soldiers were left in the bunkers to finish off their duties.

Nobody saw Steve sliding Hitler's pen off his study table while acting to be unconscious. He had gained his senses while the Germans were talking, but he'd kept his eyes closed to buy time. He glanced at his timer, which was perfectly hidden under his sleeve, and noticed that he had 35 minutes left until the portal's reopening. He had to hurry up.

However, the mission had gone horribly wrong for him. As much as he'd planned to stay away from the major events, he had unfortunately landed right in the middle of them. Steve had not only been in the same room with Hitler, but also his private secretary, possibly Bormann. Now he could only hope that he hadn't changed the events too much.

One of the Shutzstaffel soldiers took out his *Walther P.38 Pistol* from the holster and aimed at Steve's body lying on the floor. The other two soldiers were staring out of the tunnels to see if the coast was clear. He loaded the gun and the sound of its recoil was the signal that Steve was waiting for. Time slowed down for him immensely as he prepared himself for the assault.

Within seconds, Steve had opened his eyes and kicked the knee joint of the soldier, who lost his balance and crashed to the floor. With his right hand, Steve rammed the sharp point of Hitler's pen in the soldier's throat and with left hand he grabbed the gun from his hand. The two soldiers who were keeping a lookout had no time to react, as Steve shot them both instantly. It took all of four seconds, three men were dead on the floor.

It's time to finish this mission and leave, Steve thought as he ran towards the chamber that housed Hitler's art collection. There was an eerie silence in the tunnel, and it looked rather frightening. The dark and the cold made the whole place feel desolate. However, these concerns were too minor to perturb Steve.

Next to Hitler's chamber was the room Steve was looking for. But try as he might, the door wouldn't budge. It seemed that the door handle was jammed.

Time was running out for Steve, and he had to take extreme measures. Three shots from the *Walther P.38 Pistol* at the door's lock made such a racket that the sound reverberated through the tunnel. But he couldn't be bothered about noise now, he was literally racing against the time. With one big push using his right shoulder, the door banged open and crashed on the inner wall.

As Steve entered the chamber, the first things he saw were European classical paintings stacked on top of each other. The famous painting of *The Astronome*r was resting quietly on the floor. Another famous work by Hans Makart called *The Plague* in Florence hung on one of the walls of the chamber.

There were sculptures too that stood in the corner watching Steve intently. Prominent among them was *Madonna of Bruges* by Michelangelo. Other sculptures by famous artists like Arno Breker and Josef Thorak were also among the collection. Along with it, there were some Japanese swords that ranged from early 16th to late 18th century, and some Mesoamerican artwork from the pre-Columbian era.

Steve stood aghast, looking at the huge compendium of art. More than a chamber, it was a museum housing art worth millions of dollars. The worst thing was that most of it was destined to turn into ashes in some hours. *I wish I could take all of them,* he thought as he felt bad about leaving it all behind.

In one corner, there were laminated papers and books, stacked neatly on a table. *This has to be it,* Steve thought and leapt at it.

The stack included the 1918 Armistice of Compiègne, which

marked Germany's surrender to Allies during World War I. As Steve went through the stack, he also came across a handwritten letter by Charles Darwin to Alfred Russel Wallace, sometime in 1858. His eyes also fell on the lost manuscript of Margaret Fuller's history of the 1849 Roman Republic and poems by William Blake.

And then there it was ... precisely the thing he had been looking for, kept right in the middle of the stack. The handwritten manuscript by Albert Einstein stared back at him. It was of the size of a notebook, in which there were handwritten equations. Steve extracted the manuscript and safely placed it inside his uniform, clasping it to his chest.

Time to get the hell out of here, Steve thought as his timer informed him he had 12 minutes to go before the portal reopened.

***

The tunnels became darker and colder as Hitler and Bormann proceeded. One Shutzstaffen soldier with them was there to make sure the Führer reached the destination safely. The noises of shells and howitzers were going on in the background and insides of the tunnel were faintly shaking as well. The artificial lighting fitted across tunnels, showed the way as Bormann's eyes were fixed on a single ray of light at the end of the tunnel.

Hitler clearly remembered the day he'd ordered the construction of an extensive underground pathway in the late 1930s, when the threat of air raids from the Allies became closer to reality. Goebbels lobbied for the construction company Hochtief, which had the most impressive designs for Führerbunker, to get the contract to develop these tunnels under Reich Chancellery. It was only in late 1943 that the underground chambers were finally developed, protected by approximately 13 feet of concrete. The exits led into the main buildings, as well as an emergency exit up to the garden, which these three men were about to take.

Bormann had arranged everything for the Führer in such a

discreet manner that even Goebbels had had no inclination about the escape. All of them had made the sacrifices necessary to make the suicide look authentic for Hitler. *My lovely Eva,* thought Hitler, remembering her still body. However, not a single shred of guilt surfaced in Hitler's mind. His singular objective was propelling him forwards.

Hitler knew the road ahead was difficult and surely, intense grit and determination was needed to resurrect the Third Reich. The reassembling of the Third Reich needed sacrifices and having Eva by his side made Hitler weak. *Your sacrifice won't go to waste, my love,* thought Hitler as the faint natural light at the end of the tunnel was becoming visible.

Bormann suddenly stopped walking. There was an echo in the tunnels – a repeating sound that was becoming louder each second.

'Somebody is following us!' he said as the other two stopped. Hitler stood still, listening intently to the faint noise of rhythmic footsteps, as if someone was running towards them.

Hitler looked at the Shutzstaffen soldier and signalled him to take care of this incoming nuisance. The soldier nodded, removed his Luger pistol from its holster and aimed it in the direction of the sound. The other two men stood behind to look out for the mystery man.

The steps became louder as the soldier loaded his gun. Everything stood still for a moment, the darkness adding to the mystery. In the dark, he shot one bullet a bit too early in his nervousness as he sensed someone's presence. But the bullet ricocheted in the tunnel, with sparks flying as the bullet hit the metal. And then there was silence.

'We should move,' the soldier informed Bormann, advising him to continue the journey. And then out of nowhere came a kick that sent the soldier crashing against the tunnel wall. Before he could retaliate, a punch on his face knocked him unconscious. As the artificial light fell on him, Bormann realized that it was the Russian spy again. He had been shot on the left shoulder, and blood was gushing out of the fresh wound.

The bullet wound was excruciating for Steve, but the pain subsided when he realized that Hitler had indeed safely escaped, fooling the whole world. *And they thought he shot himself.* So Dr Gilbert was wrong, Hitler did escape. Disappeared into thin air. But where? How did a personality so famous just vanish?

As much as Steve tried to avoid running into major events that shaped world history, he was obviously failing. *Landing back into the soup,* he thought. Not one bullet grazed him while serving in Kandahar, and here he was, in a simple extract-and-run mission, and he had been shot. *Crazy!*

Steve had only one option left right now, to get back to the surface in the remaining two minutes. He shouldn't interact with any of these historical figures more than he already had. He must sprint out of here.

Steve was still lost in these thoughts when Bormann came forward, suddenly in attack mode, and threw a punch. But Steve, anticipating an attack, crouched in time and Bormann missed him by a foot. A left jab on Bormann's abdomen was enough to neutralize him. He fell down on his knees, writhing in pain, but not unconscious.

Steve looked at his timer. *Only ninety seconds left,* he thought. He got on his feet, only to find the Führer holding *Mauser C96,* which he had removed from his ankle holster.

'Your little game ends here!' Hitler warned, pointing his gun straight at the spy.

'You don't know what this is,' Steve replied in German. 'I mean no harm. Just let me pass.' He slowly extended both his hands forward, gesturing to him to calm down.

Thirty seconds left!

After a brief moment of silence, Hitler pulled the trigger. The poor lighting didn't give him a clear view, but he shot the bullet nonetheless. The bullet missed Steve's hip by mere inches, and before Hitler could pull the trigger again, Steve had already leapt at him.

Irritated and tired, Steve now held Hitler by his collar, and banged his back on the cemented wall of the tunnel. It was easy to overpower him because of his short height. The man about whom Steve had read extensively in school, and watched numerous Hollywood films made on his life, was now breathing inches away from him.

'Get your filthy hands off me, you American!' Hitler shouted in volcanic rage. He had a firm grasp, which illustrated his military background. A scuffle ensued between them, even as minutes continued to tick away for Steve.

And that's when the vibrations started. Slow at first, and then the whole tunnel trembled, with repeated waves.

Steve looked at the timer. *His time was up!*

At first, Hitler thought the vibrations were due to howitzers employed by the Red Army above. But then the tremors felt very close ... and destabilizing. The faint outline of a bubble started to appear, and the Führer shrieked in horror. 'What is happening?' he asked Steve.

Meanwhile, Steve stood there frozen, not comprehending what he could possibly do. The void, unstable at first but now completely firm, eclipsed both men inside it. Steve tried to push Hitler out of the bubble, but the force was too strong to let anyone leave. There were faint sparks as the void interfered with the electricity inside the tunnel. The lights began to go on and off repeatedly, giving a horrifying effect.

Steve knew that nothing could be done now. It was time to get back. He clutched the manuscript tightly to his chest as the vibrations intensified even further..

Bormann came into his senses as the clamour from the tremors and lightning filled the tunnel. *What the hell is this?* Petrified to his core, he tried standing up. It was one of the last few moments of the Führer in his present, as he was about to end up far away in future. The pressure inside the void made him faint.

And then, the void disappeared in front of Bormann. He

couldn't believe his eyes. *The Führer vanished into thin air? What is this sorcery?* He was unable to believe what he had just witnessed. At that moment, the tremors intensified. Bormann didn't have much time. The pressure from the warping of space-time destabilized the tunnel's equilibrium and it was about to collapse. The vibrations became more intense each second. Bormann dashed towards the Tiergarten exit, hoping to make it in time.

***

Back in the control room of IAU, everyone waited with knots in their stomach. Steve had stepped into the void, just a few seconds ago. The fact that it was his first survey mission had kept everyone on their toes. Everyone across the hall was busy in conversation. Some stared blankly at the ceiling, but at the back of all their minds was Steve's fate. They were about to find out whether the mission, on which they had spent many a day and night, had been fruitful.

He should be here any minute now, Nidhi thought as she counted the seconds. With every passing moment, she was passing through a wave of hope that ended with despair. *What if he has lost his timer? Or worse, what if he got shot and returned a dead man?* She took a deep breath and started counting backwards to deal with the rising anxiety within her.

Dr Gilbert was more adept at seeing the glass half full. He knew Steve would pull through. The reason was simple – he had been in more hostile circumstances than 1945. Serving in Afghanistan was no joke, and so, Dr Gilbert wasn't ready to believe that the man would succumb to an eighty-year-old redundant Nazi force.

'We have started receiving data,' the lead researcher announced on microphone as the room lit up again. This meant that warping of space-time had begun on the other side. Everyone in the room had their eyes intently fixed on the empty space behind the glass walls.

And then, the six nine-inch metallic pillars suddenly started moving, slowly at first and then adding pace with each passing moment. It was preparing itself to transfer matter across two time periods. The pressure inside the chamber slowly adjusted itself. The first readings indicated no complications in the process.

'Here we go,' Nidhi said to Dr Gilbert, without taking her eyes off the glass wall, 'This is the moment of truth.'

The metallic pillars were now at their maximum speed. The lightning had begun making noise as the faint outline of the void appeared. Everyone in the hall extended their torso out of the railing a bit further to get a clear glimpse of what lay ahead. The vibrations began as matter was finally transferred from one moment in time to another.

And then, the metallic pillars started losing velocity, and the noise started to go down. The lightning and vibrations shuddered to a stop as everyone gasped at the scene in front of them. As she saw the two figures in the chamber, Nidhi shrieked in horror.

Steve, with his bleeding shoulder, stood in front. He looked tired and exhausted to an extreme degree. Next to him, lying still on the floor, was Adolf Hitler, unconscious due the effects of the space-time warping and wormhole travel.

The dictator had just travelled to the next century, completely erased from 1945, as he opened his eyes to see people staring at him as if he were a zoo animal.

The Eternal Gene

The Sheraton New York Times Square Hotel had seen quite a pandemonium today. A huge number of people thronged to the concourse to attend an event, having waded through peak Manhattan traffic, even though it had limited seating. No, it wasn't a Hollywood celebrity for whom an army of fans would line up around the block. It wasn't even a sports personality, or an Olympic sensation, who had such a commotion created for them. Today's guest was a rarity – a celebrated scientist who had authored an incredibly popular book.

The large convention hall of the Sheraton, with a capacity of nearly six hundred people, welcomed the esteemed speaker this evening – Dr Howard Becker. A biologist by profession, Dr Howard Becker had created quite an uproar, not just in the scientific community but also well beyond, with his claims in his new book, *The Eternal Gene*. For the past few weeks, he had been on a press tour all around the world, but it was in New York's Liberty Hall that he got the first chance to discuss the theories in the book in detail.

On a wide stage, with a microphone-installed lectern, Howard addressed his audience. The room was dark and the only light came from a large LED screen behind him and a well-lit walking path cutting fifteen rows in half. The audience listened intently to what the sensational author had to say.

'So that's how microbiologists around the world have gotten really interested in this tiny fresh-water polyp called Hydra.' Howard said, addressing the people. 'Its unique abilities had been a subject of discussion for the early twentieth century, but its unparalleled potential has become a point of scrutiny only recently.'

Howard was a lean statured, forty-two-year-old man, with dark brown wavy hair and a visible jaw along with a slight hint of a chin. The humidity in the room coupled with his dark brown worsted wool suit, was enough to make him perspire. On the screen behind him, a giant hydra, with its moving tentacles, was swimming deep inside a freshwater lake. Howard continued.

'So what rare potential has the hydra shown to the scientific world? Is it the fastest swimmer in the water? No, it isn't. Is it the fiercest predator in its habitat? Not in a million years. Then what is it that makes this 30 mm organism an exceptional one? Any guesses?'

He looked around, waiting for an answer. But it was only silence and awe that he got from the audience.

Howard broke the suspense, 'The hydra is eternal ... an immortal being that doesn't age a day after attaining maturity. Understanding how it does that forms the basis of our knowledge of genetics as a whole. In the last fifteen years, not many breakthroughs have happened that could've unlocked the secrets of indestructibility that this organism showcases. But our recent scientific endeavours have managed to give us some answers that can satisfy our curiosity, for now. And those answers are what I've managed to compress in this book, *The Eternal Gene.*' On the screen came the image of his book, with a double helix structure on the front cover.

The lecture went on for another hour, at the end of which Howard's ardent fans all stood up, clapping and cheering. It was his controversial scientific theories and avant-garde predictions that tickled the mass's brains, making him quite a sensation.

After the speech, a book signing event was scheduled by his publishers in the Sheraton's basement. Becker, seated on a revolving chair behind a heavy wooden table, spent the latter part of the evening signing copies of his book for his readers. The room was full of people queuing up to get pages signed and talk to the author.

Howard just couldn't understand the euphoria around him. *My writing satisfies the curiosity of a certain section of the population, but I just can't put my finger on what exactly tickles them,* he told his wife Caroline once. Meanwhile, his wife would laugh reading all the bizarre fan mail that he got on a daily basis. *Your fans are nothing but high-school nerds,* she would tease him occasionally.

At the book signing event, he met readers from South-East Asia, Japan, Ukraine, Poland, Malaysia – from all over the world, really – who had come especially to listen to him today. During the interaction with Howard, most of his readers would confess that his books had changed their perspective towards science and made it more palatable for them. In his last book, which eventually became a New York Times bestseller for nine weeks straight, Becker talked about the future of *Homo Sapiens* as a species in a world full of virtual reality.

Nearly two hours of constant signing, congratulatory wishes and compliments on his scientific endeavours made him realize how hard it was to keep a smile on his face for so long. His cheeks were aching now. The constant flashing of cameras had already temporarily blinded him. The commotion around him had begun to make him slightly claustrophobic.

He was in the middle of attending to one of his readers when two men cut the queue and walked right up to him. Howard noted their natural sense of authority as one of them leaned towards Howard to whisper something in his ear. He turned to hear what they had to say.

'Do you have a place where we can talk, Dr Becker?' one of them asked Howard. He looked like a government agent in his thick black suit. *Maybe they want selfies,* Howard thought but immediately realized that that wasn't the case.

'And who are you people?' he asked while he continued to sign a copy of his book for an eagerly awaiting fan.

'We are from the government, Dr Becker ... from the Office of Scientific Studies,' the other agent spoke now. He looked quite a bit younger than his bald partner and was similarly dressed. His companion turned towards the people waiting for their turn and announced with an air of nonchalance, 'The book signing event will not proceed any further. Thank you all for coming.'

The people were miffed. Some of them started murmuring amongst themselves while others protested. Howard heard a woman arguing with the agents in Italian. The bald agent handled the disagreements that ensued effortlessly, and eventually the crowd started thinning. The bald agent pushed out the stubborn stragglers and emptied the whole room in no time.

Howard had no idea what was going on, he simply watched as the crowd started thinning. Only three men were left in the basement now, apart from the marketing agent, who seemed helpless amidst the commotion but was insistent on staying next to Howard. No amount of threatening would make her leave. The two agents dragged steel chairs and sat opposite Howard at the table.

'Dr Becker, for your book, *The Eternal Gene,* what is the source material you used to support your claims regarding superhumans?' asked the bald agent bluntly. The nature of the question startled Howard, as he failed to understand why the government was interested in his book.

The younger agent, probably in his late twenties, was sitting silently and observing Howard. He had a lean physique and dark brown hair that was combed back. There was a hard-to-miss mole on the left side of his neck. His scrutinizing stare annoyed Howard a bit.

'It is just a statistical study, based on the intensity of genetic drift. The effects I've mentioned in the book are yet to be seen, at least in the human race,' Howard replied calmly, but the agent was already prepared to shoot another question.

'But the scientific concepts relating to static ageing couldn't have come without observing or experimenting on someone.' The agent was looking directly at Howard, as if trying to read his thoughts and guage what he was feeling.

'I don't think people like these exist, sir. As you can see it is just a prediction based on probabilities. Individuals with these chromosomal anomalies can't be there in the real world, or we would have known about them,' Howard replied, now stressing his point. His tone had suddenly become defensive, as if he was standing in a federal court proving that he isn't guilty.

'The scientific phenomena you've discussed in this book around cell renewal and static maturity has attracted our attention. If you are in contact with any person like this, you should inform the government at once to avoid an interference like this from the government, Dr Becker,' the agent said, in a threatening tone this time. It was a tactic used by federal agents to intimidate their suspects into submission, especially when they have nothing concrete to detain them.

'People with static ageing don't exist. It is just ... a theory!' Howard retorted in frustration. His voice was raised now. He couldn't understand why such a simple fact had to be explained repeatedly. It was always annoying when people began to discuss science with him without having a background in the subject.

'Never say never, Dr Becker.' The other agent spoke finally. He seemed to carry a certain cool-headedness and maturity that his companion lacked. 'Well, I think you've made your point pretty clear. Thank you for your time, Dr Becker. Have a nice day.'

Both agents got up from their chairs and took their leave. The basement was suddenly empty, as Howard sat alone for some time not knowing what to make of this conversation.

***

The next couple of weeks were busier for Howard. In recent meetings, the publishing house insisted that Howard increase his visibility across various streaming platforms. Their PR team ensured that Howard was seen collaborating with Instagram influencers including his appearances on numerous YouTube videos and podcasts.

As the book featured on the New York Times bestseller list, Howard was brought on as a guest to talk about his new book on a late night show with Jerry Spencer as host. Being a camera-shy person, Howard had initially refused to feature on the show, but his publisher insisted, since they were looking to tap into a more global audience. Later, it was decided that Howard's appearance would be broadcast live, adding to his dread.

The insides of a TV Studio looked very different from what Howard had imagined. He'd never in a million years thought that such a huge crew worked behind the scenes to make a production like this possible. There were teams of production managers, set designers, lighting technicians, sound engineers and light boys. It was all too overwhelming. There were monolights installed everywhere, to keep the whole set illuminated.

While coming to the studio, Howard was given a set of questions that the host was going to ask him. *So all of the talk shows are actually scripted?* Howard was startled, as he'd always believed that the questions asked to the celebrities were spontaneous. He took a quick glance on all the questions, realizing that he had been answering most of them for weeks now. This put him a little at ease.

Howard arrived on set and shortly after, they went live. The host, Jerry Spencer, introduced him as he came in front of the studio audience amidst loud cheering and applause. He made himself comfortable on the couch and waved at the crowd. Howard had watched the show on Saturday evenings often, and had seen film celebrities, politicians and NBA stars on the very couch he was sitting on. It was surreal to be here.

The drum rolls and jazz continued till the cheering went on, and then slowly faded. Spencer gave a small monologue to open the show and as always, the comedic elements in the monologue made the audience tickle.

The ambience was lively and animated when the interview finally began.

'So, what is the book about Dr Becker?' Spencer asked. He had a long face, curly hair, and a paunch that was well hidden behind the desk, although he was dressed neatly in formals.

'Well, *The Eternal Gene* talks about the variations in average lifespans on an interspecies and intraspecies level. It addresses our long quest to achieve longevity and how science comes into play to make it a reality,' Howard answered, as calmly as ever.

'It won't be incorrect to say that this touches the sensitive topic of *immortality*,' Jerry Spencer said questioningly, picking up the book and inspecting its cover front to back.

'If you want to simplify it, then yes, it does talk about it,' Howard replied. He was resting his left leg over his right, and was at ease with himself at that moment.

'That is a fascinating topic. I believe this hasn't been discussed before in detail.'

'Scientifically, no. But religions around the world have talked a lot about it. Roman and Greek mythologies are cases in point. The folklores in Indian and Chinese traditions have elaborated on immortality also.' As Howard spoke, he found his host nodding at him quite a few times.

'So Dr Becker, which species that you've mentioned in your book have shown near-immortality traits?' Spencer asked, trying to keep the conversation engaging for his audience.

'The freshwater polyps, hydra, has been the only known immortal being. But apart from it, the bowhead whale is seen to survive for 200 years. The Galápagos tortoise have clocked the 400-year mark consistently. So if we take such cases into account, many species on this planet have gone closer to immortality.' Howard was dumbing down the facts to make it palatable for his host and the audience.

'And you linked immortality with humans also?'

'Yes, the last two chapters talk about it. But it was just my calculation. Of course, no proof of this has been found yet,' Becker said, suddenly remembering the conversation that he had with government agents the other day, where he had to reiterate this very point many times.

'How is such an immortal human different from us? Genetically speaking,' Spencer asked, genuinely curious about the contents of the book.

'Well, if I put it into simple terms, the FOXO3A gene, a gene that governs longevity in organisms, would have undergone mutation. The genetic drift, which is a sampling error by DNA, must have affected this gene, and senescence or simply, cell ageing, might not occur in that individual,' Howard said.

There was complete silence on the set, and everyone was listening to Howard intently. He realized he had to explain further, in layman terms this time.

Howard continued, 'The tissue in such an individual would renew itself faster than in regular humans. The individual would definitely show self-healing in the body, the immune system would be trained to resist pandemics such as smallpox and the plague. Their bodies would exhibit rapid blood clotting, auto organic repair and quick-learning antibodies. Such an individual would be humanity's hope for a brighter future. More individuals possessing these abilities would solve most of humanity's current problems.' He saw his host listening keenly to what he had to say. For people, *The Eternal Gene* was less science and more a plot straight out of a science-fiction action flick.

'Problems like what?' Spencer asked. The conversation was going deeper than Howard expected. 'Don't you think people possessing such a huge longevity period would induce population explosion? The resources on these planets would become scarce, resulting in war and destruction,' Spencer was now asking questions he'd been asked for several weeks now.

'You must understand that such kind of a mutation would be a rarity. As rare as one in ten thousand. Having such insignificant numbers of individuals with these abilities would never have any effect on the population.' Howard took a slight pause for people to understand what he had said. 'As far as resources on the planets are concerned, I think we may have a unique opportunity on our hands if we could ever find individuals with a huge longevity period. They can undertake long-term space travels, explore earthlike planets that are light years away and help us expand resources. Another opportunity would be in the field of medicine. We could study their genetic and immune systems and figure out how to fight off cancers, tumours and immune-deficiency syndromes. Chronic diseases could be eliminated.' Howard explained as he already had grappled with questions like these while writing the book. There was a whiff of confidence in his tone, that the interviewer noted.

'One last question, Dr Becker. If a human is known to be immortal, how do you think it will affect the concept of God? Do you think it threatens the existence of religion?' Spencer now treaded dangerous territory. This question wasn't in the list given to Howard some hours ago.

'The existence of a human who is indestructible to the test of time will definitely be compared to God. I believe if we surpass the barrier of immortality, there are no superhuman abilities left for humanity to conquer,' Howard replied as cameras zoomed in on him. 'We can fly already, talk to anybody anywhere on the planet in an instant, lay to ruin any area with advanced weaponry, and if immortality is added to the list … there are no powers left for us to achieve. What else makes God all powerful? I truly believe the faith in God will dwindle as humans become divine.' Howard instantly knew he should've dodged the question.

'All right. Thank you, Dr Becker.' The host turned to the camera. '*The Eternal Gene* is in the bookstores near you and the sales are through the roof. It is hot property these days, so get your copy today!'

***

Howard woke up the next morning to see himself all over the news. He hadn't even got a chance to have his coffee when his cell phone started buzzing without break.

On the early morning news show, *Good Morning America,* an archbishop had spoken about Becker's *disturbing* views on the future of religion. Snippets of Dr Howard Becker answering Spencer's question flooded Instagram, Twitter and Facebook overnight. As more and more people woke up to these clips, a massive wave of negative publicity hit *The Eternal Gene* on Monday.

'Does Dr Becker think humans can take the place of God?' the Archbishop demanded, facing the host and folding both his hands on the table. He was wearing an omophorion, he must have known his garb added weight to the questions he raised. 'What does it mean that the need of God would end in the future? The presence of God gives us hope, endurance and a path through adversity amidst a world full of poverty, hunger and war.' There was a hint of sternness in his tone.

The archbishop took a deep breath. 'Lately, scientists trying to debunk religion has become a trend. Science cannot quantify the pain and suffering in humanity, and the indispensability of God in relieving it. It's high time that the so-called know-it-all personalities understand the function of religion in modern society.' The other guests on the show nodded to show their agreement.

The archbishop's interview sent shockwaves through the print and electronic media. It became the breaking news of the day. He had opened a pandora box of controversies as the news spread like wildfire.

Howard had expected this, but he couldn't quite fathom the quickness of the reaction. When this continued for half a day, his wife, Caroline, hid his cellphone. Caroline was a news presenter and she knew that negative press was sold like hot cakes. Keeping her husband away from this volcano was the only way to handle the situation.

Caroline Becker's job required interviewing film celebrities who come on her show to promote their films. Her own show had recently been greenlit by a prominent news network, promoting her from a weather presenter on the 7 a.m. slot.

She couldn't have been more wrong in assuming that the controversy would die down soon as most scandalous news does. The next day, a lawsuit filed against Howard and the publishing house to ban the book (on the basis that it hurt the sentiments of the Christian community) was breaking news across the channels. Clips of protesters, in many eastern European countries, burning the book publicly and chanting slogans condemning Howard, surfaced on YouTube. The controversy was ballooning every day, and Howard Becker became a name that regularly features in newsrooms across the world.

The book was branded as sacrilegious literature, for it questioned the role of God in the modern world. The idea of immortality in humans was said to be blasphemous. The outrage against the book was now building up, and the danger of vandalism became apparent for the stores that offered copies of it.

The book was cleared out of bookstores in the upcoming weeks. The demand for the book also suddenly arose, as it became a rare piece of literature. However, the news of many governments, especially in France, Australia and India, moving to ban the book, surfaced. The government spokespersons explained that this was done to ensure peace and harmony amongst their nationals.

And then, Howard's own scientific community took sides against the book. Dr Jeremy Drake, a leading anthropologist, had written a long op-ed criticizing not only the book but also

Howard's intentions.

'*The Eternal Gene* is a pseudoscientific study as it uses scientific facts to reach exaggerated results. It has vague and untestable claims that aim at creating a sensation to sell millions of copies. The mythological and philosophical discussions aren't what a scientific study targets. Obscure language and technical jargon has been used to give it a superficial scientific veneer. What *The Eternal Gene* ends up being is science-fiction. This makes Dr Howard Becker not a representative of science but an entertainer.'

The book had made a significant profit for the publishers, but now the dirt had started smearing their reputation. They were initially reluctant to be concerned with the negative publicity, but the controversy refused to die down and had become an international issue. Surely, it was too much of a price to be paid over a single bestselling book. Several corporate meetings and deliberations later, the publishers finally decided to pull the plug on the book.

For Howard, who had by now experienced enough mud-slinging in a matter of weeks, the news of discontinuing production of the book wasn't news at all. Nothing came as a surprise to him. He had seen the controversy expanding rapidly like the universe post Big Bang. *Why did I decide to write this book,* was the only question that bugged him during those sleepless nights.

With regret came deteriorating mental health. Howard started getting less and less social. Even Caroline's repeated efforts to take her husband to movies and dinner dates wouldn't cheer him up one bit. *He is lost somewhere,* she realized when her husband didn't pay attention to her as she talked to him about her office gossip. They would usually drive in silence now if he ever agreed to step out of the house. She would often come home to find him depressed and he would start having food only after staring at his plate for an eternity.

Caroline then decided to sign him up for therapy. His mental health was taking a beating even after the whole controversy related to his book had eventually died down. She saw Howard having second thoughts about every decision now. However, after slight persuasion, he accepted Caroline's idea of therapy, and did attend two or three sessions.

It was around this time that Caroline had to attend a film premier of Robert Downey Jr's latest action flick in Los Angeles. The storyline had been kept under wraps, and there was a frenzy among the fans regarding his comic book superhero portrayal. No way could she send anyone from her team to interview the cast. *It's just four days,* she convinced herself.

She put Mrs Jefferson, their housekeeper, in charge of taking care of her husband. She had made a schedule for Howard to follow, which included his therapy sessions. She contacted Howard's friends and told them to check up on him every evening. She even disabled the house's router, making it harder for Howard to look up news on the internet. Everything that was needed to distract Howard from thinking about his book was arranged by Caroline.

'I will be back on Friday, Howard. Don't do anything stupid,' she warned her husband as she left for the airport.

And then he did something stupid mere hours after Caroline left. He went out of the house, hailed a cab and left. It took half an hour for Mrs Jefferson to realize that Howard was no longer in the house, and she called Caroline as soon as her flight had landed.

'What do you mean Howard left a note?' Caroline asked in frustration as she waited for her luggage at baggage reclaim at Los Angeles International Airport. *This is so Howard,* she thought, annoyed.

'There is a note attached to the fridge magnet, Mrs Becker,' Mrs Jefferson explained in a panicked tone. 'It says "Heading to Tennessee to clear my head."'

***

Tennessee was the place where Howard grew up. During his

formative years, he hardly ever got out of the countryside. He was just seven when his father succumbed to a prolonged neural illness, and his mother single-handedly raised him there. Just on the outskirts of Nashville County, Howard spent his childhood centred around corn and hay farms, along with the ripe, tangy odour of cow manure. He belonged to a family of people who've been farmers for the last seven generations.

But when he graduated from Greenville High School in the nineties, he earned a scholarship and did something unprecedented, – at least as far as his family was concerned – he went to a college and not just any college, it was Columbia University. Since then, he had hardly visited his home in Tennessee for more than two days. All these years of having a thriving career, Howard barely had time to miss his home. However, the past had started to catch up as he started to burn out.

For some time now, Howard had contemplated going back to Tennessee to get away from the frantic New York life. It was all-consuming, and too fast-paced for Howard, who now in his forties, missed the country life. This looked like a perfect time to go off the grid and live a quiet life away from all the clamour.

It took him two hours of flying and then a taxi ride to find his way back to those farm fields and a neighbourhood full of pine, maple and oak trees. His eighty-year-old aunt, who had been sitting in her rocking chair on the porch, overlooking the corn fields, was excited at seeing her nephew back home. She visited Howard's mother, Martha, every weekend as she lived just across the town.

'Martha, look who's here?' she called out loudly, trying to get up. Her painful knees severely restricted her movements.

His mother opened the aluminium mesh door, which made a creaking noise upon opening. She was wearing denim overalls, and a red check shirt along with yellow garden gloves and a farm hat.

'Howard?' his mother said, elated and dumbstruck at the sight of her son. 'Why didn't you tell me you were coming?'

'It wouldn't be much of a surprise, Maa, if I had told you.' Howard smiled and hugged her. She looked fragile, Howard noted her wrinkled neck and hands.

'Where's Caroline?' Martha asked, looking behind Howard to see if she was there.

'She's away for work,' Howard replied, realizing how unchanged his home was. Pretty much everything was in the same place as it had ever been. 'I needed some time away from some stuff that has happened lately at work,' he said, hugging his mother once again.

Meeting up with his family after such a long time was indeed revitalizing for Howard. *This is where I started,* Howard thought, taking his luggage to the room he'd spent his childhood in. The same hand-carved, brown teakwood cupboard, the squeaking wooden floor, the grey panelled curtains, all of it brought back a flood of memories. The room had one more thing that his urban life didn't have – a sprawling view of the giant farmland along with a gravel road cutting through it.

Howard spent the next couple of days helping his mother on the farm and spending quiet evenings chatting with his aunt on the porch. The long strolls across the farm, grocery shopping from the local store and Steve McQueen film marathons with his mom on weekends made him value his childhood more.

Having himself involved in this life helped Howard make peace with what had happened with *The Eternal Gene.* Life had finally slowed down for him. The kind of life he'd always wanted, making eggs and bacon for his family early in the mornings and bathing dalmatian cows at the ranch, was inherently fulfilling for Howard.

'It's like turning back the clock,' he said to Caroline on the phone. She was happy that her husband had finally decided to take a break from his gruelling professional career, but she had started missing him since she got back from Los Angeles. She was still mad at him for leaving abruptly though – an old habit of her husband that she couldn't stand any more.

'When will you be back?' she asked.

But Howard had no answer to this question. That world, that city, had nothing left to offer him. He did miss Caroline and wanted to go back to New York just to be with her, but the idea of being in a city where everybody knew him was repulsive to him at the moment. He knew at some point, he'd have to go back to work. He knew he couldn't just decide to keep living in Nashville. But for him that time wasn't here yet.

On a quiet Sunday noon, Howard joined his mother in clearing out the attic. Termites had wreaked havoc on the antique furniture that had been stowed there for years on end. Some of the boxes hadn't been moved since Howard's father had died. Thick dust had settled on the three-feet cardboard boxes, retro electronic appliances and various antiques.

A Vietnam war veteran, Howard's father, Captain Allen Becker, had been a part of the 4th Infantry Division stationed at Binh Duong Province in 1967–69. The boxes in the attic contained memorabilia of his, along with some personal items that he'd carried with himself.

Howard took out his father's uniform, neatly wrapped in plastic in one of the boxes. He also discovered some framed medals from his training days, a military canteen water bottle and a laminated cutting of the front page of the newspaper *The Evening Star* with an article 'US Quits Vietnam'. Some of the books that his father was reading were stored in another box and it seemed that Captain Allen Becker was a fan of historical fiction.

All the things were removed from those dusty boxes, wiped clean and washed and then finally laid out in the sun to dry. In one of the boxes, Howard had found a framed photograph. It was his father, looking happy in a close-up with his friend. Sitting on a rock, both men were wearing uniforms and must have been either in their late twenties or early thirties. The sharp jaw, protruding Adam's apple, the red cheeks ... everything in the picture pointed towards fearless youth. Military dog tags hung around their necks.

As Howard observed the photograph closely, the earth shook

beneath him. He could swear that the man in the photograph with his father was present at the book signing event at the Sheraton a little more than a month back. *That's the government agent from the Office of Scientific Studies,* Howard reminded himself. He was the younger of the two agents, or so it had seemed. Howard remembered how keen they had been on knowing about the contents of the book and had kept grilling him. *But he was so young, how can it be?* Howard scratched his head, questioning the possibility of it all.

The man in the photograph had the exact same facial features – the squarish jaw, bushy eyebrows, brunette hair and sluggish smile. *How is this possible?* For a moment, Howard thought he was confusing the two persons as one. It was preposterous to think that a man hadn't aged a day for fifty years.

And then, Howard remembered seeing an unusual mole on the left side of his neck. He concentrated hard on the photograph, and there it was! Exactly in the same spot. He felt a sudden headrush and looked for a place to sit. Howard's father would have been eighty, if he'd been alive. *This man still looked young! How can it be?* Howard stressed his mind hard as he rested his forehead on both of his palms.

'This is Derek ... Derek Hauserman,' Becker's mother said when Howard showed the framed photograph to her.

'Derek who?' he was startled that his mother knew this man well.

'They were in Vietnam together ... and became really close on the battlefield,' she said as she cleaned the dust off the glass frame. 'You know, they kept their friendship when they came back from the war.' Howard saw a hint of teardrop on his mother's face, as her voice cracked.

But Howard couldn't sleep that night. Lying in his bed, he thought about the possibility of that man coming to meet him at the Sheraton. *Still young? Late twenties? No ... no, it can't be!* Howard was restless in his bed, like a fish in a frying pan. He knew he was getting confused between two different people. It just didn't make any sense. *But what if?*

At 2 a.m., Howard found himself back in the attic, rummaging through the remaining boxes that belonged to his father. But there was nothing in them besides some old family albums and some political magazines from the seventies and eighties. There were some music records too, of bands like *Led Zeppelin* and *Black Sabbath*.

Howard remembered that some of his father's stuff was also lying in another property of theirs, lying across the fields. Officially, that land belonged to their property dealer and his father's friend, Darryl Wilson, but only on paper. In reality, Allen Becker used that house on the property for his personal work.

After his father's death, some US government agents had come to their house, with a permission letter to search their premises for some 'documents' that his father had kept since his Vietnam days. They explored everywhere but couldn't find what they were looking for. Since Darryl's property was not registered on Allen Becker's name, they left without searching it. *Could it be that his father knew they'd come for those papers after his death and hid it?* Howard played with the thought.

Whatever the answers were, it was up to Howard now to find them. His curiosity was taking over him. .

In the dead of night, Howard revved the engine of his mother's 2004 Chevrolet Silverado.

***

As he drove along the gravel road, he remembered the last days of his father. For some years before his death, Allen Becker's memory had weakened tremendously. The tests came negative for both Alzheimer's and Parkinson's diseases, and the reasons for memory loss were never fully diagnosed. In his final days, Allen started having hallucinations, visualizing past moments, started talking to himself and believing that he was living in the seventies.

Eventually, Howard's father's motor nervous system failed and was soon declared brain dead. In June 1990, he was pronounced dead by the doctors. It was not really bad news, for he suffered a lot in his final days. He would forget to wear pants in front of guests, and started urinating in public places. The memory was so on and off, that he would even find Martha and Howard, strangers in the house.

The truck tires screeched to a stop and the engine was shut down, as Howard rotated the key backwards. He got off the truck, with a flashlight in his hands. It was a one floor single family residence, with three bedrooms, four bathrooms and two garage spaces. Allen purchased it in 1983, and never bothered to register it in his name. *He had trust in his friends, and it always paid off,* Howard remembered his mother's speech at his father's funeral.

Howard inserted the house key, and the front door unlocked with a click. The squeaky hinges on the door brought a creaky sound as the door opened. It was not at all furnished, and almost empty as Howard's footsteps started making an echo. There was some stuff lying in store rooms that belonged to his father and Martha hadn't moved anything an inch.

Howard noticed his father's old typewriter, baseball bat, unopened envelopes and cigarette butts lying exactly where he left it. *They remind me of his presence,* Martha would say while justifying why she didn't move stuff out of the hallway. The carpeting and walls still looked well kept, as his mother was coming every month to scrub on them.

He stepped down into the basement and tried switching on the lights only to realise the electricity connection in the basement wasn't installed. Using his flashlight, Howard could see many large cardboard boxes lying in the corner. *This has to be it,* he thought as he started tearing apart the tapes that closed the lid of the boxes. The silence all around was a little creepy.

With a flashlight in his mouth, Howard started arranging stacks of papers, which had become yellowish with time. Most of them were journals that his father had written during his days in Vietnam. He realized soon that they all were very well-kept notes, with proper dates and stapled photographs. *Is this classified information,* he asked himself while arranging typed journals.

After being at it for hours, all the notes were finally stacked on the floor, dates wise. One of the documents contained information about the disappearance of a photojournalist Stephen Carron, in Cambodia under strange circumstances. He was declared 'killed in crossfire' by the government, but in reality he was 'removed' by the US Army as he had uncovered some 'battlefield secrets'.

Howard turned to another document, which had listed information about a mission, in which the US Army helped in arranging the chemical weapons for the *Army of the Republic of Vietnam* (ARVN) against the People's Army of Vietnam. There were stapled photographs of *sarin* and *phosgene* cylinders, carried by US soldiers in ARVN camps.

A different document indicated about a failed mission of 1971, in which a crashed landing of *EC-121 Warning Star* at Da Nang Airbase took place, killing 31 soldiers. The mission was shown as a success to the media by the Nixon government, but in reality it was not only an embarrassment to the US government, but a huge waste of taxpayers' money as well. The debris and fire, along with dead soldiers, were photographed.

It took hours for Howard to go through these documents one by one. They were definitely scandalous, and worth seizing for the government agents. But these documents were not the answer to the question, which had the name Derek Hauserman in it. How come the same man remains young, for fifty years?

And then Howard found what he was looking for. On the top of that file, it was stamped *Classified.* The photographs inside the file featured Howard's father in the uniform, along with his crew. Looking closely at the photos, Howard found Derek Hauserman, grinning in one photo while busy having a conversation in another. The file contained information about Operation Dessert, a covert mission, given to Task Force 121, to extract one of the most important documents that could change the course of the Vietnam War.

As Howard continued to read, he found out that Captain Allen Becker led the operation, with fifteen 'elite' soldiers to get their hands on *Lệnh chiến đấu khẩn cấp số 1,* which translates to *Urgent Combat Order No. 1.* It was a North Vietnamese Army plan to conduct a series of bombing attacks in Pleiku district, to annihilate US army bases. These documents featured exact dates and timings of the attack. The covert plan was successful, but many crewmates, including Captain Derek Hauserman, were gravely injured from grenade. Some were declared dead on the spot.

Howard was still at the file as the first ray of morning sun entered the basement's window. His heart skipped a beat when the file mentioned that the members of 'elite' *Task Force 121* crew had 'come back from the dead'.

***

Seated on a flight to New York on the same day, Howard checked his watch and realized he'd be landing in thirty minutes. The decision to head back to New York was taken abruptly, as deeper digging couldn't be done by staying back in Nashville. The classified documents he found this morning had only made the mystery murkier. Howard needed to get to New York as soon as possible to get to the bottom of this.

Saying goodbye to his mother was hard. He had had an amazing time in Tennessee, seeing his mother and spending time with her, revisiting his childhood and working on the family farm. Tennessee was both calm and detoxing, but he couldn't have remained there for long, not when a larger game is afoot. *The government was trying to hide a secret that involved my father,* thought Howard as he watched clouds drift past the aircraft. He should've found out about his father's past long ago, instead of immersing himself in his New York life so much.

Who are those elite squad members of Operation Dessert? How did Hauserman mysteriously survive those brutal injuries? And most importantly, why hasn't he reached senescence after half-a-century? For Howard, *The Eternal Gene* didn't look like a theoretical and speculative work now.

With thoughts like these swirling in his head, Howard fell into an uneasy nap until the aircraft touched down at JFK airport. Exiting the airport in a hurry, Howard hailed a cab. By the time he reached his home on 14th Avenue, beating the evening rush of NYC, it was already dark.

Caroline opened the door and was relieved at the sight of her husband standing at the door. She was wearing her black rimmed glasses and hair was knotted into a bun, which meant she had been working at her laptop. Howard felt nice seeing his wife after so many days. He knew Caroline was miffed with him, for not telling her before leaving for Tennessee. But before he could say anything, Caroline began.

'When were you planning to tell me that you're coming back?' she snapped at him as she snatched his luggage and disappeared inside. Howard entered and settled himself on the couch.

'I couldn't keep myself away from this city and you.' He smiled when Caroline returned. She rolled her eyes.

'How's Martha?' she asked.

'She's good. But more about that later.' Howard zipped open the bag he had been holding and removed a file from inside. He handed her the file and saw her confused expression.

'What's this?' She looked at the file. 'Have you been working still? I thought you went there to have a sabbatical, Howard!' she snapped at him again. She couldn't understand why her husband acted like a child sometimes. And then she noticed the red stamp that said *Classified* across the folder.

The next half hour was spent in explaining to Caroline what Howard had been doing back in Tennessee. The classified documents about the horrible things that had been covered up by the US government in the past along with the Derek Hausermann riddle. It was too much to absorb for Caroline in so little time.

'You mean this man, Derek whatever, looks the same today as he is in this picture?' She looked at the photograph, and then at her husband who nodded. 'And this photo is fifty years old?'

Howard nodded again. 'I've met the man, Carol.' he said, almost pleading.

'Come on, Howard. You can't possibly think this is true,' she said, as she was not at all convinced. 'Conspiracy theories? Cover-ups? Since when have you started believing in these things?' She waved her hands in the air aggressively.

'I know it sounds ludicrous,' he said as he pacified his wife. 'But you need to trust me on this. I have a hunch. Even if I have gone completely wrong on this, I will sleep peacefully knowing I have checked every nook and corner.' Howard said while holding his wife's hands.

Caroline looked at the photograph in her hands and then looked at her husband. She took time to think. 'Okay, fine. But once we are done with this, I want you to stop with this and continue living the life you were living before you decided to write that goddamn book.' She took a deep breath. 'Okay, how can I help with this now?'

'I want you to run the name Derek Hausermann in your WNB archives. Any piece of news we can find to link him with it.' Howard said, in a serious tone.

The company for whom Caroline worked, had been a news network since the sixties. Its archive was likely to be exhaustive, covering the latter half of twentieth century extensively.

'All right.' She got up and went to the bedroom.

Meanwhile, Howard went to the refrigerator and poured himself some beer in his mug. His mind was so exhausted due to the mixture of travelling and overthinking. *Maybe he is making too much out of thin air? Maybe Caroline was right in thinking that this was just a conspiracy theory, miles away from reality?*

Caroline came back with her laptop and sat on the couch with her husband. She opened the WNB archives webpage and logged in with her employee code number and with numerous security checks. A white search bar opened up on the screen.

'All right, let's see what it's all about.' She said as she typed Derek Hausermann's name in the search bar. The webpage started loading as both of them waited with bated breath.

And then, the database spit up exactly four results.

One result was of a news video dated 31 January 1990 in Kuwait.

First result was a four-minute coloured interview clip of a British army major, Harold Dean, who talked about Hausermann and Task Force 121. He explained how he had seen these elite forces expelling the Iraqi Army from the soil of Kuwait in less than 100 hours of landing in the Middle-East. 'I can't describe the things I've seen these men doing ... simply superhuman,' Major Dean confided in the interviewer in the clip.

The next search result was a photograph of Derek Hausermann, who was looking down at a body, which appeared to be of Saddam Hussain's. The captor was lying on the floor with his eyes closed. The photograph contained members of the elite Task Force 121, that carried out *Operation Red Dawn* – a mission to find Saddam Hussain. He was ultimately found at ad-Dawr in Iraq, hiding in a spider-hole.

The third search result was a printed news article, dated 10 October 2002. In the article, Major General Frank Durand was quoted saying 'Operation Enduring Freedom was successful because of Hausermann's men.' This covert operation was a mission to topple the Taliban government in Afghanistan.

And then, the last search result was also an article from August 1984, in *The Globe.* It was related to a man named Hausermann, arrested in Ukraine by the KGB, who claimed their captor to be a US spy. It was a very small article that ran at the height of the cold war and nobody took notice of it.

Both Howard and Caroline analysed these four search results, one by one. After they had gone through each one of them, there was a silence for ten minutes as Howard closed the flap of the laptop.

'You see?' He said while pointing at the laptop, and looking at his wife, who was now lying on the couch and looking at the ceiling.

'See what? This doesn't prove anything, Howard,' she said, 'We are looking at a man who served in Vietnam, in the Cold War, Iraq and Afghanistan. Come to think of it, it is not unimaginable to see a man serving the government for forty years. He must be a highly skilled soldier for all we know.' As she was speaking, she realized how unlikely this was to happen.

'A man conducting covert operations for forty years? Even if he was thirty years old in Vietnam, he must be seventy by that time he is conducting operations in Iraq,' Howard retorted, trying desperately to convince Caroline. 'Old men aren't sent on dangerous missions.'

'All I am saying is that this isn't impossible,' she said as slurped some beer from Howard's mug. 'Stories like these don't hold up in newsrooms.'

Both of them stayed silent for what seemed like eternity.

This can't be it? Howard thought as he opened the laptop again and this time, opened the online directory of soldiers that served during World War II. A web page was opened, with a white colored search bar on the top left. Howard typed the name in the search bar, with zero hope of finding anything. However, there was one search result that popped up.

```
Hausermann, Derek, 29th Infantry Division, Omaha Beach, Normandy (1944)
```

Howard couldn't believe what he was seeing. He was on the right track all along. *Derek Hausermann* doesn't age! He couldn't believe he was right all this time. His peers in the scientific community ripped him apart for his claim of 'possibility of some humans defying the law of cell-decay' in the book. *I was right all this time,* he took a moment to rejoice.

Howard turned the laptop screen towards his wife.

On reading what was there on her screen, it was like a truck load of bombshells just dropped on Caroline. *He fought the second world war too,* she wondered while being spellbound with the possibilities of this piece of information.

And then Howard's cell phone rang, distracting the couple from what they were doing. It was Martha's call. Howard picked up the call, thinking that his mother had called to ask if he had reached safely. He couldn't be more wrong.

'Yeah, mom,' he said, as he put the call on speaker.

'Howard, there are some government agents at Darryl's place.' Martha sounded helpless and panicked. 'They are taking away all of Allen's stuff.' She was on the verge of tearing up.

'What?' Howard asked, baffled, and looked at Caroline, who seemed equally confused. 'Mom, did they have a search warrant?'

'They did, Howard. I am fretting at the sight. These agents are searching the house and putting everything upside down.' Howard sensed that his mother was crying on the call. 'Allen had set up the house himself, and these people are ruining everything.' Her voice was cracking.

Caroline tried to console Martha and calmed her down. She advised her to comply with the demands of the agents, as there was no other option.

'We are coming to Tennessee by next flight, Martha,' she reassured her.

And then, there was a knock at their own door. The couple shared confusing glances, as Howard got up to open the door. He saw two men in black coats, trousers and navy-blue skinny ties standing there.

'Yes?' Howard asked. And then he saw shiny badges buckled to their belts.

'Dr Howard Becker?' One of the men asked.

'Yes, I am.' He replied. 'Is there a problem?'

'You need to come with us, sir. We have a warrant in your name.' Behind them, Howard could see there were numerous other agents.

'And who are you, if I may ask?'

'We are the CIA, Dr Becker. You have the right to remain silent.'

***

Howard was pushed in the backseat of a Chevrolet Caprice Classic, and on both of his sides, two agents adjusted themselves. Caroline was terrified of what had been happening around her and why her husband was being taken away. But none of the agents bothered to give her the answers. They didn't even tell her where they were taking him.

'Call Terrance,' Howard said loudly as the doors of the car were being shut by the agents. Terrance was Howards's attorney. However, Howard already knew that the CIA wouldn't let the lawyers interfere. They were above the 'innocent until proven guilty' principle that the US judiciary was proud of.

As the engine revved and throttled, Howard gave one last look at his wife. Caroline was crying, with both her hands on her mouth. She saw them take Howard away as she started dialing on her phone as soon as the car was out of her sight. One of the agents, however, was left behind who walked up to Caroline. The agent removed a pen-sized gadget from his pocket.

'Can you please look here, ma'am?' The agent said while pointing towards his gadget.

***

In the car, Howard sat still between two agents. The uncertainty was killing him.

'Where are we going?' he asked, but no one bothered to answer. Howard looked outside as he realized that they were moving towards the North Brooklyn area. *They're not going to CIA headquarters,* he thought as he discarded the option of going to prison. Going to prison meant that a judicial process would be involved, which would attract media and civil society groups. *Whatever they are going to do now, it would be extra-judicial,* he thought as he realized that the option of getting killed was also on the table tonight.

It was almost midnight when they entered a neighbourhood in Bushwick, through Grove Street. The car then took a right turn into Knickerbocker Avenue. The car finally pulled up in front of a shop named Kerry's Drycleaners.

Are they going to do my laundry? Howard thought. The doors of the car were opened as he was frisked again and taken inside the shop. It was a large hall with clothes, covered with transparent plastic sheets, hanging and rotating on a conveyor rod. The owner and the workers of the place turned a blind eye to the federal agents walking inside the shop with another man.

Howard followed the agents towards the back end of the shop, where there were two elevators . One agent clicked the down button to call one of the elevators. In a matter of twenty seconds, the doors slid open and the three men stepped in.

The elevator travelled downwards for what seemed like two levels. Once the doors dinged open, Howards saw a large office with cubicles and people, mainly agents, running around. *CIA's secret office,* thought Howard as he stepped forward. There were agents sitting on their desks, making reports on computers, the printer machine beeps filled the entire office space along with the coffee machine buzzing. It was as full as any corporate office at 11 a.m.

Howard was led into a room that only had a table in the middle with two chairs facing each other. He sat on one of them as the two officers left the room and closed the door behind them. The walls in the room were white and one of the walls had a large black glass. Howard was pretty sure someone was watching him from behind the glass.

It was clear to Howard that the only reason he was here was because he had uncovered one of the deepest secrets of the US government. *I have pissed off some powerful men in the government,* thought Howard. But how did they know I was doing some investigation on my own on classified files? There had to be only one explanation. He had been under state surveillance.

There were so many questions that Howard needed answers to. First was Derek Hausermann, who had been with the US Army from 1945 to 2006, conducting covert operations with a stagnant age. Secondly, what was this Elite Task Force 121 that Hausermann commanded? And finally, how was his father connected to all of this?

It was a twenty-minute wait, a standard CIA procedure that is done with a person who is brought in for questioning. Howard spent his time thinking about his mother and Caroline, who had been worried back at home. *Will I ever get to meet them again,* he was lost in these thoughts when the door suddenly opened, and a man walked in.

A familiar tall, lean figure with brunette hair and squarish jaw in a fitted suit stood in front of Howard. It was Derek Hausermann.

***

The tension in the room was palpable when Hausermann sat on the chair opposite Howard. Hausermann placed what seemed like a file on the table between them. There was silence for some seconds for both of them had spent the last couple of days thinking about each other.

Hausermann placed one leg over the other, and now looked straight at Howard.

'Do you know how advanced the CIA has become in its operating procedures, Dr Becker?' Hausermann spoke suddenly.

Howard was silent.

'Consider the Closet 8 surveillance technology, for example,'

Hausermann began. 'The Weeping Angel malware infected the smart TV installed in your living room. The owner, that's you in this case, falsely believes that his TV is off, but in reality it is recording the conversations of the people around it. Not only that, it transfers the audio over the internet to a CIA server.'

Howard didn't respond but kept looking at Hausermann.

'Fascinating, isn't it?' he began again. 'Another marvel is this VulturePro bug, which safely jumps the encryption layer of all social media applications on your cell phone. Which profile have you been stalking? Who have you been chatting with? What are you googling? What is your geolocation? It even records whatever you've been uttering to people around you. All of your activities over the past six weeks are in this file.' Hausermann said, pointing at the folder on the table.

Hausermann opened the file and started thumbing through the pages.

He began again. 'Naturally, this stuff wasn't there when I was born.' He shrugged his shoulders. 'Belief in science could get you killed back then. I was ten when Galileo was refused stately burial by Pope Urban VIII, simply because he said Earth revolves around the sun. And look where science has reached today.'

It was becoming harder for Howard to control his emotions now. The man just admitted to him that has been alive since the seventeenth century. He wanted to say something when Hausermann spoke again.

'The first thirty years of my life were spent in Marseille. I do have some faint memories of that era. The grand processions of Louis XIII, the play *Andromaque* running at Hôtel de Bourgogne, the famine of 1636 ... Ah, and the Thirty Years' War … One of my very good friends perished in that war. I remember the frenzy over La Varenne's, *Haute Cuisine,* sometime in the 1650s, a dish only the bourgeoisie could afford, for I tasted it only a century later,' Hausermann said, waving his hands in the air while looking up at the ceiling, recalling all the times gone by.

'How on earth are you alive—?' Howard tried to speak but he was cut off midway.

'You already know the answer, Dr Becker. *Mutation* ... what else? Your book is a phenomenal study in immortality. Who says your work doesn't show concrete proof? Here I am, a being who withstands the test of time, no ageing,' Hausermann said with both arms wide open. 'Your chapter on amelioration, about how a mutated organism would show self-healing early in his life is an accurate calculation. I developed self-healing in my teens, when my deep cuts while dueling with my friends, would disappear within minutes. The Spanish Flu of 1919 infected the whole town of Guimarães, but I was unscathed.' He was deriving pleasure from showcasing his abilities.

'Thanks to the shackles of serfdom that the French Revolution broke, I was able to rise through the ranks in Napoleon's army. I have talked to him, you know, 'Le Petit Caporal' ... he had the gravitas that no other leader has been able to showcase since. I commanded the Battle of Austerlitz in 1805, under his leadership, and after his death I sided with Metternich and commanded the Tricolour's army ... until I got tired of politics. Some people had begun to question the fact that I was simply not aging. At first, it was a compliment and then they said it's ... witchcraft!' Hausermann started laughing. A painful laugh.

'They don't understand science, Dr Becker, unlike you and me. Only science can explain how I could've attended Beethoven's *Fidelio* at Theater an der Wien in Vienna's fall of 1808 and The Beatles' concert at The Washington Coliseum in summer of 64'. Only science can explain how I could've fought in the Jacobite rising of 1745 and in the Cuban Missile Crisis of 1962. Only science can explain, Dr Becker, how a man looks thirty for more than three hundred years!' Hausermann's intensity had reached a peak as he spoke.

'Seems like you've settled with the CIA now, for more than eighty years I suppose?' Howard asked.

'Ah … right! The land of opportunities ... the United States of America. They made me an offer I just couldn't refuse. The CIA was called the Office of Strategic Services then. I disclosed my abilities to a government organization for the first time in my life, and they didn't believe me at first. They sent me to fight at Normandy, the Nazi blitzkrieg. I had shrapnel scattered all over my body, from the *Stielhandgranate*, and I reached the French medical camp on a stretcher. Then the shrapnel pushed themselves out of my body on their own. That's when they knew,' Hausermann explained as if he really wanted to share what he had gone through.

After being silent for some time, and flipping through pages on the file, Hausermann continued. 'It was in 1946 when they did tests on me to find out what was causing this superhuman effect. They couldn't find any success. But what they did find out is that there were more people who possess abilities that are similar to mine. There was one from Brazil, another from Ukraine, there were two from Algeria ... both twins … and many more. The US Intelligence made a team of thirty men who were valuable assets in most dangerous missions because they just couldn't die. We were initially called *Supersoldiers*, but later it changed to *Task Force 121.*'

'And you are their commander?' Howard asked.

Hausermann nodded. 'Simply because I am the eldest and most experienced of them all. The CIA has been managing us since its inception, allocating us missions as well as covers and fake names to live normal lives in the modern world.'

'You also knew my father?' Howard posed another question. This one was personal.

'Allen? Of course, I knew him. He talked about you so many times.' There was jubilation in Hausermann's tone, suddenly. 'We were in Vietnam together, and he was assisting Task Force 121 in 1972–73. I was injured during one of the operations, and the blood loss and internal wounds were at critical levels. Allen saw me getting back to my feet in less than six hours and he was spellbound. Ah! It's a tragedy what happened to him.' Hausermann shook his head thinking about Howard's father.

'His death wasn't natural, was it?' Howard asked. His tone was getting defiant with each question that he posed now. Hausermann's calmness was bothering him even more.

'Noell, the then CIA director, wanted to poison your father. He was quite adamant. It took me God knows how many weeks to persuade him not to do it. Hell, I even vouched for your father to be inducted in the CIA, but that son of a gun, Allen, started siphoning off classified documents from the inventory. That's when it was out of my hands. Noell had been given orders from higher up, to use ERASER on your father,' Hausermann replied.

'ERASER?' Howard was confused.

'Oh! I forgot you aren't aware.' Hausermann had shown no remorse for what he had done. It seemed he had made peace with everything he had seen in his life. 'ERASER is a photo-optical device that uses light beams of certain wavelengths to erase memories. One of the earliest versions of ERASER was in use then. I think it was the ERASER SPECTRUM series. They were crude technologies then, and that took Allen's life. It affected the neurons in his brains.'

'So, my father's wasn't a natural but a state sponsored death? You people are sick!' Howard raised his voice in anger and thumped his fist on the wooden table.

But Hausermann didn't react. He just kept still. Although he appeared younger to people, centuries of experience had calmed him down. Nothing ever rattled him any more.

'We get the work done, Dr Becker and that's what matters,' he said with a faint smile on his youthful face. 'People sleep under the blanket of security that we provide. We have special abilities, but unfortunately, we have to keep it under wraps.' He took a deep breath. 'Imagine the frenzy if people came to know that superhumans are staying amongst them. It will, just like you've written in your book, make old gods redundant. New gods will rise, and change the world order. It will be utter chaos.' he said as he removed a pen sized gadget from his breast pocket and held its one tip between his forefinger and thumb.

'Now, I want you to see where I am pointing, Dr Becker,' he said as Howard looked at a specific point on the gadget where Hausermann had been pointing.

A series of quick flashes erupted from the pen-sized gadget towards Howard. The sensitive light entered his brain via his retina and reset the information contained in the neurons of his temporal lobe.

The Representative

PART I

It had started snowing outside when Dave Hughes looked up from his desk. He stole a moment from his back-breaking work schedule, to rejoice looking at the tiny snowflakes falling on the street, which was twenty-seven floors down. *Only a few more minutes of slogging left,* Dave thought as he looked at a stack of papers, still lying untouched at his desk.

Dave Hughes was a sales executive at Frank & Griffin Inc., a company that sold printer's ink. His job included pursuing a list of potential customers and convincing them that buying ink from Frank & Griffin Inc. would significantly cut their office's annual spending in the procurement and supplies.

Dave's day would begin with calling people from the list and asking the question, 'Which ink do you use for your printer?' Some would slam the phone down immediately, some would politely say no before they hung up. Then, out of the blue, one of the callers would be found waiting for exactly this call and they would readily buy ink in bulk. Whenever Dave found this rare caller, for at least that day, he would grow a little less scared of losing his job.

Dave's desk phone rang as he picked up the receiver. 'Mr Livingston is calling you to his office,' came a lady's voice, whom Dave recognized as his boss's secretary.

'Right away,' Dave replied, unsure about why he was being summoned. He got up to stretch his back, which had become stiff due to hours of sitting in one position. As he walked across the hall, he realized that almost all desks were empty. The urge to get back home overwhelmed him too, as he glanced at his watch. *Just five more minutes,* he consoled himself.

His boss's chamber was a familiar colossal cabin with wine-coloured, carpeted floor, a view of the city and expensive furniture. There were blinds covering the wide glass walls, and it looked a very spacious and comfortable place to work in. Dave stood at the door for a few seconds while his boss was busy on his cellphone. With slight hesitation, he knocked on the door to get Livingston's attention.

Barnard Livingston was the regional manager of Frank & Griffin Inc., and extracted a salary equivalent to fifty sales executives, with privileges.

'Oh, come in, Dave,' Livingston said as he gestured towards the chair opposite to him. He was now poking his fingers on the keyboard of his computer. His long face, with a visible jaw and frameless glasses, in contrast with his brown straight hair, gave him a 'corporate success' look.

Between them was a large office table, with fewer things on it. Dave remembered his own messy table and wondered if his boss ever got any work done himself. A photograph of the boss's wife with their seven-year-old kid was among the few things on the table.

There was an awkward silence between them for two minutes, until his boss finally began.

'What is this, Dave?' Livingston turned his laptop screen towards Dave, who could see himself on screen entering the office. It was CCTV footage from that morning. His stomach knotted for a brief second.

'I … I … don't understand what you mean,' Dave said while stuttering. *What have I done now?*

'You were two minutes late to work today, Dave. Two minutes!' Livingston stressed. 'Were you not?' He looked into Dave's eyes.

'I … was … surely … on … on time, Mr Livingston.' Dave's confidence started plummeting drastically.

'Ohh!' Livingston said, looking at his laptop screen again. 'Then I must fire Simmons. If you are right, then there is something seriously wrong with our surveillance system.' He picked up the receiver of his phone. 'Someone has to pay the price, right.'

Simmons was the IT guy who looked after the internet and surveillance system in the office.

'Wait …' Dave interjected, frightened to the core. 'I may have been late, the tube was running late today,' he said apologetically.

'So, you lied to me?' Livingston was now livid. He took a deep breath. 'Our partnership doesn't work if I can't trust you, Dave. I think I may have been protecting you from my superiors too much because you are turning into a useless employee who is just a liability to the company!'

'I … I …' Dave tried to explain, but the stuttering eclipsed the point he wanted to make.

'Shut up!' Livingston pointed his finger at Dave. 'Mend your ways, Hughes. This is the last warning,' he said as he pulled out a chit from his pocket, still maintaining eye contact with Dave threateningly. He slid the chit across his table towards Dave. The code *H-42* was scribbled on it. 'You want to prove you are a good employee?'

Dave nodded, looking down at his shoes like a school kid.

'Go to the basement and remove the documents from the box H-42. Shred all of them before the day ends,' Livingston said as he got up to fetch his overcoat.

'Don't disappoint me again, Hughes,' he said in a strict tone, pausing at the door of his office. 'I will come in the morning to check, and you better be done with this task or face the consequences!' Having said his piece, he left.

Dave, scared and frustrated, trudged back to his desk. All lights were off except a small light over Dave's desk. From the glass window, he realized it was already getting dark. Christmas lights were lighting up across the city. Down on the street, Dave saw the secretary Eline getting into Livingston's car. She shut the door behind her and the car sped away.

It was suddenly silent across the office. Dave was the only one left in the building, perhaps a cleaning guy or two. Lately, he had been doing a lot of overtime, and taking the same pay for the last five years. The screaming and yelling had become quite a norm in the office. And Dave didn't protest when other employees dumped their work on him to enjoy an extended weekend themselves.

In the basement, Dave looked for the box of documents he was ordered to shred. *H-33, H-36, H-40, H-41 ... here it is.* He picked up the box from the shelf using the sliding stairs and chopped the tapes that glued its lids. There was no one in the basement, and it was eerily silent. A slight metal clanking noise echoed across the basement, with nothing but huge shelves stacked on top of each other in six large lanes.

Lonely and humiliated again, Dave thought, questioning his self-worth. For as long as Dave remembered, he had always been a pushover ... *a loser that must be taught a lesson.*

You are a weakling, Dave. A wimp ... that's what you will remain all your life, he remembered the words his stepfather had once said to him. These words never stopped following him since childhood. He was lost in his thoughts as he took out the papers from the box and stacked them on the floor.

I am not made to do anything significant in my life, Dave almost said to himself,. He knew what the contents of these documents were. Frank & Griffin Inc. had been struggling with rising embezzlement incidents, amounting to millions of pounds among the employees.

The board had initiated an investigation, and it had been asking for account books from regional offices to ensure grassroot scrutiny. Livingston, in the last financial year, had stolen company funds that he faked as vendor payments in account books. These papers were evidence of such fraud, which could eventually expose Livingston. This explained his urgency to shred these papers at the earliest.

Dave picked the papers, which were very heavy bundles, and took them to the shredder on his office's floor. He switched on the shredder, and a loud noise from rotating blades pierced the silence in the room. He was about to feed the papers into the machine's teeth, when all of a sudden he started to feel dizzy. Maybe it was due to a lack of air in the basement or lifting the heavy bundles, the dizziness started increasing. He started loosening his tie, but it didn't help much.

He now stood holding on to the desk's edge, as his vision became blurry and foggy. *What is happening,* he asked himself as his limbs started to get weak. He fell on the floor with a thud, and the smell of white marble was the last thing he remembered. He was unconscious the next instant.

He must have been out for an hour or so when he woke up suddenly. He was seemingly tired as his vision took time to adjust to the sudden light. He found himself in a white room with very bright lighting. 'Where am I,' he murmured as he got up and walked around. There was nothing in the room, except a white recliner and a window.

Dave looked outside the window, only to see an advanced technopolitan city with slender buildings touching space and large spaceships floating in the air at high speed. The dark space up above was visible with glistening stars that never in his life had looked so close. He rubbed his eyes, hoping to snap out of the illusion, but it was all very real. *Am I dreaming?* he asked himself, refusing to believe the reality in front of him.

***

The Group of Seven, or simply G7, leaders were on video call with each other. The leaders, especially the US President and his Russian counterpart, were intensely worried. A new viral strain, with no *earthian* link, had started infecting certain sections of the population. The death rate had started to climb up, attracting attention from across the globe.

Although the government agencies in these nations had worked tirelessly to keep all of it a secret, it was just a matter of time before someone figured out the threat. *It would create panic and bring everything to standstill,* a thought that weighed heavily on every leader's mind.

The governments around the world had managed to keep the existence of extraterrestrials a secret. It was necessary to keep the world running, and to avoid conspiracy theorists spreading doomsday messages, pushing human societies towards anarchy. In a world of high-speed internet and camera cell phones, it was a colossal task of keeping this contentious information under wraps. A huge force of bureaucrats around the world worked tirelessly to ensure that the public never found the answer to the question – *Are we alone in the universe?*

'Someone was selected just now for the council, from England,' the UK prime minister informed the others as he sat in front of a laptop reading a document. There were six other people joining him on the video call.

'Finally! I was beginning to get tired of waiting,' the Russian president admitted. 'So, what's so special about this person?' His voice was cracking, with a slight lag between the audio and the movement of his lips.

'Nothing much. A salesman from Frank & Griffin Inc., hails from London.' The prime minister replied. 'It seems he had no significant talents, a pretty normal human.' He sounded confused.

'Do you think this can change things? It's really putting stress on me. I am hardly able to sleep these days,' the Canadian prime minister asked.

'It's the only hope,' the US president said. 'We are in dire need of *external* support.'

Everyone nodded along in silence as they seemed to agree with the last sentence.

***

A knock on the door took the attention of an already startled Dave, who had apparently found himself in an alien world. On the shiny white walls, Dave couldn't find the door anywhere. *This is not a reality,* Dave reassured himself. But even if this was a dream, it was a weird one. The detailing of the world was exceptional and was very close to reality. When Dave pinched himself, he felt the pain. *Marvellous,* he said to himself.

He was lost in his thoughts when the speakers in the room blared.

'Hello, Dave. This is Artemis speaking. I am the one who is knocking the door,' A voice spoke, a seemingly friendly one, and of someone who would have answers to his predicament.

'Where are you speaking from?' Dave asked, muddled. He looked around in utter confusion. All the walls looked the same, and there was no hint of the door.

'Through the microphone installed just outside your door.' It was a calm voice and didn't get worked up, sensing Dave's panicky tone. It sounded smooth, with a kind of clarity evident in the speaker.

This is surely a dream, Dave thought. 'I can't find the door,' he said, exploring the walls with his hands to figure out where the door was.

'I am sending you an instruction manual on how to interact with matter here.' The speaker took a pause. 'Do you see it, Dave?'

At that instant, a hologram appeared in front of him, floating in air and showcasing a set of instructions. It took a moment for Dave to understand that they were a list of hand gestures to move things around.

Dave read the instructions on how to open the door. He swiped his right hand in the left direction. A portion of the wall slid in the left direction to expose the other side.

This is incredible, he was bewildered and looked at his hands in astonishment as if he was the possessor of some supernatural powers.

'On Alhadra, you can interact with inanimate objects without even touching them. That's how things work here,' Artemis said as he entered Dave's chamber. 'My name is Artemis and I am an android.'

Artemis was a human looking, clean shaven, blonde man with a square shaped face. With an average height and athletic build, Artemis wore a white uniform with a mandarin collar and a small, inverted triangle printed on the right side of the chest. He looked like the perfect specimen of a human that ever existed.

'Android?' Dave asked.

'It means I am almost a human – I am basically an operating system but my shell is organic, human. I am designed and assembled, unlike you who took birth twenty-eight years ago at Charing Cross Hospital in London,' Artemis explained. 'I am created specifically to assist you.' He smiled.

For Dave, it was hard to believe that this was not a human but a machine. Artemis was so lifelike just like humans, the walk and speech delivery was exactly the same. *How far has this civilization progressed,* Dave asked himself in bewilderment.

'Can someone explain to me where I am?' he asked while looking outside the glass window and realizing that this world had two suns in the sky. 'What is this place?'

'This is planet Alhadra, Master Dave … present in sector 4C381 of the revised Nova Maps released by Cordova Security Council,' Artemis explained, as a hologram appeared between the two men of a galactic map marking planets with complex life forms. Different sectors were labelled on the map, and each sector contained one or more galaxies, multiple star systems and asteroid belts.

'How far away from Earth are we?' Dave asked, beginning to believe that this might not be a dream after all.

'Earth is here, in sector 4C208,' Artemis zoomed the map and showed the blue earth revolving around its star, ever so slowly. '*XERXES*, the most powerful artificial intelligence system created by humans, has chosen you through its algorithm.'

'Chosen? For what?' Dave asked, unsure of what Artemis was talking about. At that moment he realized that he was wearing the same uniform that Artemis was wearing, including the inverted triangle logo on the chest.

'To represent Earth, Master Dave in the CSC or Cordovian Security Council that meets once in almost three earth-years. The CSC is a legislative and executive body that takes decisions through voting on security issues concerning the Cordovian group of species,' Artemis explained.

All of this sounded like gibberish to Dave. *A galactic version of the United Nations?* he thought. Last he checked, he was in his office shredding company documents and now he was on an alien planet talking to a humanoid. He was never chosen for anything in his life and so, it was impossible for him to believe his Android companion.

'Cordova-what?' He enquired.

'Cordovian species, Master Dave. It is a name for the group of species that have evolved from a similar single-celled organism called Cordovan, found in the Drezoid asteroid belt in north-western galactic centre.' The hologram now depicted a slow-moving belt of asteroids, perfectly arranged due to the action of a giant star's gravity on them.

Artemis continued, 'In the last billions of years, the asteroids from this belt have gone offcourse, and bombarded themselves on different planets … kickstarting complex life on barren planets. There are a million Cordovian species today, however only a handful of them are intelligent. Humans, Tardenians, Adronians – to name a few, all are part of Cordovian habitat and formed a galactic alliance after Kerakin Age, the time when Cordovian species were fighting amongst themselves,' Artemis explained as the hologram depicted different Cordovian species standing side by side. The hologram then featured an inverted black triangle that was the logo of the Cordovia Galactic Alliance.

'Why me? I am sure that algorithm could find a better choice to represent Earth. The president of the United States perhaps?' Dave asked.

'The short answer is that we don't know, Master Dave. But XERXES is a highly advanced system, and if it has chosen a particular being for a particular task, there will be a reason for it that we don't know yet. XERXES' algorithm is based on the genomic database of every human on planet Earth. According to it, you are the best option to represent your civilization, in the current scenario.' Artemis had answers to every query that Dave had thrown at him.

Dave suddenly felt good about himself. *These guys think I am best suited for a job … Well, this is a first,* he thought buoyantly as a spaceship passed by the window and he ran to get a glimpse of it. It was a gigantic piece of technology, having an arrow-like shape and being propelled by purple-coloured blasters. It had four enormous wings that gave it stability while it flew across space. *Incredible*, Dave thought.

'So who represented Earth at the CSC meet during the last session?' Dave asked as reality started sinking in. He was now convinced with everything that Artemis had said.

'The last one was a man named Minamoto Yoshimitsu, a construction worker from Osaka. He was teleported to Alhadara for CSC, thirty-eight earth-years ago. He died on Earth last year and so, a new representative was chosen for the next council.' The hologram showed a man who was talking to another extraterrestrial being, possibly after the session was over. He was shaking hands with other members of council and looked incredibly ecstatic at having fulfilled his responsibilities.

Artemis continued, 'Before him, the representative was a man named Omar Sayyid from Doha. That was sixty-five earth-years ago. There was a war of succession going on between rulers of planet Gaia, plunging the whole kingdom in a civil war. Omar Sayyid helped the Cordovian Galactic Conference to peacefully resolve the matter.' The hologram now showed a man, sitting in a meeting and listening attentively.

Dave scrolled down the hologram screen using the hand gestures detailed in the manual he'd been given before, and the list went as far back as 13,000 earth-years ago, when a prehistoric man was made the representative of Earth. *This is real,* thought Dave as his doubts started to dissipate. He was not dreaming after all ... he is really on an alien planet!

'Master, there are a few issues you need to understand before you step inside the Security Council's premises tomorrow,' Artemis said gravely. His tone had become serious, as if it was imperative for Dave to listen intently. 'There has been a significant threat facing the Cordovian species in recent times. That makes this session of the Security Council a paramount convention.'

'What kind of threat?' Dave asked, as he was trying gestures with his hands to see how things moved in the room.

'We are under attack by a different galactic species, known by the name of Echidna – a parasitic species that is known to enter the bloodstreams of Cordovians, killing them instantly. It has spread among the populations exponentially and has been touted as the primary threat to the Cordovian survival and advancement,' Artemis explained. 'Earth has been a victim of Echidnan terrorism for last few months, but Alhadran, Kalzonia and Adronia have been severely affected for many years now.'

The hologram now showed a few shots of Echidna. It seemed like a thick black mass of indefinite shape, with hundreds of moving and vibrating tentacles. It was indeed a ghastly creature.

A lethal parasite among humans? How have governments managed to keep this a secret? Dave asked himself as he focused all his attention towards the hologram.

'This tablet contains more information on the security issues that will be discussed in the session tomorrow,' Artemis handed him a rectangular glass screen. As soon as Dave touched it, the screen came to life. There were digitally illuminated alphabets embedded on it, and the screen flipped from one page to another like a book. 'In addition, I will be accompanying you to the council as your deputy.'

***

Dave was sure he was going to wake up in his office, when he went to sleep in Alhadran. But when he opened his eyes, the black space stared at him from the windows. The spaceships, hovering around like butterflies in space looked like stunning scenery created by a painter. *This is incredibly calming,* he thought as he got up. A part of the sky was lit up by the illumination of one of the two stars.

Last night, he had spent his time learning about the Cordovian species, which were not only extremely advanced, but often mated with humans as well. It was a revelation for Dave to realize that human evolution was the result of external interference, possibly Adronian, around two hundred thousand solar years ago. During one of the ice ages, Earth had received an Adronian visitor who induced genetic changes in the Neanderthalian population.

The fact that the governments on Earth know about extraterrestrials was a revelation for Dave as well. The Adronian and Tardenian premiers had been regularly in touch with the presidents of US and Russia. Not only that, they even had visited Earth and the White House on many occasions. Dave saw photographs of political leaders meeting with alien races on a regular basis. It was brilliant the way they have kept all of this a secret, in an era of information boom.

Conspiracy theorists were right all along, thought Dave as he pulled on the blue uniform of the Cordovian Security Council . The blue signified Earth, and a small inverted triangle logo on the chest for the Cordovian alliance.

Artemis had arrived right on time, and within moments, both were sitting in a covered space-pod-like structure. For the first time, Dave saw the Alhadran atmosphere, and it was the purest form of air he had ever breathed. 'All the Cordovian planets have similar atmospheric compositions,' Artemis had explained when the pod, powered by twin nord engines, took off towards the exosphere.

The elevation was gained pretty swiftly as Artemis aligned it in what seemed like a traffic lane in the air. With each passing second, the acceleration rose exponentially, without the slightest discomfort to Dave. However, the enthralling view of the planet was too grandiose for the new visitor to be bothered about travelling hassles.

The high rising buildings, with the pitch-black background of space, sprang up as far as the eye could see. It looked like an endless jungle of iron and steel, with flying mosquitoes in the form of numerous space pods, like the one in which Dave was travelling. Alhadra looked like a bustling economy that had already achieved a hyper-advanced societal outlook, a stable level of well-being for its citizens and connections that reached far beyond their own orbit.

Dave was yet to recover from the galactic enhancements in his general awareness when the first hazy and foggy glimpses of the Cordova Security Council building became visible. *A technological marvel,* thought Dave as he saw the outline of the building even before reaching the edge of the planet's atmosphere.

The CSC was a colossal building that was floating in space and revolving around the planet of Alhadra. The shape of the building was like a collection of five concentric circles around a giant metallic rod, both steadily rotating on their own axis. The internal system would use energy from enormous nord power backup, which ensured that the giant structure never goes off course from Alhadran orbit. It was an extremely stable structure, a symbol of Cordovian advancement over all the species in the universe.

The space wasn't a quiet place for Alhadrans, as orbit around the planet had been used to develop the trade transit system. The rush of space pods entering and leaving the border of Alhadra made it look like a congestion in outer London during the peak hours of Monday. Dave had already figured out the fact that trade must have been the backbone of Alhadra, but the nature of the trade was yet unknown to him.

'The Alhadrans are one of the richest civilizations among all the Cordovian species,' Artemis said as he navigated through the toll plaza system installed at the edge of the Alhadran atmosphere. 'Under the Alhadran lands is an abundance of the most sought-after resource – duranium.'

'Is that like … a metal?' Dave asked curiously.

'Not just any metal, but the strongest metal in the universe. A critical metal that is used in manufacturing of nord cells,' Artemis said as he overtook a space pod that had been flying way too slow on a high-speed lane. 'Not only that, the sophisticated weaponry, advanced automobiles and even androids like me run on nordic technology, which is an expensive commodity around the universe because of the rarity of Duranium. Duranium has been the primary cause of Cordovian advancement since last century.'

Artemis's pod zipped through a curtain of blue laser beams at the toll plaza, electronically deducting three *kurds*, the Alhadran currency. The laser curtain had also done a bio-scan of the people in the space pod – a process of copying the travellers' genomic composition in their systems. It was done to calculate how many people exited the Alhadran atmosphere through their pods, a brilliant way to calculate population at any given time.

'The Alhadrans have become a truly advanced civilization by exporting duranium all over the universe for centuries. They are one of the few societies that have stabilized the ratio between population growth and resources available,' Artemis explained. But Dave was now too busy staring at the spectacular space that spread out before them. His eyes were glued to two concentric rings of asteroids around Alhadra, which gave the planet a truly majestic look. The space jam of thousands of nordic pods, passing through the transit system amid two suns, rising and ebbing, gave the look of a truly exceptional civilization. *Earth is primitive compared to what extraterrestrials have managed to build,* thought Dave. The pod now entered the giant CSC building, as one of the entry doors opened and the pod was sucked inside the building with an invisible force. Artemis initiated the landing mode, making the pod ready to be parked, slowly descending as automatic landers came out, sensing the proximity of a hard surface.

Dave got out of the pod and stepped into a different world altogether. It was a giant chamber, encompassing thousands of pods that were entering and leaving. One could see three colossal sculptures of the current Alhadran king and his predecessors; they looked majestic. There were numerous teleport stations on the left side of the chamber, made for the visitors who came to attend the CSC event from millions of light years away. The holograms were everywhere and looked so lifelike that it was impossible to differentiate them from the real-life objects. Only when someone passed through these holograms, it became clear that they were just photons hanging in mid-air.

There was a huge crowd of strange looking people, or aliens, recording Dave's entry as he stepped on what seemed like a blue carpet. He was being photographed, and the broadcast travelled to numerous other planets where their denizens were watching the CSC proceedings intently. As he halted to take in all the clamour around, Artemis pushed him gently from behind to keep moving. For the first time in his life, Dave felt like a celebrity.

At the entry gate stood an Alhadran security personnel who was checking everyone's wrists. Alhadrans had a purplish face with rough skin that had slight protruding points like on an alligator's body. The ears were long, with a helix extended backwards, and had no hair on their head (and possibly their bodies too). Their build was broad, with two upper and two lower limbs. *They look more like goblins,* thought Dave, observing the security personnel.

The Alhadran gestured to Dave to show his left wrist. Confused and dazed, Dave pulled his sleeve up and showed him. To his dismay, there were a couple of markings on it that appeared out of nowhere. *When was it marked?* Dave asked himself in amazement.

《『Δ』》

He touched it and found that it had been engraved on his wrist.

'This is Alhadran script and it marks your identity as a representative in CSC,' Artemis explained. 'It was marked upon your entry into Alhadra.'

The security personnel signalled at Dave to put his hand through a hollow circular gadget, embedded within the wall. Dave acquiesced, and the scanning was completed in an instant. He realized that the markings on his wrist had started glowing. The door opened, and both Dave and Artemis stepped forward, into what looked like an elevator.

The elevator seemed to move upwards, as the space looked magnificent from the glass window. *This has to be the greatest moment of my life,* Dave thought. The planet of Alhadra gave a hint of reddish-yellow colour from above, and Dave enquired why it was so.

'The Alhadran soil has rich deposits of *ghrogh* spice, an ingredient that makes food taste delicious, but excessive intake makes a person belligerent. Some say that is the reason behind Alhadrans' heightened aggression as compared to other Cordovian species,' Artemis said, taking a small gadget out of his breast pocket. 'Master Dave, that reminds me that you need to wear this just under your ear.'

He handed Dave a gadget that looked like a small ear pod, no longer than two inches.

'What is it?' Dave sounded confused.

'Akoúo is a Gaian technology gadget … It not only converts the speech of the people around you into your own native language but also the foreign script that you'll come across will automatically be converted into the one that is familiar to you. Akoúo twitches the thalamus in your brain and tricks your cerebral cortex into seeing what is not there.'

Dave attached it just beneath his right ear. It illuminated a bluish-green light to show that it had been connected. He took a look at his wrist, where the Alhadran script was engraved. Dave's cerebral cortex processed the data into his own native language of English. It read:

CSC: EARTHLING

Brilliant, thought Dave.

And then the elevator opened. Both men stepped forward. On the glass door in front of them, there was a circular engraved writing – *Cordova Galactic Alliance Security Council,* and in the middle of the circle, Dave could see the familiar logo of a giant inverted black triangle.

***

It was a large hall, with seats arranged in three concentric circles, and every seat had seating cards placed on it. On the walls hung framed photographs of various Cordovian leaders who had made significant contributions in forging the Cordovian Galactic Alliance and helped mark an end to the gruesome Kerakin era.

Dave's perspective had shifted suddenly, as he became increasingly familiar with the new world. He had now begun to believe that all the petty skirmishes among the nations of Earth, along with the border disputes, invasions, political inclinations, religious propagandas, ideologies … everything was too insignificant in the larger scheme of things. Humans were currently swimming in a sea of delusion, of imagined self-importance, that they were the centre of the universe. As Dave walked through CSC's assembly hall, he realized humans were nowhere near the centre of cosmic reality.

Dave read the seating cards – Adronia, Octavia, Gaia, Tardenia, Abraxas and many more were written on the cards. As Dave and Artemis reached the seats that had the card with 'Humans' written on them, they saw three people already standing by the chairs. They were humans and immediately took Dave's attention.

As they saw Dave approaching, they came forward, as if someone important had just arrived. One of them eagerly shook hands with Dave.

'So good to finally meet you, sir,' said one. He wore glasses and his baldness was more conspicuous than his facial features. 'POTUS sends his best wishes.'

Another one, sensing the opportunity, came forward and shook Dave's hands. 'A human at the big table … A historic moment.' He had a thick moustache and curly hair. His accent was peculiar and the body language signalled that he must have had a military background.

Dave looked at Artemis, baffled.

'This is United States Defense Secretary, Mr Garrett Hansley,' Artemis said, pointing towards the bald man. 'And this is Mr Mikhail Manturov and he is the Deputy Minister of Defence in the Russian Federation.' Artemis pointed towards the man with the moustache.

Behind them was a third human, who now came forward.

'And this is United Nations Policy and Mediation Division Director, Mariana Sanchez,' Artemis pointed towards a woman, who looked slightly senior than the other two. She was of medium height and wore black formal clothes. It looked as though there were years of experience behind her.

'I don't mean to put you under any pressure, young man, but the future of Earth rests on your shoulders,' she said. 'We are going through a very difficult time, and the solution lies in the success of this conference.'

'All of them have teleported especially to meet you,' Artemis told Dave. 'They can't be here when the council begins and so, they will leave for Earth shortly.'

Dave had started to get cold feet now, after realizing how contentious this whole set up was in which he had been chosen to represent his civilization. *Why was I chosen for this?* The question that had been plaguing Dave's mind since he woke up in Alhadra. The reality of the situation was sinking in slowly as other representatives had started arriving.

As Dave took his seat, present in the innermost concentric circle, his humanoid companion took the adjacent seat that was reserved for him. Dave saw someone already seated on the highest chair of the podium.

'That's Director-General of Cordovian Security Council. He is Tardenian,' Artemis pointed out.

In a few moments, the seats of the council had started to fill slowly, as Dave could see the short-heighted Kalzonian representative adjusted next to him. A green coloured species, with what looked like tiny horns on their heads and enlarged nostrils, Kalzonians had a little reptilian feel to them.

'On the planet of Kalzoid, the age of reptiles, similar to the Triassic age of Earth, never ended. They developed into an intelligent life form,' Artemis whispered to Dave, whose jaw had dropped. He stared at these beings unabashedly for a few minutes. They looked like larger versions of geckos one could find on the walls of a house and in corners breeding during the summers back on Earth.

The Tardenians were a unique turquoise-coloured species; instead of having hair on their heads, had thick extensions of skin itself. Their eyes had large dark circles, a human-like nose but no ears, and they seemed to have teeth with over-extended canines. The Tardenian representative took the seat and had been busy talking to his deputy.

Then came Adronians, who looked exactly similar to humans. *Even better forms of humans,* thought Dave as an Adronian representative took her seat and gave Dave a quick look. She looked taller and sturdier than her human counterparts. They were perfect beings, with sharp facial features, athletic build. Dave heard a couple of the Adronian men walking behind her.. They were having a conversation and Dave noticed that they all had a thick baritone voice.

'They think themselves to be a better species than humans ... they're certainly advanced. The evolution has gone in similar directions on both planets. Some theorists believe that the evolutionary line of humans can be traced back to Adronians, but in absence of any concrete evidence, the theory is nothing but a conjecture,' Artemis said to Dave, noticing that he had been staring rather too long at the Adronian representative.

Next came the Abraxians, who were truly unique in appearance. The Abraxians were tall, with what looked like webbed hands and eyes protruding backwards and had outlining of lips that gave a circular look to their mouth. The Abraxians had a look similar to some of underwater species on Earth. Instead of only one deputy, the Abraxian representative had arrived with four deputies, along with an infant.

'Time moves faster for Abraxians, which impacts their aging. In the course of this conference, most of the young Abraxians that we see right now would turn into adults and grow old in front of us, before turning into dust. As they perish, the infant Abraxian will take their place and carry forward the representation,' Artemis said.

Incredible, thought Dave.

The Gaian and Octavian representatives entered the council together and sat next to each other at their designated seats. It was apparent that the representatives from both species were close not only culturally but also genetically.

The Gaians were similar to humans in facial structure, but the three lines on the forehead protruded outwards like granules on rocks. They had a pinkish tinge to their skin. That coupled with an extremely pointed nose and bluish-green lips gave them a multicoloured look. 'There is an absence of a human-like throat,'

Artemis said, 'due to the fact that the Gaians had stopped using speech to communicate for some millenia. Their vocal cords eventually became redundant and was weeded out by the forces of evolution.'

On the other hand, their counterparts – the Octavians – looked similar to Gaians, but were more broadly built, taller and rugged. Because of similar cultures and biology, the intergalactic relationship between governments had been the strongest among the Cordovians. They would usually formulate policies in tandem.

Many more species arrived to attend the council session, filling the second and third concentric circles. The Cordovian group of thirty, finally packed in the entire room, almost an hour after Dave's arrival. There were other seats too, separated from concentric arrangement, towards the other end of the hall, where the members of the media seated themselves.

The session finally began when a hologram suddenly appeared in the middle of the concentric seating arrangement. It showed the full body of Alhadran king, Tritus, in real time. His rough, purplish face showed that he was quite aged, and was an experienced leader of an advanced empire.

'I welcome every representative, from the Cordovian group of thirty, to the humble habitat of Alhadrans. We feel incredibly proud to host the Cordovian Security Council as it aligns with our vision of peace, security and cooperation among the advanced civilizations of the known world,' the Alhadran king began his address.

'I would start the conference by highlighting the imminent concern that requires our attention. Peace, as we know it since the end of the Kerakin era, is under the gravest threat today. Many representatives sitting here are familiar to the Echidnan terrorism that has already been unleashed on our innocent people. Their terrorism has developed into a full-blown pandemic, which spreads faster from one person to another than any other parasite previously known.'

'Their attack on the Alhadran military battalion at Drogh is testament to their barbarism.' The hologram now showed a video of Alhadran forces in the desert, fighting with what seemed like black sands flying in the air. The sands rose from the ground like blood in veins, somehow entered the suits of the Alhadran soldiers and burst them from within. The soldiers popped like crackers, with thick masses of blood released in the air with each pop. The loud screams of soldiers was filled the entire assembly hall and showed the torture that they had been going through while battling the Echidna.

The representatives sitting in the room gasped at the sight. There was an apparent horror on their faces, along with a tinge of disgust towards their common enemy.

'This is the Massacre at the Mount of Stin on Planet Drogh, where during a peaceful Alhadran-Kalzonian military exercise, the Echidna launched an attack and killed around twelve hundred soldiers.'

The hologram now showed a somewhat worried king again. 'They enter the bloodstream, crush organs from within and eliminate their enemies in a flash. We all know the dark times of the Kerakin Age, when warcries and bloodshed filled the Cordovian skies, when mercilessness and barbarism were the ways of our ancestors. We don't want those times to return, for the Eirini Age values of cooperation and mutualism have given us technological advancement and unprecedented prosperity,' Tritus said, as the members of council were listening with utmost attentiveness. 'However, the threat of the Echidna cannot be taken lightly … they can't be reasoned with … can't be negotiated with ... and most importantly, their expansion can't be halted … especially if we bind ourselves to the Eirini Age principles to fight against this parasite.' The king took a deep breath.

'The leader of the Alhadran Royal Society of Scientists, Dr Aldrodh, has analysed the relationship between Cordovians and Echidna for decades, and only recently, released her evaluation of it in her study, the 'Two Species Theory'. It says that these two species, *us and them,* are designed by the cosmos in such a way that their interests are perpetually opposite to each other. Both species are biologically encoded for competition against each other, to fight for galactic dominance and to end up at the top of the galactic hierarchy. Our origin, heritage and intellectual prowess are in direct contrast with what the Echidnan culture stands for – savagery. They are a slowly growing cancer ... a direct threat to the survival of the Cordovian prosperity that we've achieved. We need to act fast, for they have not only entered our skies, but have also drawn the first blood.'

After a pause, the king continued, 'With this threat in mind, I announce the start of the Cordovian Galactic Security Council. May we achieve what we set out to, respecting our commitment towards peace, security and collaboration.' The hologram faded slowly and steadily with his last lines.

There were some faint voices of appreciation for the king's speech. The representatives had started to mumble among themselves, and the Director-General announced the initiation of discussions on the security issues concerning the Cordovians.

It took a moment for Dave to analyse what Tritus had just said. The video of the massacre of Alhadran soldiers had shaken him from within. He was now aware of the gravity of the situation and was eager to hear the views of the council members on this.

With apparent hesitation, Dave reached out to his Octavian counterpart, who was taking notes on what seemed like a tablet, to strike up a conversation. The being didn't respond. Dave tried to speak a bit louder, only to be ignored again. Dave decided to come closer to the being to whisper a greeting in his ear.

'You don't want to do that, Dave,' Artemis spoke from behind him in a low voice. 'Unless you want to start a diplomatic crisis between Earth and Octavia, you must restrain yourself.'

Dave backed off instantly. He was just about to explain his actions to Artemis when his voice faded, as a council member got up to begin the proceedings.

The Gaian representative initiated the discussion by highlighting the immigration crisis that they were currently facing. 'The Holthain refugee crisis, stimulated by fear of Echidnan expansion, has stretched our resources to the limit. The refugees have been pouring illegally into our boundaries, breaking border rules and flouting the restriction of movement norms in our refugee camps.' The representative sounded very serious. 'We are in no position to contribute towards a joint Cordovian military effort against the Echidna. The resettlement of refugees remains our first priority at the moment.'

The Octavian representative, while supporting the Gaian representative, toed the same line of not being much concerned about the Echidnan threat. 'The Octavian Empire understands the grave threat of Echidnan terrorism. However, the recent climate changes on our planet remains the centre of our focus. The hardening of permanent ice across all continents has severely shortened our food resources.' She took a pause before adding, 'We would want to wait and see how this Echidnan situation develops before we decide to take any steps towards joint military effort.'

The Alhadran representative wasn't shy in showing his disgust towards the Gaian and the Octavian representatives, for taking the Echidna threat too lightly. The intergalactic relations between Alhadra and Octavia had also hit a rough patch in the recent past, which was spilling into the Echidnan issue now.

Meanwhile, the Tardenian's representative was more direct in his messaging. 'The Tardenian Empire hopes that the council would adhere to values and commitments that define the Eirin Age, and doesn't take a inflexible approach towards a species about which we have little or no data available. If the Kerakin Age has taught us anything, it is that overt and extreme military actions must be avoided, especially when there is little or no ground intelligence available.'

The liberal Tardenians, as always, banked upon their wait-and-watch approach, much to the irritation of the Alhadran government, who seemed to be running out of time and patience.

As far as Dave was concerned, he'd just realized how difficult it was to arrive at a consensus in this council.

However, the Kolzonian representatives supported the Alhadran cause of military action against Edchidnian terrorism. 'The threat is apparent, and it is here. The Massacre at the Mount of Stin led to four hundred of our rangers perishing.' The representative was stern in her speech. 'And for those who are taking this threat lightly and aren't contributing enough, I give them an opportunity to visit the Mount of Stin and see the pile of dead bodies themselves,' she spoke with a hint of aggression in the tone.

There was a thumping of tables from Abraxians and Adronians, who also believed in the gravity of Echidnan expansion. The council was visibly divided into moderates and extremists, with no concord in sight.

'Why do the Alhadrans need approval from the council for military action?' Dave asked Artemis in a hushed tone.

'The Alhadrans are targeting a particular species in order to establish peace. In literal terms, this specific action is called Specism, an act prohibited under the Cordovian Code. The code declares that if the circumstances force us to deviate from principle of the Eirin Age, an absolute majority is needed in the council to legalize any military action. The conflicts during the Kerakin era have taught Cordovians to have stops and checks on any kind of effort that involves attacking a lifeform,' Artemis explained in a calm demeanor.

'And what happens if the Alhadrans manage to get the majority in council?' Dave asked.

'If the Alhadrans succeed in getting absolute majority, all the thirty races of Cordovian species would have to join the Alhadran war effort, contributing their last soldier to exterminate the Echidna from Drogh.'

Dave nodded as he processed the information.

The session continued for another hour with back-and-forth discussions on the Cordovian future and survival. In the final hour of the session, the Alhadran representative had announced that King Tritus had arranged a visit for the CSC representatives to the Mount of Stin at Drogh, where the Alhadran forces had secured the parameter.

'Zeki, our intelligence system, will ensure that all representatives are safe during the travel to Dorgh. General Aldarish would receive the convoy at the Dorgh's exosphere and take you around the perimeter we've captured. I believe, after perceiving the grave danger that our soldiers are serving in everyday, we all can be on the same page during the vote at the next season of the Cordovian Security Council,' the Alhadran representative declared.

The discussion finally ended as all the representatives stood up, after what seemed like a drawn-out, gruelling session. Dave could see how the representatives now indulged in casual conversations with their counterparts. It was truly a sight for Dave: diverse beings stood on a single platform, discussing the most contentious issues. It was something that humans were yet to experience.

***

That evening, all the representatives had gathered for the voyage to Planet Drogh. It was mandatory to take this trip as representatives have the primary duty of ensuring a stable galactic diplomacy at the council. Dave, as a representative of Humans, had no option but to accept the invitation, even if that meant leaving Artemis behind.

Strapped on a ship they called the Provecta-Navis VII, flown by an Alhadran squadron leader, Dave looked at the unlimited space that was in front of him. Next to him was an Octavian representative who was poking at her cell phone screen, which was floating in mid-air. For Dave's eyes, that display was blurred, for the Octavian had installed some kind of privacy setting to limit her content's viewing.

There were eight rows, with four seats in each row. All the representatives had occupied these seats. The Tardenian representative had some kind of virtual reality device strapped around his head, and he was lost in another world. The Kolzonian representative fell asleep as soon as the spacecraft took off, while his Abraxian counterpart had pasted some kind of rectangular device to his chest that activated his muscular tissue.

The journey to planet Drogh had begun an hour ago. Only the representatives had been allowed to visit the battlefield. It was easier to manage the security for these many people. If the assistants and deputies to the representatives were also to be allowed, it would be a huge risk to ensure their safety on the Mount of Stin.

Inside the spacecraft, there were Alhadran military personnel incharge of handling the emergency situations if the need arose. The Alhadrans were leaving no stone unturned in making this visit safe and impactful to their larger cause of having Cordvian Joint Force to limit the Echidna expansion.

The Provecta-Navis had made a steady course. On its way it had surpassed a giant nebular cloud, but the stabilizing nord core helped the spacecraft to navigate through its diameter. They were just about to enter the exosphere of planet Drogh now. The pilots were commanding the ship through the omphalos section present in the front end. At the exact centre of the ship was the seating section.

The Provecta-Navis system worked on a sophisticated cooling system, using a cryostat to stabilize the temperatures of its Adronian engine from the overworked nord cells technology.

Dave unbuckled himself, only to walk around in the chambers. As he looked through the impressive design of the ship, he knew that it would take centuries for humanity, just to reach this advanced stage. Never in a million years would Dave have thought of meeting extra-terrestrial species in his life. His life had turned upside down with this experience. But why did the XERXES algorithm choose me? The thought had crossed his mind many times during the journey to Drogh.

It was some kind of logistic section of the spacecraft, combined with the service module.

Impressive, he thought as he realized that he probably had gone deep inside the rear end of the spacecraft. He looked around only to see that he was alone.

'Hello Dave,' the speakers in the corridor blared, baffling Dave.

'Who is this?' he asked.

'My name is Zeki and I am the virtual assistant installed within the communication center of the spacecraft.' She took a pause. 'My origins are Alhadran.'

'Right,' Dave said, unsure of what to be said next. 'I am currently in what part of the spacecraft?'

'This is Syntonismós, the nucleus of systemic coordination of Provecta-Navis. If you go further down the corridor, you will see the newest addition to Provecta-Navis VII spacecrafts – a separate lander for reconnaissance.' As Zeki was explaining, Dave could see the lander in sight. It was an engineering marvel, built with a mix of duranium and glass. He could see a small cockpit and a control panel in front of it.

'What is it called?' Dave asked, touching its shiny body.

'It is called Tayira Class II, the first lander that was built with space travel in mind. It can last longer than most landers out there, with minimized power waste. It is not operational at this moment and its nordic power source hasn't been installed yet,' Zeki explained as Dave took a round around the lander. 'You can step in, Dave, if you want to.' The door of the lander slid up.

Hesitatingly, Dave entered the cockpit and sat on the pilot's seat. 'Do you virtually assist this one too?' he asked, looking at the navigation system.

'I do assist with its hardware,' Zeki replied. 'Apart from it, I control advanced sensors for altitude and orbital navigation, with three-axis stabilization, to ensure it sits upright in space, rather than spin to achieve stability.'

After checking out the insides of Tayira Class II, Dave marvelled at the exceptional feat of engineering. As he was going through the control panel, he experienced slight turbulence. *I should probably head back to the seat,* he thought as the landing could be initiated any minute now. He pressed the red nozzle on the left-hand side of the door, but it didn't open the door.

'Uhhh ... Zeki?' he said after pressing the nozzle repeatedly of the insides of the lander. 'The door isn't opening.'

'We may have a slight problem here, Dave,' she said. Dave didn't know what was going on. His palms were sweaty now as he found himself panicking.

And then the system started flashing the words 'Red Alert' across all screens of the Provecta-Navis. The Alhadran military men came running towards the Syntonismós centre, followed by all the representatives.

'Can anyone tell me what the hell is going on?' Dave asked, irritated and dazed. He felt beads of sweat on his skin. He felt like a trapped rat, trying hard to escape.

'We have detected Echidnan presence within the Tayira Class II lander. I am afraid I can't allow the door to open because there is danger of contamination to other passengers on Provecta-Navis.'

You have detected what? Dave started pressing the nozzle harder, but to no avail. Anxiety started to creep in. He could see through the glass outside, as the military men were talking to each other with fast moving lips, but the soundproof cockpit had negated any noise from outside.

'Dave, I have some bad news for you.' The speakers within the lander blared again. 'The lander isn't properly sealed, and there is a danger of Echidnian granules leaking inside the Syntonismós. The Alhadran Commander present on the ship has taken a tough decision to release the lander out of Provecta-Navis. The Tayira Class II lander will be ejected in ten seconds.'

The countdown in Alhadran digits started flashing on the screen above the control panels.

'Waittt ... let me out ... you can't do this!' Dave started banging his right arm on the door, hoping that it would open. Taking two steps backwards, Dave started hitting the door with his foot now. He became drenched in sweat as he kept hitting the door. But all these efforts wouldn't put a slightest bump on the universe's strongest metal. 'Can anyone hear me?' Dave's survival instinct kicked in as he started screaming.

The countdown ran out as the screen now flashed 'Ejection in process'. The doors slid out where the Tayira Class II was parked, and the lander ejected out of the Provecta-Navis. All the representatives watched in horror as the lander containing Dave exited the spacecraft.

This is surely my end, Dave thought in panic as the lander was now floating at the edge of space and Drogh's atmosphere. Without any power source, the lander was just a small duranium box. Dave lost his balance and crashed into the control panels, and then the cockpit wall. The high-speed winds in the atmosphere, now navigating the lander. He began to expect the worst as the the lander started to descend.

The lander, upon entering the Drogh's atmosphere, sped towards the land faster under the influence of gravity. Dave needed to think of something quickly, to ensure his survival when the lander hit the ground. Summoning all his strength, he crawled on the floor, to reach the pilot's seat. The lander now speeding towards the ground as Dave buckled himself into the seat, hoping against hope that he would survive the fall.

In the middle of nowhere, in a sandy desert, the lander crashed hard on the planet's surface. The dunes of the sands provided some amount of cushioning as the sand granules rose high up in the air upon impact. It created a loud metal clunking noise, disrupting the calmness of the desert. The Tayira Class II lander, absorbing all the pressure from the fall, stood silently on a dune for fifteen minutes as Dave fainted with the sudden shock of impact.

He woke up with a throbbing head, which was bleeding profusely along with his shoulder blades and neck. *I am alive,* was his first thought as his blurry vision adjusted itself and gave way to a clear view. He unbuckled himself, as he was gasping for breath inside the lander. He saw a crack on the glass wall from where breathable air was coming. *I can breathe the outside air,* he realized.

He started ramming his soles on the glass screen, which was surprisingly not that hard. The cracks became wider and wider in the glass, and it ultimately broke enough to let Dave escape. With much effort, he came out and jumped on the sand as the air filled his lungs. Although the bleeding and headaches were enough to give Dave a concussion, the bright sky and the star's rays directly overhead made him drop to the ground instantly.

He lay there, unconscious once again, as the desert sands around him started moving on their own, encircling him as if a predator was getting ready to charge on its prey.

The Representative

PART II

…•●•…

When Dave suddenly came back to his senses, it took his eyes time to adjust. It was the darkest room he had ever been in. Nothing was visible. Horrified, he started losing all hope. It was pitch black gloom that looked like it would eat him alive.

'Anyone there?' Dave screamed, he realized he was sitting in some kind of a corner. His scream now turned into a cry. 'Helooooo?' The screams became louder, helpless screams. 'Anyone out there? Please help!'

There was nothing except the echo of his own voice. *Is this after life?* He questioned himself as the darkness gave him a chilling effect. Dave was scared, more than ever before in his life. He was grunting, frightened like a little boy. He was trying to move but some force had frozen him to his place. No matter how much effort Dave made, he wasn't able to move an inch.

'You are a weakling, Dave. A loser, that's what you will remain all your life.' The words reverberated in his mind again. In that moment, his stepfather's voice felt very real. The force restricting

his movement was overpowering him now. *It's true … I can't fight,* dwelling in hopelessness, Dave accepted his fate and halted his efforts to free himself.

You are turning into a useless employee who is just a liability to the company, his boss's words came back to him now. Dave was spiralling into an abyss of despair. The fear was engulfing him, with the realization that he had been powerless all his life. He had never stood up to anyone and had remained a victim of aggression from others. *A wimp in all seasons,* Dave remembered a bully once said to him during high school.

In that moment, he realized the invisible force that had been limiting his movement was gone. He not only felt free, but a surge of power crept within him.

'You wasted so much time being scared all your life …' A growling voice within his head spoke.

'Who's that?' Dave snapped, jumping out of his skin. Someone had definitely spoken around him, but he couldn't see anything in the darkness. *Did it come from within me?* Dave could feel something lurking and sneaking within his body, in all his senses and brain.

There was silence again.

A high-pitched noise blared inside his head again, as he screamed and covered his ears with his hands. The noise suddenly stopped. *Who is making all this happen?* he asked himself.

'I have many names, but your kind calls me by the name of Echidna,' The voice took a pause. 'In many eons, this is the first neural link I've formed with an extra-terrestrial.'

'How are you inside my head?' he asked, as fear was ebbing within him. He felt a surge of inexplicable credence and power within him.

'You don't have to talk to communicate with me, Davie.'

Dave gasped at the name by which the voice addressed him. It was what his mother used to call him. *Whose voice is this? Where is it coming from?*

'How do you know so much about me?' Dave asked, mystified.

'I can see everything. Your whole history. Embedded in your brain's neurons,' said the voice inside his head said. Dave could feel something overpowering him, crawling within his body. He felt ... stronger somehow … his wounds started to heal on their own. His shoulder blades weren't painful anymore, and his bleeding head was stitched with a brand-new skin.

And then, there was light. Dave was standing in a corner of what seemed like a backyard of someone's house. It was weirdly familiar.

Where are we, he thought, baffled at the sudden change in the scene in front of him. *Are we back on Earth? Where has this entity taken me?*

The being within Dave, had created a new reality in the latter's mind. He had extracted a memory from his brain and was replaying it. The detailing of the new world was exceptional and pointed towards extraordinary powers that Echidna possessed.

'Do you remember this day?' the voice inside him growled again. 'This is a pivotal moment of your life.'

While so many questions were knocking about within his head, Dave saw his stepfather coming out of the house to the backyard, visibly angry. He was very young, lean and had a full head of hair. He was holding a young boy of eight by the collar and he pushed him on the grass with full force. The young boy fell down, scared and petrified. He had clearly hurt his knee from the fall.

It took a moment for Dave to realize that the young boy was his younger self. *What is going on? Can they see me?* Dave asked the voice. The scene in front of him had scarred him. And here he was, about to relive it. But why?

'They can't see you. You are simply an audience to your past,' the voice said.

Dave saw his stepfather slide out his belt from his jeans's belt loops. A thick brown leather belt. His volcanic anger was apparent, a rage that he carried all through Dave's childhood.

'I told you to behave when my friends come to visit me,' the stepfather said, gritting his teeth. Holding the buckle of his belt, he lashed the other end across the young boy's back.

The boy cried out loudly, with repeated grunts and apologies.

'How many times do I have to tell you to be disciplined?' A wave of repeated trashing of the belt on the boy's back made it difficult to breathe for him. The boy writhed in pain, using his hands to defend himself, but they were no match against the fast lashing of the leather belt.

The stepfather picked up the boy by his hair and pushed him to the wooden planks that formed the boundary to the backyard. The boy landed on the planks and fell to the ground, unconscious.

Dave stood there, watching in horror and vaguely remembering this episode of his life. His eyes moistened as he looked at his younger self, abused and lying on the grass. It was a difficult episode of his life, something that he hadn't ever shared with anybody. Dave had carried the imprints of his incident throughout his adult life too.

'This is when you learnt to bow down to authority,' the voice growled. 'You never questioned anything after this.'

Dave was on his knees, crying in horror and disbelief. The pain of going through the same experience, even if watching from afar, was incredibly gut-wrenching. The voice was right, he had been treated unfairly all his life and trampled like garbage on the streets. He wondered how one incident changed his life so much.

Dave longed for the clocks to turn back so that he could change his way of life. He could change the way he dealt with people. *Wasted too much of my life in being submissive … in not speaking out,* the realization hit Dave.

'Our journey isn't over yet,' the voice said as Dave's reality changed around him once again. The backyard, fences, his stepfather, the younger Dave, everything dissipated like evaporating ink. He was entering a new reality, a new world, once again. A memory from his brain was again being extracted by the Echidna, and a fresh scene started to construct itself in front of his eyes.

In an instant, he was in a new place. As soon as the new reality was created, Dave instantly recognized the place. It was a room in the student accommodation at Newcastle University.

The room was a combination of a bed and a study table, spacious in some ways and cramped in other. Dave instantly recognized his bedsheet with a spotty green and yellow pattern, along with a teakwood study table that creaked at the slightest of weight. Michael Jordan grinned at him from his poster, which was stuck to one of the walls, and stacks of CD albums near his bed, including one titled 'Brittany Spears Hits Volume II'. VHS tapes of films like *Die Hard* and *Terminator* rested on a shelf, under which sat a fat, 30-inch CRT television. It was like the nineties were back.

So many memories came flooding in for Dave, who stood there, fascinated with powers of the creature inside him that could make him relive his memories. He was lost in his thoughts when a twenty-one-year old Dave stepped out of the bathroom.

Young Dave had long hair and kept a thick beard, wearing a trendy turtleneck and skinny brown pajamas. He sat on the chair, and opened the book titled *The Principles of Financial Accounting*, on his study table. Dave remembered it to be the time the mid-term of his final semester were going on. Setting the stopwatch on a clock, he'd just started making notes when someone knocked on the door.

As young Dave opened the door, he saw an angry Eric Jameson, the captain of university's rowing team, standing there. Jameson entered the room, and pushed young Dave towards the almirah, hurting his back. The sudden attack startled young Dave to the point that he lost sense of what was happening.

'What were you doing talking to Emma after today's exam?' Jameson said as he grabbed young Dave by his sweater. He was known around the campus as a 'tough guy'. His violent streak was well-known around the college, along with his aggression against those who messed with him. His grasp was tight, owing to his well-developed triceps from rowing constantly in the season.

'I … I … She was asking for help … on ... on ... marketing finance,' young Dave replied, terrified to the core. He didn't know what else to say, as his mind started to get foggy from the suddenness of the impact.

Jameson pushed Dave hard against the almirah's door again. This time it was nasty. It hurt the back of his head too, as dread started to surface on his face.

'You see what this is?' Jameson showed his two fists to young Dave. 'This one is marketing, and this one is finance.' He pointed towards his right fist first and then his left fist. 'If I see you anywhere near Emma again, I will be personally tutoring you on marketing finance next time,' Jameson ruffled young Dave's hair disparagingly, punched hard on the almirah's door as a loud thud noise followed. Without breaking eye contact with young Dave, Jameson left the dorm room.

Dave, standing in the corner of the dorm room, saw his past self crouching on the floor and crying. He remembered this incident as clearly as ever, but for the first time he saw it as a third person. *Deeply scarring,* he thought.

'They wanted you to yield! And they were successful. All of them. They took away your self-worth. And you never challenged any of them!'

Dave went closer to his past self. He wanted to cajole him but when he tried to touch himself, his hands went through the body. He saw himself as helpless and deplorable. It was a pitiful sight, young Dave sobbing on the floor. He remembered how the weeping would go on for hours and how he would fall asleep on the floor and get up only in the morning.

I get the point, okay! I can't relive all this, Dave thought, pleading. There had been enough of travelling through his past today, for the episodes were too excruciating to watch.

'We are not done. One last memory trip, you need to take,' the voice roared again.

Reality evaporated once again, everything around Dave was dematerialized until it vanished. The next moment, he was somewhere else. It seemed like an office, and he immediately recognized it to be Frank & Griffin Inc. There were people coming out of a meeting. *I remember this, it was only a few months ago,* he thought as he realized what was upcoming, and how the following moments had extreme repercussions on his self-esteem.

Okay okay, I know what is going to happen, I don't want to see this, Dave pleaded in his thoughts.

'Quiet!' the voice roared.

The meeting that had just finished, was an emergency meeting, called by Robert Frank, the co-owner of the company. A story of embezzlement of around two million dollars, linked to Frank & Griffin Inc., had been published by the *Guardian*. The newspaper insinuated that the company was headed towards bankruptcy, affecting the confidence of company's stakeholders. The London office had been recently put under scrutiny by an investigative committee formed by the board members.

'If an employee was found to be talking to any journalist, print or electronic media, he will be terminated with immediate effect along with a lawsuit,' Robert Frank had declared at the meeting, as a warning to every employee. There was an apparent sternness in his tone that was the result of a strenuous situation that the board found themselves to be in.

Dave knew exactly what happened after this, as he saw his past self walking anxiously to the regional manager, Barnard Livingston.

'Mr Livingston, do you have a moment?' Past Dave asked, slightly anxious. His body language exhibited hesitancy and apprehension from a mile away.

'Yeah,' Livingston replied, busily texting, not even bothering to look up from his phone and take notice of Dave. His suave and poised demeanor added charm to his overall personality.

'I had been contacted by a journalist through my office's number, for a statement on Frank & Griffin's embezzlement. They said they were going to do a story,' Past Dave reported, showcasing his loyalty towards the company he worked for.

Livingston raised his head at once. 'Okay, then?' He was observing his employee like a predator marking his prey's moves.

'The phone calls are repeatedly coming from the same person, but he ... he was using different numbers every time. So, I ... I never gave him what he wanted. But I thought I should inform you … especially after what Robert said in the meeting,' Past-Dave explained, stuttering.

'Ohh, Dave!' Livingston said, apparently disappointed with Dave. 'You are in a big mess. You should have informed me earlier,' he said, sizing up his employee's confidence.

'But Mr Livingston, I haven't said a single word. I always cut the call as soon as I realize that it is from a journalist,' Past-Dave said, frightened now.

'I wonder if you could even afford a lawyer,' Livingston said, browsing his cellphone nonchalantly again, knowing that he had shaken his employee's confidence.

'Lawyer? But for what, Mr Livingston? I haven't done anything,' past Dave stressed again, but was sounding helpless now. 'You think I am in trouble, Mr Livingston.' He was thoroughly shaken now.

'I think you are in hot soup, Dave,' Livingston said. 'There will be a lawsuit, and I hope you are prepared for it. You could go to prison for that.'

'What?'

'I will try to do something ... maybe talk to the board members about it.' Livingston had just earned himself someone who could do his dirty work in the office. Someone who could remove those documents from the basement and shred them. Of course, Livingston himself couldn't do it, as there were CCTVs covering every inch of the basement. If and when, during the investigation, this employee got caught on tape removing those documents … Livingston will deny that he had any knowledge of it. This gullible employee would be thrown under the bus then.

Dave was listening attentively to this conversation between the Dave of mere months ago and his boss when reality dissipated once again.

Dave was now back in the sandy desert where he had crash landed on Planet Drogh. Near him, Tayira Class II was parked on a dune.

'You let that guy manipulate you just because you were intimidated by him, scared of the repercussions,' the voice scoffed at Dave. 'He has made you a slave by feasting on your self-esteem.'

Dave was silent.

The voice within him spoke again. 'There are two kinds of races in the universe – the Tyrant and the Enslaved. The Tyrant dominates the Enslaved, to increase its power and control – that is the law of this universe.' Dave was listening to this inner voice intently, as it became a guiding light for him.

'The Tyrant, convinced of its intellectual and physical superiority, justifies his exploitation and keeps on plundering and squeezing. The Tyrant's might ... the Tyrant's strength … will increase by sowing doubt and a sense of inferiority in the hearts and minds of the Enslaved, making them feel powerless and hopeless. They traumatize you, scar you and are still able to utilize you for their own advantage.' The voice stopped, giving Dave time to let the words sink in. A real awareness started to grow within him, as empowerment crept its way inside Dave.

The Echidna began again, 'You and I are the same. We both have Tyrants around us. But only you are Enslaved, not me. For I've been fighting them for centuries. I don't let them invade my lands and plunder my resources. I don't surrender to their suzerainty and most importantly, I don't doubt my abilities.'

'Rise up, Human. Don't let them rule your mind and take advantage of you. Doubt is the murderer anywhere in the universe. So fight for what's yours and keep unshackling subjugated races.'

The being stopped talking and silence followed for a few moments.

Dave gathered perspective for the first time in his life. The Echidna was right. All his life, he had been forced to bow under the authority that kept him subjugated. He realized where he had gone wrong, kept quiet and swept his exploitation under the carpet. He had let many opportunities pass him by because of his inability to put up a challenge. *Fight for what's right,* he almost said to himself.

What has been your story? Dave asked after a few moments of introspection.

'See for yourself,' The Echidna said as a barrage of images flooded Dave's brain. His eyes glistened with the flow of information. The course of events that happened across species, centuries and galaxies. The origin of the Echidna, the planet Drogh receiving its first visitors, the soldiers engaged in wars, the Cordovian narrative, the speciatic cleansing, the plundering … everything!

As Dave learnt Echidna's story, he began to feel pressure tightening around his cerebral cortex. The information flow was all too fast and overwhelming, something that humans hadn't evolved enough to receive. As the pressure became too much to bear, he cried out loud.

'That's enough! That's enough!' Dave pleaded as the bombshell of images finally stopped, and he came to his senses, his heart still beating fast. The reality that he came to know now was too much to bear. *Did it really happen this way? The narrative at the CSC was entirely different and heavily against you?* he said to the being.

'To the mighty Cordovians, I am just a parasite. An obstacle to their advancement, a pest that needs to be annihilated for the benefit of galactic alliance.'

What can I do for your cause, Dave asked desperately. The reality that he had been shown by the Echidna was a horrendous account of imperialization on its lands. Dave wanted this side of the story to be heard.

'Represent me in the Cordovian Security Council,' the Echidna replied. 'Only you could do it.'

Dave took a moment to ponder over the request. *Even if I say yes to it, how will I reach Alhadran orbit in time,* he asked.

At that moment, the broken shreds of glasses on the sand, flew of their own accord and fixed themselves back on the Tayira Class II lander's broken screen. The system looked as though it was never damaged. The sand granules rose up from the ground, like a stream of blood flowing through veins, and entered the lander's control system. The communication systems and controls came to life. The door of the lander slid open.

'Shall we?' the Echidna said as the lander now hovered two feet above the air, dancing to its tunes.

***

The Cordovian Security Council was now starting a discussion on an unprecedented bill that was about to be introduced in the house. The Director-General, an Octavian, was sitting on the highest seat of the Council to oversee one of the most important military authorizations in the history of Cordovians, since the Kerakin Era.

Below him, the Speaker, an Adronian, was seated, in order to oversee the proceedings. He had led numerous councils, where his main job was keeping the discipline among the members of council. But today was different, a universal action was about to be sanctioned in this council, which could lead to annihilation in one part of the galaxy.

'I allow the Alhadran representative to put forward and table the Cordovian Species Security Bill before the council,' the Speaker announced.

'Thank you, your honour, for giving me this historic opportunity,' the Alhadran representative stood up from his seat to address the council. 'The Cordovian Species Security Bill is a reminder to us of the Cordovian Covenant, signed at the end of Kerakin era, which states that any threat against any of the Cordovian Races, will be considered a threat against the whole species.'

Everyone at the council was listening intently.

He continued, 'Ancient Alhadran texts talk about the speciatic hierarchy, that some species are superior to others in the universe. The fabric of the cosmos is designed that way. The biological purity of Cordovian Species is talked about across the galaxies for eons. Mighty empires, technological superiority, interstellar travel – all have come from the genius minds of Cordovians. We are truly an exceptional species, whose emergence has been an unprecedented phenomenon across the universe.'

The sound of thumping of tables punctured the Alhadran representative's speech.

'One threat that stands in the way of Cordovian survival today is the desert pest – Echidna. A species biologically different from our own, and murderous in its approach towards us. The Echidna threatens not only the biological purity of Cordovians, but also galactic purity. They are a vile, destructive, impure and barbaric species, and stand exactly opposite to what *we* stand for – civilization, alliance, cooperation and peace.' The aggression was apparent in the representative's tone. The successful passage of the bill had been a dream of the Alhadran government for many decades, and today they were really close to achieving that.

Some nods, indicating support for representatives from council members were visible.

'One of the most deplorable moment in the Cordovian Security Council's history had recently taken place,' the representative had turned emotional now. 'We lost a fellow Cordovian on our journey to Drogh, from an Echidnan attack. It was one of the most agonizing moments in my life when I saw my human counterpart, helpless and vulnerable, ejected out of Provecta-Navis to save others on board. A tough call that the military commander had to take. The human must have been engulfed by the Echidna, moments after his crash landing on Drogh.'

The emotional effect on the council members was apparent. The loss of a representative to a terrorist attack had steeled everyone's resolve to put all other problems on their respective planets on back-burner and attend to this ever-expanding threat.

The Alhadran representative's tone turned ever more aggressive and his speech was punctuated with exclamation points, 'Dear council members, today I ask from you all a joint military action on Drogh against the savage and vile species of Echidna! All I demand from you is justice to that human representative who lost his life to save us! All I demand is the speciatic cleansing of Drogh, so that this godforsaken species is erased once and for all! All I ask from you is to pass this historic bill, so that Cordovian might can be rained down on a species that threatens our existence!'

All the council members, including the Octavians and Gaians, started thumping their desks. It was a unanimous decision, even before voting was undertaken, to pass the Cordovian Species Security Bill. It would be the first time, perhaps, that all the members would be on the same page in a session. It was unprecedented.

'The bill shall now be put to vote,' the Speaker announced.

***

Devastated by what happened to his master, Artemis sat in Dave's chamber, on a standby, with no purpose left now. Androids like Artemis had been built to serve particular tasks. The Eirini Age, when the major Cordovian races decided to end wars against each other, heralded a technological revolution across galaxies. The collaboration of races, especially Tardenian, Adronian and Alhadran, led to the sharing of ideas and knowledge on a scale never seen before. It was during this age that androids were developed, utilized and perfected.

Created to do the menial jobs of these mighty civilizations, the androids would work as cleaners, construction workers, petty officers and assistants across galaxies. But it was in later centuries, that the use of androids by Cordovians had expanded to drug trafficking, slavery, terrorism and extortion. This rising crime rates, especially on the planets of Abraxia and Gaia, led the Empire to push for banning the use of androids, and wiping them from Cordovia.

The Galactic Union of Android Workers (GUAW) staged synchronous protests across all major empires for the protection of their liberties under the 'Right to Life', which was enshrined in the Cordovian Constitution. Alhadra was one of the few planets where the androids are still working and the population still had trust in their abilities. The Alhadran king had declared that the privileges given to androids will be within their boundaries, and the 'Right to Life' of androids will be recognized.

'Artemis, can you hear me?' Artemis's radio frequencies caught a communication from Dave. His processing unit suddenly came to life, and algorithms were initiated to perform its functions.

'Master!' Artemis said as he came out from standby mode. 'So happy to hear your voice.' He was glad that Dave had survived at Drogh. *But how?*

'Likewise, Artemis,' Dave replied. 'I am entering the Alhadran orbit in a couple of minutes.' There were disturbances in the frequencies, but Artemis was able to understand what his master was saying. 'I want you to do me a favour, Artemis.'

'Anything, Master Dave.' Artemis sprung into action at once.

'I need to enter the Security Council before the session ends.'

***

The final reading of the Cordovian Species Security Bill was finished at the Security Council. It was clear that its provisions went against the post-Kerakin Cordovian philosophy of peaceful coexistence. The tabling of this bill in the Security Council alone wouldn't have been possible, had the human representative not been attacked by the Echidna in Drogh's atmosphere.

The conservative races, those harping on about purity and endeavour to promote orthodox philosophy of 'Two Species Theory', had been dominant today in the Security Council. Alhadrans, who were leaders of conservative thought of perpetual distinction between Cordovians and the rest of species in the universe, were pushing their agenda and calling liberal notions of cooperation with other species of the universe an illusion.

'The cooperation among two species cannot happen, for there is perpetual competition between the two. Evolution works that way. Terminating the Echidna is the only path to ensure not only Cardovian survival, but also to our eventual galactic domination,' The Kalzonian representative had spoken during the discussion on the bill.

The Director-General, a Tardenian liberationist, watched the changing political landscape with great grief. Legislation on Cordovian military attack was being planned in the council, and the values of the Eirini Age were on the cusp of elimination. He knew nothing could change the dominant discourse of speciatic purity and competition now, the discourse that used to be rebutted at once.

At that instant, the door of the council opened as an android entered. The Kalzonian representative was in the middle of his speech when Artemis reached up to the desk of the Director-General and whispered something in his ears.

The Director-General, confused and dazed, was unable to believe what he was hearing. He nodded and whispered something back to Artemis. The android then exited the council in the same way that he entered.

'I request you all to pause the proceedings,' the Director-general announced. 'We have an unexpected visitor among us: Dave Hughes, the Cordovian Security Council's Human representative. Dave, please do enter and share with us how you survived your trip to Drogh.'

Every member of the council gasped at this announcement.

They turned their heads towards the door. *Did he actually survive? Nobody comes back from Drogh alive! I saw him spiralling down towards Drogh's surface with my own eyes.* The murmuring had begun, there was much perplexity and skepticism.

And then Dave walked through into the hall, alive and unscathed. The sight shook the ground beneath everyone's feet. *How is this possible,* everyone was thinking. They stared at Dave unblinkingly, unable to believe what they were seeing. They kept staring at the human representative, thinking that he might be a hologram. But he wasn't. He had actually survived the fall.

Dave walked in quietly, entered the concentric arrangement of chairs and took his seat.

'I believe our Human representative has something urgent to address at the Security Council,' the Director-General announced.

As the whole council gaped at him in shock, Dave found himself losing confidence. Beads of sweat had appeared again on his forehead. He pulled the mic towards him as his thoughts went haywire. 'I ... uh … do … your honour. Th-Thank you.' He found it hard to speak now. He saw the emotionless faces of council members, waiting. But no words came.

He closed his eyes, as he reached his innermost thoughts. He delved into his painful memories, flashes of what he saw some hours ago. The exhaustion, the victimhood, the cowering at every challenge … it was enough. He couldn't let his past define him any more … he must transform himself and his circumstances. In that moment, his eyes shone and he rose to the challenge.

He took a deep breath and began again. 'I want to … I want to tell you all that we've been a victim of a conspiracy.' He took a pause to let people digest the fact. 'My crash landing at Drogh was a revelation; I saw the reality with my own eyes. I was contacted by an Echidna at Drogh, and he sent me back to communicate his message to this council.'

There was faint murmuring among the council members.

'This is preposterous,' one of the council members yelled.

'They can't communicate with us. There is a speciatic barrier,' the Alhadran representative intervened.

'They can communicate when they want to, sir,' Dave lashed back. 'Not many people know that Alhadran scientists were the first to contact an Echidna. They were obviously very keen to make contact, because Drogh had unlimited reserves of duranium.'

There was pin drop silence within the council now. Dave's declaration had taken everyone by surprise.

Dave began again. 'The Alhadran geologists, upon marking the reserves of duranium, started mining it without the permission of the Echidnan natives. They had already been preparing for military conflict, for the first army contingent arrived at Drogh, three days after King Tritus's coronation.'

Dave took a pause before he continued. 'When the leader of the Echidna asked Alhadrans to leave Drogh at once, the army annihilated the 90 per cent of the Echidnan population with its advanced nord weaponry. It was a massacre, where the primitive natives were mercilessly blasted with high-frequency laser beams for fun. The army was acting under King Tritus's orders of *making an example* out of the conflict so that no one dares to question Alhadran power. For last two centuries, the Alhadran forces had been plundering Drogh's reserves of duranium, only to make advanced weapons out of them and quash the Echidnan population in their own home.'

The mumbling and whispering among the council members continued as Dave continued to tell them what he saw at Drogh.

'The remaining Echidnan survivors regrouped after learning the true intentions of the conquistadors. The natives started guerilla warfare in the desert, to reclaim their lands and save their planet's environment on which their survival was dependent. It was only in recent years that the natives were successful in expelling the Alhadrans, attacking the battalions with newer ways of warfare. The Mount of Stin is the last bastion of Alhadran forces and if they lose that too, they will have no duranium for their empire.

'At this point, I must inform the council that the Alhadran reserves of duranium do not exist. All of this rare metal in the empire has been imported from Drogh through invasion.' Dave took a deep breath. A wave of confidence filled his soul, something he had never before experienced in his life.

'The Cordovian joint military effort, in the name of the 'Two Species Theory', is nothing but a narrative created to expel the Echidna from their lands. An agenda to get their hands on large duranium reserves for centuries to come.' Dave paused to observe the silence in the room. He observed the Alhadran representative, who got up from his chair angrily and exited the Security Council as a mark of protest.

'But what about their airborne attacks, the Echidna bio-attack targeting the Cordovian populations across galaxies?' the Adronian representative enquired.

'The Alhadran Society of Scientists has an answer to that question. The airborne attacks are carried out by genetically engineered Echidnan copies, created and grown in Alhadran labs to be released on Cordovian planets by Alhadran army personnels. It was done to convince the more progressive members of the council of the necessity of action against the Echidna. It was done to create a sense of urgency among Cordovian races for joint military action,' Dave said as he pointed towards the vacant chair of the Alhadran representative. 'Innocent people have paid the price of the king's hunger for duranium. '

'The Alhadran artificial intelligence, Zeki, ejected me from Provecta-Navis, on the orders of Alhadran military – a tactic to push Cordovian representatives into action. I was lucky to have survived the fall but blaming all of it on the Echidna served the Alhadran purpose.'

When Dave finished speaking, the whole room was stunned. His speech had been inadvertently broadcast across empires and civilizations. A narrative created in order to strip a species of its resources – it took everyone by surprise. No one dared to speak for a couple of minutes after Dave stopped speaking.

What Dave said had made a good case against the passing of the Cordovian Species Security Bill. The Director-General had to make a call now. All eyes were fixed on him now, as he stood up from his chair.

'I order an inquiry on the accusations levelled by the Human representative against King Tritus,' the Director-General spoke, 'The Cordovian Security Council is adjourned sine die.

***

Back in his chamber, Dave was lying down. It was time to go back but he had started liking it here. *A life transforming experience,* Dave felt while looking at the last few days. He looked out of the window, only to see those two stars in space. One of them was ebbing and the other was rising.

Some moments ago, he had been injected with a drug by Artemis, to induce sleep – necessary for the process of teleportation. It was clear that the Dave that entered this world was not the same that was about to leave it. Maybe XERXES selected Dave as human representative because its algorithm calculated that only he could form a cognatic bond with the Echidna. To the AI, this must have seemed like the best possible way to establish peace over impending doom. Dave was lost in his thoughts when Artemis stepped in the room.

'Master Dave, your transport is ready,' he said.

Dave had truly enjoyed Artemis's company during his stay on Alhadra. He had been a valuable asset in introducing him to this world. There was a kind of earnestness that Artemis exhibited that made him an extremely genial person. For Dave, Artemis was more of a human than a synthetic being ... he was more human than many humans. *I wonder whether we would meet again or not,* the thought crossed Dave's mind.

He thought about Artemis and his support in toppling the

Cordovian Order. He had just opened his mouth to tell the AI about his indispensability to the mission, when the latter spoke.

'I must inform you at once that King Tritus had been found guilty of war crimes and would be imprisoned under Octavia Convention Rules. This ends his lineage's reign on Alhadra,' Artemis said.

Dave didn't give any reaction to it. *The horrible things that Tritus had done … this was the only fate that befitted him,* he thought. The Alhadran civilization must find a sustainable way to progress and stop colonizing other planets to attain advancement. As far as Dave was concerned, it was the Alhadran government and not the Echidna that had parasitic characteristics as the former was deriving benefits at the latter's expense.

'You must sleep now, Master Dave, to wake up in your world,' Artemis advised Dave as he cast a one last look out at the Alhadran space before getting into his chair and laying down. *An incredible journey*, he thought as his eyes became heavier.

And then he was asleep.

***

Dave woke up with a slight headache and a blurry vision. The light from filtering from the windows was enough to tell him that he was currently in the Frank & Griffin Inc. office, even as his vision was adjusting to the surroundings.

Was it all a dream, he asked himself. The company papers were lying on the carpet instead of being in the shredder. He realized that the whole night had passed, and he hadn't yet completed the task given to him by Mr Livingston. The sunlight filtered through the glass walls of the office, bidding goodbye to a long, drawn-out night. Dave's hair was ruffled, with a loose tie and shirt that was half tucked and half tucked out from his pants.

He got up, walked up to the coffee machine and poured himself a cappuccino. His neck was aching, mainly due to sleeping in one position. He moved his neck in a circular motion, to relieve the pain, but to no avail.

The dream felt so real, he told himself as coffee came spouting out from the nozzle into his plastic cup. He picked the cup and took a sip. There was some noise coming from the corridor, and Dave glanced at the source by standing on his toes.

He saw someone entering the office, by swiping his card. As he entered the office, Dave recognized him to be Mr Livingston, who had come to check if his employee had finished the task he had given him last night. He saw Dave and immediately said, 'Good Morning, Dave. Were you up all night to finish the task? That's like a loyal employee.' He seemed cheerful. It looked like he had a wonderful night.

Dave continued to sip his coffee, waiting for his boss to notice the mess on the floor. And Livingston saw the mess the next instant.

'You didn't shred these documents?' Livingston picked up some of them and was frustrated to see pages lying on the floor openly. 'I am asking you something, you moron. Do you even know what information they contain?' Livingston pushed Dave in volcanic anger.

Dave was listening to Livingston's rant with growing dread; all the old feelings of insufficiency came rushing back to him. But a curious thing happened. In the glass behind Livingston, Dave caught a reflection of his arm. The Cordovian Security Council's stamp stared back at him. Was it all real after all?

Livingston was continuing to curse him out, 'You are a pathetic worker, Hughes, a good for nothing, useless—'

He was cut off with a punch from Dave that landed hard on Livingston's abdomen. It tipped Livingston off-balance and he crashed to the floor. His briefcase flew in the air and fell four feet away due to the impact. Livingston couldn't believe what had just happened. *Did Dave just punch him?* And then he saw Dave walking towards him, as he tried to get up, but couldn't.

'You have been embezzling money from Frank and Griffin

Inc. for months.' Dave looked at now grunting Livingston in the eye as he spoke. 'You have been removing evidence worth thousands of pages for the past many weeks to save your arse from investigation. On top of it all, you have been cheating on your wife and sleeping with your secretary,' Dave roared like never before in his life.

Dave sat on the floor on one knee and calmly said, 'You are a pathetic human being, Barnard Livingston. And I will make sure you pay for what you've done.' Dave got up and left the office, leaving behind a baffled and shaky Livingston.

Dave took a look at his wrist. *The Cordovian Security Council's* stamp - 《『Δ』》 - stared back at him.

Down Memory Lane

He was trying to free himself, but could hardly move, strapped as he was to the chair … they didn't think twice before giving him a high intensity electroshock if he impeded their operation ... he was screaming his lungs out when the current went through his body ... In the next instant, he was forced on to a bed, with white light landing straight on his face … nothing was visible to him ... people were standing around him, but he could only see their outlines ... they were talking amongst themselves … his vision blurred, and he went into a deep sleep.

Abish woke up in the middle of the night, his pillow soaked in sweat and his heart racing. It was the same nightmare he had been having over and over again, for almost a year now. *Does it even mean anything?* he asked himself on nights like these. Trying to clear his dry throat, he got off the bed and walked to the kitchen to quench his thirst. It was hard to keep his balance; the dizziness was still there.

As he poured himself a glass of water from a nozzle embedded within the refrigerator's door, he took a peek at the sleeping city of Delhi from the window. The sprawling metropolis was silent as ever, with faint noises of horns blaring somewhere distant, a flickering street light in the nearby lane, and dogs barking in rhythmic beats. The sound of chirping crickets filled the vicinity. *There is a certain mysticism to the city,* he thought as he gulped down a glass of water.

Walking around his drawing room barefoot, Abish eyed the wall decorated with his medals and framed certificates. He never got a chance to appreciate the wall since he had moved to Delhi after his posting here, a month ago. Most of his medals and awards were due to his exceptional service in conducting the anti-terrorism operations in the region of Kashmir. However, the most prestigious medal on the wall was the Presidential medal for his actions in Afghanistan on one fateful day. He wasn't the only one, the whole unit had gotten this award on their return.

It was hard for Abish to sleep again, no matter how hard he tried. He couldn't remember the last time he had a good night's sleep. For the past few months, his brain had kept him awake every night, showing him random images in his sleep that felt far too real. Tonight was one such night.

Abish decided to turn on the TV in his drawing room, tuning in to the news. As he tuned in, a live feed from Connaught Place was being broadcast. Protests had erupted nationwide as the prime minister's popularity had reached a record low since the Herat attack that had happened a year ago and he had failed to deliver on the economic and national security front. The huge protests, going on for the past six months, demanded immediate resignation of the prime minister, followed by a re-election.

Abish saw the news channel *India Now* displaying their survey results: if at this point, general elections were to take place, Neel Raghav would surely win against all the contenders for the seat of Prime Minister, with a thumping majority. *'If these projections are true, then Mr Raghav will be the youngest PM in the history of the world's largest democracy,'* the news reporter informed the viewers. The crowd chanted for change and transformation in the system.

Neel was a charismatic young man in his late thirties and had been a popular political leader since his university days. He was tall, had a square jaw, a charming smile and an athletic build. He had become the darling of the Indian media and the urban Indian youth since his first *Ted Talk* at the age of twenty-two went viral on YouTube. But since last year, Neel Raghav became popular for an incident that not only changed his life, but also Indian politics for years to come. He had managed to get massive support from the common man, who'd given him a messiah-like status.

Major Abish Desai knew that incident very well because he was present there, deployed as a part of the *Special Operations Division,* and saw the miracle happening. *I had a front row seat to the miracle,* he reminded himself, as the news channels started discussing Neel Raghav's future. The debates revolved around Neel and his ability to lead the country in the future.

'Joining us live from Bangalore is former Indian diplomat to Iran, Surendranath Iyer,' the news representative said, as the screen was cut in half and a middle-aged man with grey hair and a moustache appeared, sitting in front of a bookshelf. 'Mr Iyer, what do you think makes Neel Raghav, a figure as yet unknown to Indian politics, the biggest contender to the seat of Prime Minister?" she asked.

'He is a symbol of security and sacrifice in India, Neha. His actions have shown him to be reliable, action-oriented and quick-thinking during emergencies,' The ex-diplomat was quick to answer. 'Consider the context while reading these projections, Neha. India is surrounded by enemies from all sides – Pakistan, Afghanistan, China – they have all been regularly infiltrating our borders in Kashmir. There is the expanding influence of the Chinese in Bangladesh and Sri Lanka, isolating India with its natural allies. We have a 4500-kilometre coastline to protect from naval terrorism, especially when our soft power has been stagnant, if not declining, in last decade or so.'

The news representative nodded along.

The ex-diplomat continued. 'With national security being a

big part of what influences public opinion in India, the rising popularity of Mr Raghav in the election season was inevitable.'

Abish gave a faint laugh. Despite Neel Raghav being a national hero, Abish had never quite liked him. The man was a strange mix of extroverted-ness and mysticism. Abish couldn't put his finger on it, but there was something about Neel that deeply irked him. *It may be because you are jealous of him,* his batchmates had once joked. But he knew that wasn't the reason.

For Abish, more than jealousy, a civilian earning the tag of *hero* on the battlefield was annoying. *It is the job of armed forces, not civilians, to prove themselves on ground zero,* he believed. Neel Raghav made trained special forces personnel look like a mere audience that day. *Deeply unsettling,* he said to himself as he switched off the TV in disgust and threw away the remote on his couch in a disgruntled manner.

But what was more unsettling for Abish was his meeting with Neel Raghav, scheduled tomorrow at Tagore Auditorium. As a guest, Raghav will be interviewed live about his experiences on Afghan soil on D-day. The more interviews Raghav gave on news channels, the more the viewership expanded. Abish was also invited to the forum, along with other members of the SOD unit, to confirm Raghav's heroic story, as they were the only ones with first-hand knowledge.

It was a gathering that would be broadcasted and streamed live as part of Neel's PR campaign amidst growing protests. After all, he was being touted by people and the media as 'the chosen one'. Abish had earlier refused to be part of it, but a phone call from Neel, requesting that he attend, forced him to change his mind. Even though Abish would get annoyed at the mere mention of Neel's name, he couldn't ignore the fact that Neel wielded the support of millions of people at the moment. On top of it all, the opinion polls made it clear that Neel could become the leader of the nation in upcoming weeks. When a political leader this powerful made a personal call, it's in one's best interest to accept.

Perhaps I can keep my annoyance at bay for one day, he thought.

Abish popped a sleeping pill, hoping it would induce sleep. After four hours, he was still wide awake, with no hint of sleep. He saw the dawn, ending the long reign of night, slowly but surely.

***

'How are your nerves holding up after seeing the pre-poll surveys, Mr Raghav?' An interviewer posed the question as a crowd of around 800 people cheered the guest.

Neel tried to speak but the cheering continued, so he waited for the clamor to stop.

'It's Neel. Just call me Neel,' he replied, as the cheering ebbed. 'It feels great to see those survey results, of course. But I am happy that I made it so far. If I win, that's good but If I don't ... well, there are many more ways to serve the public other than politics.' Neel was wearing a slim-fitted suit, which made him look more like a corporate man than an Indian politician.

'You've recently released an election manifesto outlining promises to the public,' the reporter said. 'What are your promises for ensuring double-digit GDP growth?'

'Privatization, Kanika. Being a postgraduate in business administration and with experience in travelling all over the world, I can tell you that it is more productive to produce when there is least government interference. Investments can only come with minimum red-tapism and bureaucracy, and when home-grown corporate leaders compete with each other. Telecoms, pharmas, healthcare ... everything!' Neel said as the audience responded with claps. Neel saw three sets of cameras pointed at him from every direction, capturing all his displays of emotion.

'If elected, what would be your main focus amongst all national issues?' Kanika asked. But she already knew the answer, even before her interviewee opened his mouth to respond.

'National security!' he replied without hesitance. 'I have seen the battlefield up close and it's horrifying. Terrorism is being supported and sponsored openly by some of our neighbours. I am done watching our soldiers laying down their lives due to flawed national security policies over the last two decades. The people of India deserve a safe and secure nation ... instead, the constant terrorism within our borders is making people fear for their lives. The territorial aggression is completely intolerable.' Neel thumped his fist on his lap, as if he was passionate about it.

A loud applause followed.

'Where do you get this nationalism within you, Neel? You have been a passionate speaker at world forums, be it on climate change at WEF or Millenium Development Goals at the UN, with focus on India's interests,' the reporter said.

'This deep sense of nationalism was ingrained in me by my father since my childhood. As we all know, he had been a founding member of Mesotron Inc., with a vision of making a tech enterprise so big that it competes with American conglomerates, and it does. Today, Mesotron's innovations are applauded across the globe, and so many western tech companies are eager to collaborate with it,' Neel explained, as people listened intently.

Neel's father, Kalyan Raghav, had been respected across the country mainly because of his nationalistic bent of mind. Before his death a decade ago, Kalyan Raghav, and Mesotron, helped develop new technologies of ammunition, especially weapons of mass destruction. This had reduced India's dependence on US and Russian weapon imports. India had truly become self-sufficient in the defense sector.

Neel continued. 'His vision isn't complete until India reaches the position where it is destined to be. We truly can be a world superpower. With a population of 1.5 billion and counting, we are an economic powerhouse. We need to be menacing when it comes to our external policies ... our surveillance, intelligence and diplomacy needs to be the world's best if we need to take down the enemies surrounding us.'

Another round of applause followed.

'Without having any military training and experience, what Neel has done on the battlefield is truly commendable,' the interviewer said amidst the applause. 'We have the Special Operation Division unit leader, Major Abish Desai, who saw it all happening.' She pointed towards the first row in the audience. 'Major Desai, why don't you share with us what you saw that day? We never got to hear the version of military men who were deployed there. Now that considerable time has passed since the event, I believe it's time to hear the soldiers' account.' A mic automatically flew towards Abish and hung in mid-air, one foot away from his mouth.

'Yes, fortunately for us, considerable time has passed since that traumatic event. Although I don't want to recall that day, I also think that Neel Raghav's contribution in the success of that incident must be highlighted,' Abish said. His tight white shirt was making him perspire in the Delhi heat, and he wished he had chosen to wear something looser. His old brown trousers reminded him that it had been ages since he went to buy clothes for himself.

'When did you learn that an attack was imminent?' she asked.

'We didn't,' Abish said. 'At 11:05, we were given orders that an immediate evacuation of Indian diplomats posted in Herat, North-West Afghanistan, is required. There was intel from New Delhi about the possible Mujahideen movement, and evacuation was considered the appropriate action. Officers who have worked in Afghanistan know that evacuations are part of normal routine. It is done to minimize any threat, and in all probability, there won't be a threat.'

Everyone in the crowd was listening attentively. Even the interviewer was all ears to the detailed account being presented by Abish. The live streaming relayed the interview across all social media platforms, with viewership now reaching five million people. The political landscape in the nation was changing tremendously as Abish described the battle scenes.

'Along with Indian diplomats, there were three Indian business and political leaders, who had come there to attend the Afghan Investment Conclave held two days before. Neel Raghav was one of them.' Abish took a pause. 'We were a convoy of four 15-tons M141 Defender – an armoured military vehicle accommodating two machine guns and one grenade launcher. All five diplomats and two CEOs adjusted themselves in both M141s. Neel had decided to sit in my *M141,* separated from his peers,' Abish said as he realized Neel was looking at him. It was more than a look, it was like an observation. It made him a little conscious.

'At exactly 11:42, we started towards Herat airport, and it's a narrow curvy terrain that is between the city and the airport. We were going at an average speed, quietly crawling and keeping a keen eye on blind spots. At 11:57, an RPG struck our convoy, knocking one M141 from the road. Three personnel from our unit were in it, and they died on the spot.' Abish laid out the facts calmly, leaving the audience gasping.

'Oh my God!' the interviewer said aloud, inadvertently. Abish's account made the battle look unsurvivable. The audience pictured the gruesome visuals he was narrating.

'We were surrounded from all sides. Just as we realized this, a barrage of bullets started raining down on us out of nowhere, mostly LMGs and AK-92s. We retaliated with the remaining unit, but we were too late and there were too many. We weren't able to make out the direction from which the attack was happening,' Abish explained, gesticulating with his hands. 'As if it was not enough, a G24 Chopper came up, from somewhere down south, with heavy machine gun fire. We were truly blocked from all sides. We tried constantly firing in north-east and east directions, but it was useless. The enemies came with intense preparation—'

'What were they targeting?' the interviewer asked.

'They wanted to get a hold of the diplomats alive, and blackmail the Indian government to release their leader, Zaid Shahid, in exchange.'

'Right. Go on, Major,' Kanika said.

'Now three members of my unit were dead and another one was injured, only six of us were active. It was impossible to get out of there alive.' Abish gestured towards Neel as he talked now. 'This man comes out of M141 and tells me he can help. I screamed at him to get back inside, but instead of following me, he picked up the *TAR-21 Carbine* of the fallen soldier and started shooting. I thought this man had gone crazy and was gonna get killed.'

The crowd started laughing. Neel gave a faint smirk. All cameras panned towards him; every visual of him was ballooning the network's viewership by thousands.

'And he climbed up the M141, he held the LMG amidst raining bullets and aimed at the G24 Chopper encircling us. I thought he was going to get fried ... I seriously believed that at that moment.' Abish took a pause to catch his breath. 'Now see, it is very hard to take a flying chopper down with a handgun because of its height.' Abish used both hands to show the position difference of men on ground and chopper. 'It is extremely rare to hit the guy who is flying the chopper. And that rare moment came when Neel used the LMG on a chopper, with one bullet piercing the pilot's neck.'

'Fortune favours the brave, I guess.' the Interviewer said, glancing at Neel.

'Probably a fluke. I just threw everything at it in anger and got lucky,' Neel said as faint laughs erupted from the audience.

'So what happened then?' the interviewer asked Abish.

'Yeah. The pilot lost his balance and the chopper started spiralling in the air, descending pretty fast. It hit the largest Mujahideen contingent that was firing at us from the north-east, and there was a big explosion. That was when it gave us a corner to hide ourselves properly, and we regrouped. Everything happened so fast after this. Before we could assemble properly, Neel had picked up the carbine and grenade launcher, and headed ahead to answer the incoming firing.'

Another wave of gasping and whispering from the audience

rose and ebbed.

'What was going on in your head then?' Kanika asked Neel. It was apparent that she was impressed with the guest since the event had begun and had become more enchanted over the course of the interview. As far as the audience was concerned, the magnetism of Neel was expanding every second.

'It was a fight for my life and my people's survival. I couldn't be a spectator, not when terrorism was at work,' Neel said, and people cheered at the strong reply.

The answer rankled Abish a bit, but he let it go.

He continued talking. 'We had no option but to give him cover. Suddenly we heard a blast taking place. The firing from the other side had stopped. I later found out he used a grenade launcher, by catching them unaware, from behind. I gathered strength to move forward, taking cover behind our M141 and the scene I saw was something that I couldn't forget. A hand-to-hand combat was taking place between him and two Mujahideens. Before I could step forward to help him, Neel shot them both point blank. I joined him finally and found that he was charged up. By now, I had realized that either bullets were repelling him or he was incredibly lucky.'

Sounds of laughter erupted from the audience again.

'The firing had frizzled by now. They had accumulated far more casualties, which counted to be around twenty with chopper clash and eight more alone by this man sitting on stage. The trained SOD unit hadn't killed a single enemy, and all kills, along with the credit of us being alive, went to Neel. And rightly so.' Abish blurted the last sentence with reluctance. 'There was almost zero chance of coming back alive from that situation.' Abish took a deep breath, and out of nowhere, he said, 'I think Neel Raghav is the most selfless and valiant soul I've come across in my life.'

He couldn't believe that he had said it. He knew he didn't believe in this statement, but it was almost as though he had no control over his mind.

The crowd applauded vehemently, and this time even the interviewer joined in.

When Abish's version of the story was finished, the mic automatically floated away from him. The interview went for another hour or so; Neel was asked about his childhood and the policies he would undertake regarding the agriculture and mining sector.

That was truly excruciating, Abish thought once it was finally over. He somehow threaded through the interview with a mixture of disdain and vexation.

It was almost dark, and Abish wanted to head home fast. Seeing such a large crowd today was enough for him. He wanted to spend time alone in his apartment now. On his way back to the parking lot, Abish saw a familiar figure waiting next to his car. He became attentive when he saw Abish coming towards him.

'At ease, Lieutenant Neville Mistry,' Abish said cheerfully as he unlocked his car. He already knew that Mistry had taken voluntary retirement from the army four months ago.

'Sir.' Mistry managed to answer in a cracking voice. He looked dishevelled, with his wrinkled clothes, beard growing like a bush, dark circles under his eyes and long but ruffled hair. Even his shirt was only half tucked in.

'Everything all right at home, Mistry?' Abish asked, now concerned for his junior. Lieutenant Mistry was one of the survivors from the SOD unit that was ambushed in Herat. His performance of military duties had gone down considerably since the attacks.

'You've got to help me, sir. They are killing me,' Mistry cried, grabbing Abish's arm. He almost threw Abish off-balance. Mistry sounded weak and helpless, a version that Abish had never seen in the three years they had served together.

Abish was stupefied. 'What? Who is killing you?' he asked, liberating his arm from Mistry's grasp.

'These dreams, sir. It has been days since I've slept properly or eaten anything. These dreams go around in my head … they seem more real than reality,' Mistry said, in a frightened voice. A jovial character in the SOD unit and incredibly funny, Lieutenant Mistry was never down with his mood. Today, he looked deranged and unstable.

'Dreams? What dreams?' Abish asked, not understanding what Mistry was trying to say.

'That I am strapped to a chair and they are operating on me. They cut me open on a hospital bed. They shock me, these doctors, if I am out of line. I feel the pain in my head when I dream about this. Pain ... real pain! Help me, Major ... HELP!' His voice suddenly went loud and eventually became a cry.

This shook Abish's world as he couldn't believe what he was hearing. Mistry had described the exact dream that he was also having. *How is this possible,* he thought. Abish didn't know what astonished him the most, seeing his military mate in such a state or this uncanny similarity in their dreams.

Meanwhile, the people in the parking lot were starting to stare, owing to loud cries of Mistry.

'Sit in my car,' Abish ordered.

***

It was late evening when Abish and Mistry sat down in a shady bar in Daryaganj. It was one of the few places where the probability of someone recognizing Abish was really low. They both sat down in the corner where the lighting was very dim. There was loud music too, and it seemed like no one would bother them for a while. He ordered a pint of beer as his companion adjusted himself.

'What do you mean things hadn't really happened the way we remember?' Abish asked, now very inquisitive.

'Things don't add up, sir,' Mistry said, stuttering. Abish looked at the lean boney fingers of his ex-subordinate and realized how physically weak Mistry had gotten. 'If I ... If I remember correctly,'

Mistry coughed a bit while speaking, 'It all happened exactly like you described today ... at the event,' Mistry said as he looked around him before speaking the next sentence, 'But when I think about the Herat attack, these dreams ... they ... they play out in my mind instead of what we believe has happened …'

Abish gave him a confused look.

'These dreams, sir … they seem more real than the reality itself,' Mistry stressed again, holding his head in his hands. 'It's like ... the Herat attack ... never happened.' The sentence sounded bizarre as soon as it came out of his mouth.

'Now that is a stretch, Neville,' Abish said, shaking his head. 'You mean the rest of the unit survivors, the diplomats, business leaders, Neel, everyone's lying? You've lost your mind.'

'I am not mad, sir,' Mistry shouted, raising his voice in frustration. 'Do you know Lokhande is in a mental institution? He was ... he was ... also having these dreams. He confided in me long before I started having them. If you think I've lost it ... then ... then visit the Army Base Hospital in Delhi Cantt,' Mistry said, now weeping.

Lokhande is in an asylum … Abish thought. He sorely regretted not remaining in touch with his SOD mates since Afghanistan.

Abish didn't know what to believe now. He was surely having the same dream that Mistry was having but claiming that whatever happened in Herat … hadn't actually happened … was nothing but fiction … It sounded like one of those conspiracy theories shown on the History channel every weekend.

Mistry continued. 'How can a civilian, with no military combat and weapon training, fight the goddamn terrorists? That man doesn't even have a licensed weapon and never shot a round in his entire life? The truth just doesn't match the facts!' He thumped his fist hard on the table, as people sitting near the table turned their attention towards them for a second and then went back to their conversations

'Don't you have those dreams, sir?' Mistry asked, whispering in

Abish's ear.

Abish gave a faint nod. 'Exactly like you've described.' He knew this was the strangest thing he had ever heard in his life.

'Then that confirms it, sir.' Mistry said.

On the TV just above the bar counter, Neel Raghav was giving a speech to the protestors. The day before, around 50,000 people joined in a candle-light march in Delhi alone, asking for the prime minister's resignation. Everyone, especially students, were chanting his election slogan of *Nation First. Security First,* as Neel waved his hands towards the crowd with numerous yellow garlands over his neck.

'Only he deserves to be our next PM ... India needs him,' the bartender said, also watching the speech on TV as he poured whiskey for one of the customers.

Abish kept staring at the TV and thinking what if all that made Neel Raghav, a national hero, never actually happened. *But how is that possible?* He immediately negated the thought.

Sitting in another corner, beneath the staircase of the bar, a man was looking intently at both men, reporting their every movement to someone.

***

Abish woke up the next morning with thoughts full of conversations with Mistry. He kept talking of this political conspiracy, and at one point Abish thought that he was acting as a borderline lunatic. He had dropped Mistry off at his apartment late at night, but his revelations never really completely left Abish's mind.

It was getting hard for Abish to sleep, and in the morning, he woke up with a headache. Last evening, at the event, he remembered how observant Neel Raghav had been as he watched him as he described the Herat terrorist attack incident. *How can a civilian, with no military combat and weapon training, fight the goddamn terrorists?* Mistry's voice reverberated in his head now.

There was something that was clearly not right. Those dreams also seemed real to Abish, and if the other members of the SOD unit were also having them, there had to be a possible explanation to this. *I have to get to the bottom of this,* he made up his mind.

At 11 a.m., Abish found himself visiting the Delhi Cantt Hospital, to check if Mistry's story actually held true and that he hadn't gone mental. Beating Delhi's peak-hour traffic, winding his way through Green Park and Hauz Khas, he entered the premises of Delhi Army Cantonment.

Made during the British era, the army cantonment was actually a mini town in itself, made by keeping in mind the comfort of British officers. It not only had Indian Army headquarters, but also the army golf-course, military residential area and most importantly, Army Hospital Research and Referral (AHRR) for tertiary care of defense personnel.

It was in AHRR that Junior Commissioned Officer Ravi Lokhande was admitted and undergoing mental treatment. Abish reached Block 8 and Ward 4, to find his once brawny SOD unit member, lying lifeless on a wheelchair. It wasn't pleasant for Abish to see his ex-colleague, a friend, in this condition. A nurse was getting ready to take him for a spin across the lawn, for fresh air, and Abish decided to accompany them.

'What exactly has happened to him?' Abish asked the nurse, as she dragged the wheelchair into the elevator.

'The doctors have diagnosed his condition to be schizophrenia. The recurrence of delusions, abnormal motor behavior and hallucinations, have been observed even since treatment began. He is in a catatonic state right now, and it appears his health is worsening,' the nurse said as the elevator began to go down. Her short hair with red streaks alluded to a devil-may-care attitude. She was in the early half of her twenties, and it looked like she had problems of her own..

'Can I try talking to him? I was his senior in the army. We both served in Afghanistan together,' Abish said as the elevator opened and all three walked towards the lawn opposite the hospital building. 'He might respond to me.'

She shrugged. 'He has difficulty interpreting reality and speaks gibberish whenever he wants to speak. But you can always try.' They were on the lawn now, as the fresh air breezed through Abish's hair.

Abish bent down on one knee to be on the same level as his junior, who was as still as the eucalyptus tree behind him. 'Hey buddy, how have you been?' he asked, holding Lokhande's right hand.

Lokhande didn't even move an inch of his body. Not even his eyeballs.

The nurse watched this with a look on her face that clearly said 'I told you so.' Abish looked at her embarrassedly and decided to try once again.

'Cheeku,' Abish called Lokhande by his nickname, in a hope that he would respond. 'I too have those dreams,' he said, whispering in his ears. But there was still no movement, not even the slightest twitching. Abish tried one more time, but there was nothing that could indicate that Lokhande would respond.

He ultimately gave up and got up to his feet. 'How long has he been unresponsive?' he asked the nurse.

'Four months now. Hardly ever moves, stays still all day long,' she replied, but Abish wasn't even focusing on what she was saying. His eyes were now fixed on Lokhande's left hand, which was moving ever so slightly. Lokande wasn't completely inactive after all. He was responding, though it was quite a subtle response. But why?

It took a moment for Abish to understand that Lokhande was signalling something. His left hand was communicating in three recurring rhythms – a fist, two fingers out, then again a fist. It was a standard signal for 'raid and search', among infantry units deployed in forward areas. If Abish had deciphered the signal right, then it meant Lokhande wanted him to look for something. But search for what? And most importantly, search where?

Bidding goodbye, the nurse slid Lokhande away to saunter around the lawn, leaving Abish confused. *What does he mean by that,* he thought as his eyes fell on the sprawling building of AHRR. *His hospital room!* Abish hoped that he was on the right track.

He ran up the building, through the elevator and into the room where he had found Lokhande some moments ago. It was a typical hospital ward, with three beds placed side by side and green curtains between them. The smell of the disinfectant solution, typical of every hospital, was omnipresent. Behind every bed, on the wall, there were sensors placed that were used to monitor vitals of the patients. There was no one else in the room, except a patient on the bed.

Abish started looking through the drawers near Lokhande's bed. There was nothing except medicines, syringes and medical equipment. Then he moved to the closet at the end of the ward, checking each and every cupboard. *Time is running out.* The thought crossed Abish's mind as he looked outside from the glass window to find out that the nurse was done with Lokhande's strolling and was entering the hospital building. He started rummaging through the closet rapidly, but there was nothing except a pair of folded surgical gloves, a patient's gown and cotton ... too much cotton.

Maybe I've read his signal wrong. Abish was having second thoughts now as he looked under Lokahnde's mattress, which was as clean as the tiles on the floor. The nurse could be entering the ward any minute now. *What more hidden places are there,* he thought as his mind wandered around the room. There was nothing that could act as a secret compartment of some kind. Abish still continued to rummage, with hope diminishing every second.

And then it struck him. *Under the bed!* He immediately looked under Lokahnde's bed, and there it was – a black pen drive taped under the bed, well-hidden from anyone who came looking for it. *That is such an SOD tactic,* Abish smirked as he removed the pen drive.

As soon as he was on his feet, he heard the nurse entering the ward with Lokhande. Abish hid behind the swinging door. As the door opened and the nurse came barging in with the wheelchair, Abish snuck out of the ward without her noticing him.

In the next few moments, Abish found himself in his car. The adrenaline flow was on its peak within his body. He removed the tape off the pen drive and plugged it into the car's infotainment system. The screen flashed a 'A new input device detected' message and it processed the device successfully. The screen showed that the drive had only one audio file. *A recording?* Abish tapped on the audio file and it started playing.

Abish was right, it was a recording in Lokhande's voice. But he was speaking gibberish. The words he spoke made no sense at all! *What the hell is he saying,* he thought as he strained his brain hard to understand a single word that Lokahnde spoke, but he couldn't make it out. *It doesn't even sound like another language,* he thought as he unplugged the device. Another dead end. Disappointed, Abish turned his key, and the car came to life.

At that instant, his cellphone rang. It was an unknown number.

'Yes,' He answered.

'Is this Mr Abish Desai?' A hoarse voice spoke from the other side.

'That's right.' Abish sounded confused. But he could make out that something was amiss.

'Mr Desai, this is Station House Officer Monojit Roy speaking. You need to report at Connaught Place Police Station today,' the voice said. "It is pretty urgent.'

'Is there a problem?' Abish was confused. He'd had too many surprises in the last twenty-four hours. He wasn't expecting any more of them.

'Yes, in fact there is. A man named Neville Mistry was found dead in his apartment last night. We need to ask you some questions.'

***

A human body looked more sinister when it had no soul within it. This was exactly what Abish was feeling when he saw photographs of his SOD junior, Mistry, lying lifeless on the carpeted floor of his apartment. In the next photograph, his torso had a large diagonal cut, maroon in colour, starting from his right underarm and ending where his left lung would be.

He was found lying flat on his back, and it seemed like it was a sudden attack that caught him unawares. A closer look at the photographs showed no cuts or bruises anywhere else on the body, indicating that there was no struggle from the victim's side.

'If you think that it is the work of a blade, you are mistaken,' Officer Roy said, looking at Abish. 'There are burns around the injury, which means whatever has cut him has also smouldered his insides.'

Abish kept staring at the photographs. He was feeling a mixture of outrage and discomfiture. His body language had suddenly transformed from a confused to cautious state, as he became aware of the peril.

'The CCTVs on the street showed us that you dropped Mr Mistry at his home at 11 p.m.,' Roy said as Abish looked up. 'Did you see anything wrong with Mr Mistry?'

'He looked dishevelled, but nothing looked out of place as far as he was concerned. He had been depressed for quite a while, but that is very common with people who had served in the army in high-risk areas, especially overseas,' Abish replied and went back to looking at the photograph.

'Had he talked about any threat to his life?' Roy asked.

Abish shaked his head, 'No, he hadn't. He wasn't in any danger at all. It was just a casual meeting. We served in Afghanistan together and since I was recently posted to Delhi, I decided to meet him. It's surreal to know that someone wanted him dead. He could hardly offend anyone,' Abish said and went quiet for a few moments. 'Any break-ins at his apartment?'

'His apartment's back door was unlocked. He must have been keeping it that way; the intruder didn't have to break any glass or lock to get in,' Roy explained. He was observing Abish's reaction intently. As an investigator, it was his job to take everyone's word with a grain of salt.

Almost all day was spent at the station, answering questions about Mistry's army record, his past and his reasons for early retirement. It was beginning to get dark when Abish recorded his statement. Before finally letting him go, Roy told Abish that he could be called back to the station if there were any new developments in the case.

While driving back home, Abish tried to connect the pen drive again to the infotainment system, hoping that the recording would make sense now, miraculously. However, it was still gibberish in Lokhande's voice. Abish was now facing a series of dead ends, with the awareness that someone must be wanting him dead too. In a sudden fury, Abish thumped his right hand with force on the car's roof and ended up hurting his fingers. *Mistry is no more,* the thought was overwhelming him, making his eyes wet. *If only I had trusted him earlier.* The regret was surfacing.

It was clear to Abish that Mistry's had been on the right track. *Was the Herat attack a dream? A dream they all had at once? And he was murdered the same night he contacted me. Is that a coincidence?* These were the questions that flooded Abish's mind as he drove home. He checked his watch when he reached his apartment, it was already 10 p.m.

Abish had no appetite left after seeing his junior's body lying on a white sheet like a piece of wood. He went straight to bed without removing his clothes or shoes. He had been awake for the past thirty-six hours and fell into a deep sleep at once.

***

'This is Kanika Rao, reporting live from New Delhi. The protests on the outskirts of Raisina Hill, the prime minister's office, had intensified in the last twenty-four hours. The numbers in the protests were swelling as we speak, and we are close to 1,00,000 people, marching together to protest against the incumbent government. The environmental activists and human rights campaigners have also given their allegiance to the protest.'

'Neel Raghav has just initiated his speech, for which protesters were waiting for the whole day. We are taking you straight to Raisina Hill, for the live speech.'

The news channels across the nation broadcasted Neel's speech as he stood on a podium, addressing the crowd:

'The public's anger is at its peak. Why can't the government just accept that it has not been able to keep up its promises? I demand the resignation of the prime minister at the earliest, and new elections are announced as soon as possible so that the people's will can be expressed. The country needs a new leader, a younger face, and someone that is relatable to youth … a leader that is reliable when the crisis hits! If we don't get the prime minister's resignation in the coming days ... prepare for a nationwide civil disobedience movement.'

The chanting of the slogan, which began with a bunch of passionate people, had been picked up by the entire crowd. As a politician, Neel had a finger on the pulse of his supporters and knew exactly when to end his speech. The moment he stopped speaking the crowd erupted with loud chants of 'Nation First. Security First.'

***

They plug something on his brain … his hands are strapped and his feet are tied ... when he resists, the doctor frustratedly barks an order at his assistant in French … they inject something into his right arm … on his right he sees that Mistry has fainted from the high voltage shock ... the vision blurs again and he sees only the outline of the people around him ... they switch on a surgical light that shines brightly on his face ... they start operating as he loses consciousness.

Abish woke up again, breathless. His heart was beating like it was going to break his ribs and erupt from his chest. He wiped off the sweat beading on his forehead and neck. The dream had brought with it pain and anxiety, which Abish felt was happening in real life. As he got off his bed, he froze in one place to minimize any sound from his movement. A metal clanking sound from outside took his attention and the source seemed very close. It immediately alerted Abish.

The barking of the dog was out of rhythm tonight, and very hurried. The sound of crickets was muffled. *Something is out of place,* thought Abish as he tiptoed towards the window that overlooked the entire front area around the house. It was all quiet as usual; he thought the sound might've been in his head instead of coming from outside. And then, the sound came again. This time, the sound was closer than before.

Abish saw four men in black outfits and masks walking stealthily in two-by-two crouched formation. They were dressed in military guerilla style, with the only thing visible in their body was their eyes. *What are these guns,* Abish thought, looking at strange looking guns, which had giant butts and operating pads, with no magazine holder or handguard. It had the weirdest looking barrel. But there was no doubt in his mind that they were here for him.

The sight was enough to propel Abish into action. Their complacency was the only weapon that Abish had, for they will be entering inside thinking that their target is fast asleep. Hiding in the corner where the front door opened, Abish waited for the assassins to enter. There was silence everywhere now. Even the dogs outside had stopped barking. It was like time had slowed down.

Abish saw a bright beam of light burning through the lock of the front door. The doorknob, with some part of the wood still attached to it, fell on the carpet, just a few inches away from his feet. Smoke hissed out of the wooden part and the steel knob was glowing hot red. The door creaked opened and four men in crouched positions stepped on to the carpet. They were making minimal noise, and their body language indicated that they had great expertise in whatever they were doing.

Instead of giving them a moment to take their positions, Abish drew the first blood, with a kick on the chest of one of the intruders, knocking him off his feet. He collided with the wall from the force of the kick, injuring his chin and nose in the process. The man then promptly fainted. The intruder behind him pointed his gun, which produced a high frequency sound, as if loading something. Before Abish could react, a high intensity laser beam missed his left arm by mere inches and struck at the refrigerator door, boring a hole into the metal. The refrigerator's inside was now visible, including the circuits and hanging copper wires.

What the hell is that, Abish asked himself in bewilderment while the rest of the intruders pinned him to the floor. One of them had a large stick, which they activated and touched to Abish's body. Electric waves ran through his body and he screamed as they waited for him to pass out. *They are going to kill me, just like Mistry,* the thought passed through his mind as his body began to tire. He made one last effort to save himself.

One of the intruders who held his legs was close to him. The trigger of his blaster gun was within Abish's reach. The constant electrocution was sapping his energy, and he had to make his efforts count. He slid his right hand out, and pulled the trigger, as the laser beam flashed out of the barrel. A beam, hardly a millisecond long, tore a hole in the intruder's abdomen. The man's intestines rose in the air from the sheer pressure and splattered themselves on the ceiling.

Abish used his legs to get himself to his feet. Holding the blaster gun in his hands, he pointed it at the remaining two intruders.

'Who the hell are you working for?' he asked, trying to catch his breath.

There was silence for a second. One of the intruders, who had been lying unconscious till now, was beginning to stir. Seeing that his team was trapped, the man reacted quickly; he removed from his back a handgun type of gadget. He triggered it to release sonic shockwaves that caught Abish unawares, blew his body away like a piece of paper and crashed his ribs into the wall behind. Abish instantly fell unconscious.

There was silence again. Everything was quiet except the sudden barking of dogs that began again. Their high-pitched noise was cutting across the night sky.

The three intruders were now preparing to slay their target just like they had slain their last target, twenty-four hours ago. That one didn't struggle and was cut with a high intensity laser at once. But this target seemed more skilled, and he had managed to eliminate one of their highly trained assassins. They couldn't remember the last time a target of theirs had challenged them this much. But in the end, they had managed to overpower him and that's what mattered.

Cervical dislocation was the most preferred way for them if their target was unconscious. One of the basic techniques an assassin should know is how to disengage the spinal column from the skull. *An instant death ... no bloodshed, no evidence.* One of the intruders put his arm around the prey from behind, to give Abish's neck the 'ultimate twist'.

At that instant, three men barged in with silencers fitted on their Beretta M9 handguns. Before the intruders could react, the new entrants started firing. There were two headshots and one shot to the chest. The intruders were neutralized at once.

***

'Good morning, this is Kanika Rao, presenting the biggest news of the day. A statement from the prime minister's office has just arrived and it acknowledges the nationwide protests as well as public anger toward its recent decisions. I am going to read the statement that has just been released. India Now is reporting it first:

The prime minister's office has acknowledged the mistakes caused by the administration and is open to talks with any leader that the protesters select. If the will of the people governs that the prime minister should resign from his post, then the PMO would not only accept but also carry out the will. At 9 p.m. today, the prime minister will welcome protesters' leader to Raisina Hill for a talk and deliberate on the future of the current administration along with a possible re-election at the earliest.'

***

Abish woke up somewhere underground. The bruises on head and arms had been attended to, and surgical tape was wrapped around his back and torso. But as he woke up, the pain in his body was too much to bear. *Definitely a fracture,* he almost said it aloud. He didn't remember anything except passing out at his apartment, late at night. *How long have I been sleeping?*

He looked around to see people running around, busy in their own work as if they were short on time. The sound of running feet echoed across the hall, the architecture of which looked very ancient. The artificial lights were installed for lighting. *Looks like a government department,* he thought at once after observing the ambience. But how did I get here?

He tried to stay on his feet but couldn't because his ribs and back were excruciatingly painful whenever he tried to move. He sat down again and realized he had been sleeping on a couch all along. All he remembered was the intruders breaking in, and the advanced technology they used to capture him. He remembered crashing on one of the walls and getting knocked out. *Who are they working for? Why did they want him dead? And what is that other-worldly tech they had?* He was lost in his thoughts when a man, around fifty years of age, wearing a white cotton checked shirt and black trousers, entered the room. He sat on the chair that was placed near the couch.

'How are you feeling now?' he asked Abish as he folded his one leg over the other.

'Doing better,' Abish replied. 'Can you tell me exactly where I am?'

The man looked to the ceiling. 'We are exactly below the Mutiny Memorial of New Delhi. This large safehouse was built underground by the British to ensure safe escape for the viceroy in the event of a repeat of the 1857 revolt.' He paused. 'And this now is occupied by RAW, to carry out clandestine operations.'

Abish looked around the large hall and nodded. 'And who are you?' he asked as he eyed his companion.

'I am Bhaskar Sangma, Deputy Director of RAW.' He smiled and shook hands with Abish.

'How did I end up here?' Abish asked, touching his ribs just below his left underarm. It was throbbing in pain! He tried moving his leg to analyse what other parts of his body were injured. It was all right everywhere else.

'There were four mercenaries who were sent to kill you last night, Major Desai. We had been expecting an attack, and it did happen. It was a narrow miss for you,' Sangma said, his eyes glistening behind frameless glasses. He was lean, heavy chested, clean shaven and had a full head of hair with a single white streak. 'We have been keeping an eye on you and the others for the past six months.' he said unapologetically.

Abish gave a confused look. 'I was under RAW's surveillance? Why?' He tried to recall if he had noticed anyone suspicious in the past six months. He couldn't come up with anything. *These people are pretty good at surveillance,* he thought.

Sangma took a deep breath and was now sitting attentively. 'We believe the Herat attack, of which you were also a part, never happened. It's a conspiracy to topple the current government,' he explained. 'We already knew the members of the SOD unit were in danger. Still, we couldn't prevent the murder of Neville Mistry.'

How weird it sounds when you're told that one of your memories is fake, thought Abish. 'How is this even possible? I remember being there … the shootings, the chopper crashing … retaliation … everything.' Abish placed his hands on his chest, the muscles in his ribs were aching when he spoke.

'We don't know yet how it is possible. We've got nothing concrete even after investigating for many months. But there are some facts that make the whole affair quite murky. That is when the government decided to investigate deeper and we have some pretty solid findings that tell us that the Herat attack were nothing but a lie.' Sangma was cleaning his glasses with a handkerchief as he spoke.

'Like what?' Abish asked. One of Sangma's assistants then came in to hand him a file. Abish took it wordlessly.

'Firstly, there was no intel from New Delhi about an imminent Mujahideen movement. A technical glitch, a rare one, from the army's communication system released the evacuation orders. We have reason to believe that someone hacked it. Someone from the inside.' Sangma took a pause. 'Tea?' Abish shook his head in refusal.

Sangma continued. 'Secondly, all three diplomats that accompanied SOD units showed varying degrees of dementia in later months – dreams, seizures, hallucinations. We believe this couldn't be a coincidence.'

Abish took in the information and began browsing through the pages of the file. There were reports of PET and SPECT scans of the diplomats in it.

Sangma paused as one his assistant whispered something in his ears and he quietly nodded. 'And finally, the terrorist outfit that released the video claiming responsibility for the Herat attack… they were recognized as Uzbek and Turk theatre actors,' he said as Abish saw a photograph from the video released by the terrorists who took responsibility for the attack. There were red circles drawn around their faces, labelled as Uzbeki actor Rafiq Gikalo and Turk actors Devlet Arikan and Hikmet Cem.

Sangma continued. 'The actors were in a disguise, with fake beards and hair. But the RAW's artificial intelligence Falcon-24, scanned the video and established their real identities through facial recognition software.'

So the plot thickens, thought Abish as he flipped through the remaining pages of the file. 'So you think Neel Raghav is behind all this?' he asked. It was natural that he would be part of this as he was the one gaining the most from this activity. No one else came to Abish's mind. Although, in his heart of hearts, he was relieved to know the truth behind the Herat attack.

Sangma nodded. 'But he isn't alone in this. The intruders that attacked you had some extremely advanced weaponry. Pulsars are guns that shoot high intensity lasers and cut human tissue like a piece of cardboard.' He showed him a photograph of the weapon that all the intruders were carrying the previous night. 'And these are Sonic Shockers, they shoot high frequency soundwaves that can knock anyone off their feet when it hits.' Sangma showed Abish another photograph of a handgun type of weapon, with a steel body and expanded barrel. 'We have reasons to believe that the tech giant Mesotron is behind it.'

Abish thought he couldn't be shocked anymore, but the facts still managed to catch him unawares. It was too much for one night. There was silence for some moments.

'All right,' Abish said, nodding slightly. 'Then what are you waiting for? Stop them ... arrest them—'

'Major Desai, it's true we are an intelligence agency and do a lot of covert work,' Sangma cut him off. 'But we still need evidence to go after people we think are behind certain mischief. Especially when the man we are after is currently an extremely popular personality and could become our leader in the near future.' He paused to gauge Abish's reaction. 'Anything done without concrete action can take away everything we have strived for.' he said, as calmly as ever. 'And if we can't prove what we believe is the reality in the next few hours … it's over.'

Abish was still absorbing the revelations just made to him when Sangma spoke again. 'What we want from you, Mr Desai, is any detail you can remember ... any clue ... that can help us crack this case. The prime minister is under too much pressure, and he may be forced to resign today unless we get something concrete ... something that can break Neel Raghav's messiah image.'

Abish remembered Lokhande's pen drive and wondered if he still had it in his jeans pocket. He sifted through the contents of his pocket and felt the cool steel of the little device.

'Found this in Ravi Lokhande's possession,' he said, brandishing the pen drive. 'He wanted me to find this. But it's useless ... when I plugged it in, the audio in it didn't make any sense.' He threw the pen drive on the table. 'Lokhande was also having dreams to the point that he developed a mental disorder.'

'Well, something is better than nothing. Let's see what we've got.' Sangma signalled to his assistant to bring a laptop and he ran to get it.

Abish had almost forgotten about the pen drive and the audio file in it. He strained hard to figure out what the balderdash meant and why it was important to hide it in a manner that Lokhande did. *It has to make sense,* Abish thought as he focused his attention towards cracking Lokhande's code.

Meanwhile Sangma connected the pen drive to a laptop and played the audio file. The gibberish threw him off a little too. He asked his assistant, who had started scribbling whatever Lokhande was saying, to decipher his language. But Abish knew Lokhande didn't know any other language except the one he spoke. *Its solution has to be simple ... like Lokahnde's personality,* he thought.

Abish remembered the time when Lokhande was recruited for his SOD unit. They had developed a bond when stationed in Panjshir valley. A fan of Urdu poetry, Lokahnde would be a pain in the arse, reciting the couplets all night long. Even during reconnaissance missions or patrolling the base, he would keep blabbering lines from the poems. Abish smiled, remembering that time, reminiscing about his days in the rocky mountainous terrains of Afghanistan.

The only regret Lokhande had was that he couldn't read Urdu, and desired to learn the language while stationed in Herat. *The beauty of Urdu lies in the fact that it is written backwards,* he would often say.

'Backwards!' Abish whispered to himself, as his eyes shone. *That has to be it,* he thought.

'What?' Sangma asked, seeing Abish murmuring to himself.

Abish ignored him and asked one of the assistants to play the audio file backwards.

'Backwards?' The assistant looked at his partner, who nodded ever so slightly. 'Yes, it can be done,' he said as Sangma looked around, confused.

The assistant, a lean man in his early twenties, picked up the laptop. While they poked about the keyboard, Abish waited nervously. If this didn't work, then it was surely a dead end.

'Sir, we have inverted the audio. Shall I play it?' the assistant asked.

Sangma nodded in response. The assistants clicked on the play button and the audio began to be processed by the system.

'Hello, Abish sir. I am glad that you cracked the code. I knew only you could do it.'

Abish couldn't help but be excited. He looked around to share this euphoric moment with Sangma, but the latter was listening intently to what message Lokhande had left. One thing that had to be admired was Lokhande's clever tactic to camouflage the information. He had perfectly applied the tools of military intelligence to his advantage.

'For the last many months now, I have been having dreams. Dreams of being operated on, of being cut open and injected, of shocks running through my body ... and pain. Real pain! It was clear that things haven't happened like we think they have. The survivors from our unit were slowly getting eliminated. In order to save myself, I am acting like I'm a victim of acute schizophrenia. I have tampered with my reports to show that my lifespan is severely reduced. When they found this out, they actually moved on to the next targets.

'I have done some digging on my own, sir. I have found some

irrefutable proof that what happened with us was a part of a larger conspiracy. Using my sources and skills that I gathered during my long service for the Directorate of Military Intelligence, I have found that some incredible technologies are at play to create an illusion for us and the people. All of the protestors are living in fear of a false threat – a threat that is created to control the world's largest democracy.'

'Sir, I am about to give you coordinates of the exact location of where I have stashed all the data. I know you will make good use of it.' There was a moment of silence before Lokhande continued to dictate the coordinates.

Sangma looked at Abish, who was listening to the audio with utmost attention. He checked his watch. *We have just a few hours left,* he thought as he signalled to his men to ready the vehicles.

***

Somewhere near Raisina Hill, a reporter, amidst a huge protest, was talking to the news presenter, 'Will the prime minister resign today? The protesters certainly think so. And they seem very excited today, Kanika. Sources say that Neel Raghav will be sent to Raisina Hill for one-on-one talk with the prime minister. Considering the amount of public support Mr Raghav has, he can pressure the prime minister and the cabinet to resign with immediate effect.' He was finding it hard to speak amidst all the sloganeering.

The news reporter replied. *'All right, Rishabh. Keep us posted on all the latest updates from ground zero.'* She paused and then continued. *'We will take a short break. On the other side of the break, we will take a look at some exclusive childhood photographs of Neel Raghav and try to understand the beginnings of this great leader. Stay tuned!'*

***

The coordinates lead to somewhere in East Delhi. Two Ford SUVs, consisting of ten men, raced towards the coordinates. *When you reach the coordinates, look for Tower 4 and Flat 26,* Lokahnde had informed them in his recording.

Sitting with Sangma, Abish's excitement had reached a point where he forgot all about his aching muscles and possible rib fracture. *What irrefutable proof can there possibly be?* His mind was racing. The Delhi traffic at the peak hour of 6 p.m. had made it impossible to reach the place without wasting hours. The race against time had begun.

'Switch on the sirens,' Sangma instructed the driver. With the sirens blaring, the driver crossed the divider and now drove on the, comparatively emptier, wrong side. *We might crack this when it's too late,* Abish worried as he checked his watch.

The coordinates pointed to the Commonwealth Games Village, a housing society built around forty years ago to house athletes participating in the 2010 *Commonwealth Games.* The society was now abandoned for more than two decades. They entered the premises and saw a huge residential area, completely vacant like after a nuclear bomb had just gone off here. They could see cracked buildings, overgrown lawns, broken glasses, rusted swings and see-saws.

The cars stopped in the middle of the area, and as Abish stepped out, his feet made an echo that travelled far into the premises. *What the hell is this place,* he thought while looking at high rising buildings but totally empty. Even the fluttering of crows' feathers was making a loud noise. Abish's eyes moved fast as he read the tower numbers one by one.

'There it is.' One of the assistants pointed to a building. 'Tower 4.' A building stood tall at the end of the street. It had a large, faded blue board, on which was written *Tower 4.* The four assistants, Sangma and Abish ran towards the tower. The other men stood outside the tower, holding weapons and wireless communication devices.

Inside the tower, there were pigeons flying about and the floor was full of their excreta. Spiderwebs greet the new entrants at every door. Abish clicked on the elevator's button, just to check if it was working. It wasn't.

'It's on the second floor,' Sangma said as he read a chart pasted on the wall behind the reception. All of them hurriedly ran up the stairs to the second floor. Flat 26 was locked, but two bullet shots to the lock caused it to creaked open pretty quickly. They entered the three-bedroom, now completely empty except for the hall, which had a study table with a computer on it and a wall full of information pasted on it.

The rooms were dark, and the only source of light was a single glass window that illuminated the wall on which all the information was pinned. But getting the information wasn't enough, especially if they were too late in preventing the conspiracy.

'This is it,' Sangma said as Abish marvelled at the amount of research Lokhande had done. There were clippings of news articles from various countries, spread out on the wall, almost hundred in number.

The assistants immediately started working on the computer. Meanwhile, Abish and Sangma started looking at the truckload of information on the wall. One of them was a *Times of India* article from a decade ago, it spoke of Mesotron conducting the world's first successful memory implantation experiment on a rodent.

'The injection of Cholecystokinin (CCK) in the hippocampus region of the brain stimulates the neurons. The scientists used optogenetic techniques to produce a similar effect that may be equated with false memory creation. With the targeted electrocution at a specific point of the cerebellum, memories of pain and fear were injected in the mice. Dr Eric Schimdt, head of the scientific research wing of Mesotron said that calculated direct electrical stimulation of the lateral temporal cortex can not only insert the memories they wanted but can also erase the memories by tampering with the neurons in the brain.'

There were other cuttings too, from newspapers across the globe.

One of them was an article from the *Guardian*, which accused Mesotron of using Syrian refugees as human test subjects in its research. There was another article from the French newspaper, *Le Parisien,* stating that the French government had cancelled Mesotron's research permits due to their track record of human rights violations.

The next article was from a Canadian newspaper, *National Post,* revealing that some human subjects, under the Project INSERT of Mesotron, had developed permanent neurological damage. There were activists protesting Mestron's unethical practice of forcing the homeless population to volunteer for their projects in lieu of cash money.

'These people are sick,' Abish said, reading the articles. Mesotron, it seemed, had been involved in quite a few controversies in the recent past. But they needed something more concrete than these articles to prove the conspiracy.

'That's capitalism for you,' Sangma replied as he removed his glasses to rub his eyes. He knew that a lot of time was required to process this abundance of information that Lokhande had accumulated. They needed a clincher ... and they needed it fast. Sunlight was already fading, slowly but surely.

'Sir, you've got to see this,' one of the assistants, who'd been working on the computer, said. Both Abish and Sangma turned their attention towards him. 'I think this is what we were looking for.' He played a video on the computer.

It showed a black screen on the bottom of which was written:

Project INSERT 142-E
This video is the Property of Mesotron Inc.

After five seconds of showing black screen, the first picture appeared. The visuals shook everyone who was looking at the screen. It was a grim sight, and this was exactly what Lokhande was talking about. It was what Abish had seen in his dreams.

In the video, Abish saw himself on a chair, with strapped hands and feet. On top of the screen was written *'Subject-68'*. Three wires were connected to his head, and a person in a lab coat, possibly a doctor, injected something in his arm. He then nodded towards someone who was not in the frame. Behind the doctor, Abish was resisting, moving his hands and feet aggressively.

And then, a high voltage electrocution transferred through the wires in Abish's head. He screamed his lungs out, but doctors around him kept observing as if it was a normal affair for them. The camera now panned in another direction, and the whole SOD unit could be seen strapped to similar chairs. Some had fainted due to constant electrocution while others were still receiving it and being tortured. Abish saw Lokhande, Mistry and other members on the chairs. The diplomats were also faintly visible within the frame.

The black screen appeared again and the text on the video changed.

Subject Number 69, 77 and 81 didn't survive the insertion

The visuals appeared again and now the subjects were strapped on to a bed, and it seemed that their head was being drilled into. Abish, while looking at the video, touched upon his head to see if he could feel any mark that was left after the operation. There was nothing. *These visuals are exactly what I was dreaming of,* Abish thought. They were real, broken memories of the past that refused to erase themselves.

In the frame now, everybody could see Neel Raghav loitering around the lab. He was accompanied by some doctors, who were busy explaining to him about the process of memory implantation. It seemed like Mesotron was giving him a tour of the facility.

The video went on for a few more minutes, and when it was finally over, everyone was silent for a few moments.

'Extract this file and transfer it to a laptop,' Sangma said. 'We are going straight to the prime minister's office.'

It's enough to get that bastard, Sangma thought as he removed his glasses and wiped it with his shirt. He looked through the window to find that the sun had gone below the horizon, and darkness was descending.

***

For Neel Raghav, this was the moment he had been waiting for all his life. As he walked alone on a cemented path, on both sides of which were lush green gardens, the prime minister's office was in his sight. Raisina Hill, on which PMO was built, was truly breathtaking architecture. Built by the British imperial government, the architecture was neither Greek, English, nor even Indian. It was a strange mix of everything created with extensive use of red sandstone.

A dome on top of the building, an Indian feature, gave the premises a magnificent look. Neel noticed there was extensive use of elephant heads on pillar capitals, perforated screens and eaves. The carving on the walls looked spectacular. The architecture became grandiose as Neel came closer to the entrance. *The world's biggest democracy is within my grasp now,* he thought as he took his first step on the stairs.

All the news channels had been reporting the same thing all day: 'Is the prime minister going to resign today?' The protests had intensified over the last few days, since the candlelight march first began in Delhi University. Neel Raghav, who had been the backbone of this march, was considered by the people, especially the youth, as a beacon of sacrifice, security and hope in Indian politics. His charisma was enough to convince other parties to rally behind his leadership.

For the past few weeks, Neel had been on the front page of every newspaper. He must have attended a thousand interviews in the past few days, attracting attention from all sections of society.

The international media had already declared him the next Indian prime minister.

And now, he had finally been called into the PMO, where he would put forth his demands, including a resignation of the current PM and calling of new elections. *Victory is just a few yards away,* he rejoiced in his thoughts as he was being scanned by the PM's security personnel for the possibility of him carrying a weapon.

He wasn't allowed to keep his phone, even the currency in his pockets wasn't allowed inside. 'Turn right and take the stairs at the end of the hall,' the security person informed him and Neel followed. *Should I be full of authority or should I be respectful?* he thought as he finally arrived in front of the PM's door. Two security personnel were guarding the door.

'He's here,' one of them relayed the message through his wireless earbud and then immediately opened the door for Neel to enter. For Neel, the moment was surreal. It was finally happening, and he was beaming with excitement.

It was a large room at the end of which was a huge desk, where Neel could see the prime minister sitting. The room had an expanded sitting area that had to be crossed first to reach the PM's desk. On the wall, huge oil paintings of all the ex-PMs of India hung.

It was extremely overwhelming for Neel, but he had to control his nerves today, for he knew the PM was under pressure today. He couldn't afford to look weak, especially when he was going to demand the resignation of the leader of a country of 1.5 billion people.

He shook hands with the PM, who greeted him and gestured to him to sit on the chair. The PM looked old and wise, his white hair shining from the light of the lamp from the desk. He was wearing a sleeveless light khaki colored jacket, over a white kurta. There was silence for some moments between the two leaders.

And then, two men entered through another door, on the far

left of the PM's desk. It was Major Abish Desai and RAW Deputy Director Bhaskar Sangma. They stood behind the desk, next to the prime minister's chair. Neel was confused, but he greeted Abish with a smile. *What is going on,* he thought to himself but he couldn't afford to look confused.

Neel was expecting respect from the prime minister, because of the people's support that he was wielding. But instead, the prime minister looked unflappable, as if all the protests and opposition against him hadn't shaken his resolve. The air in the room wasn't exactly what Neel had expected. He remained seated, nonetheless.

The prime minister nodded at Abish, who took out a laptop, opened its lid and placed it on the desk facing Neel. *Something isn't right,* Neel thought as Abish played the video. As soon as the video played, his world shook beneath him. The prime minister was quietly sitting in his chair, observing his guest's expressions.

Two minutes into the video, Neel suddenly got up and started walking brisking towards the exit. Sangma sprang into action and went after him. As soon as Abish started to follow, the prime minister held his hand and said, 'Be gentle with him. He shouldn't be humiliated.' Abish nodded, gave a brief smile and followed Sangma.

Neel exited the prime minister's chamber and started walking towards the stairs at the end of the hall. Meanwhile, Sangma chased after him, alerting all the guards on his wireless com, to seal all exits.

The whole premises was now on full alert as Neel exited the PM's chamber. The CCTV surveillance room was now actively looking for Neel. All security personnel were now chasing actively, with Abish and Sangma a few yards away from the target.

Reaching the end of the hallway, Neel saw guards closing in on him from all sides. In that moment, Neel's thinking ability plummeted, and the smoke of confusion engulfed him from all sides. He didn't know what to do. *So close, yet so far from power,* Neel thought.

'The target in sight, sir.' The security head buzzed Sangma.

'Neutralize and arrest the bastard,' Sangma ordered his men on wireless com. Even though the PMO was a fortress in itself, if somehow Neel managed to reach the balcony or worse, got out of the building, the crowd of protestors might resort to violence to protect him. Sangma knew the stakes, and the gravity of nabbing him inside the building.

Abish ran from one corridor to another. For him, the moment had slowed down and he was living a life in each passing second. This danger, the peril, the threat … this was exactly what he was trained to do. He was glad that he wasn't just part of an audience today, like that fake memory of Herat.

They were close to the finish line …

***

'This is Kanika Rao, reporting live from Raisina Hill. In a dramatic turn of events, Neel Raghav has been arrested by the CBI due to unknown charges. The news is currently breaking the internet, while the opposition has started calling this act as unconstitutional and draconian. The protesters, who were waiting for the PM's resignation, are not only disappointed but extremely agitated. Everybody is asking the same question – what are the charges?

'The security has been tightened across the city, as more battalions of paramilitary forces have been deployed by the government, but looking at the protesters, it seems as though they are at the edge of their patience. The threat of the situation getting worse is becoming apparent every passing second. The danger of resorting to violence—'

She cut herself off from speaking, as she was getting information straight from the news control room through her earpiece.

'I've just received fresh information. It seems the government has called a press conference. But before that, the prime minister's office has uploaded an official video,' she spoke with her right hand on the earpiece. 'We are streaming the video live on our website.' The giant screen behind her was now playing the video as all the protesters' attention was now fixed on it. Some were already watching the video on their phones.

The first words appeared on the black screen:

Project INSERT 142-E
This video is the property of Mesotron Inc.

A wave of confusion, bewilderment and a sense of hopelessness erupted across the whole nation, as the video streamed. Social media platforms buzzed with activity as international media adjusted their schedules to put Neel Raghav's real story on priority.

For Abish, the reality needed some patience from people to make sense. The public, which had always held suspicion towards their governments, had to believe them this time. *It was absolutely imperative.* If they failed to believe the evidence, then we would be looking at a gruesome chapter in Indian democracy.

While people wrapped their heads around the new reality in front of them, Abish reached his apartment in the dead of the night. He felt worn out and jaded, but it was a good kind of fatigue. A sense of satisfaction overwhelmed him, something that had been missing for the past year. *Perhaps the nightmares will end,* he hoped as he went straight to the bed. The dogs were still barking in the night, out of rhythm.

Abish got up to check his windows before he went for a long sleep. There was no one outside now. Nothing that can threaten him.

Cryosleep

PART I

The numbness that I felt in my body ... I had never felt before. I could feel no circulation within me as I drifted in timelessness for what felt like an eternity. My bodily fluids were frozen, and life had been squeezed out of me. The icy cold sensation that I could feel around my body felt distant but at the same time, it was all around me. My eyes were closed and wouldn't open even if I wanted to. I was dead but somehow alive ... for what seemed like an aeon.

Had I travelled months, years, decades or centuries in this steel cylinder? I had absolutely no clue. I could sense neither space nor time. I was just floating through eras, unaware of what was happening out in the real world.

It was true that I had chosen this path. My chance of success was very bleak, and it was becoming bleaker as the arrow of time progressed. I could have been buried, like any other human of my time ... but with the kind of resources I had, I could choose to indulge myself ... toy with the thought of beating death at its own game.

There was a part of my consciousness that was awake, everything else was in suspended animation. I was dead seconds before they put me in this container, amidst temperatures that were not possible for a human to survive.

I was barely surviving. My limbs, nervous system, lungs and even heart were inactive. The electrical signals in my brain were somehow functioning and I had access to faint memories floating around my brain. Voices from these long gone remembrances echoed in my mind … over and over again. The most frequently played conversation by my brain was the one I had had with my fiancé Anne.

17 January 2025

'It won't work,' she had said. 'This is a mad obsession.' She was crying, her voice cracking and tears flowing down her beautiful cheeks.

'You don't understand,' I had replied, calm as ever, even though there was fire burning within me. 'We've been over this again and again.' There was a sprawling view of the city in front of me. I was wearing a blue gown with little black spots on it. 'Beverly State Hospital' was embroidered on to the gown where the breast pocket would have been.

The silence in the isolation room was too much to bear, followed by occasional sobs from Anne. There was something deeply disturbing for her in this whole arrangement. She was not able to make sense of what was going on. *How could she refuse to understand something this simple?*

'It is a stupid … stupid decision. You can still unsubscribe from this program, George … right?' she asked. Her eyes were red, and the area around her nose had turned pinkish due to excessive crying.

'Yes, but I don't want to, Anne. I paid a fortune to be a part of this.' I replied, devoid of any emotions. I had quite firmly made up my mind.

'You didn't even think about me, our future … before choosing to do this.' Her voice was harsh now. 'How am I supposed to go on without you?'

'I am leaving my estate in your name, Anne. It is worth billions of dollars, and growing. Don't tell me I am leaving without fulfilling my responsibilities. I have thought this through—'

'It's not about the money, George. What about us?' She was infuriated with her husband's determination. 'Do you want to spend the rest of your youth in stasis? Completely frozen and barely alive?

'If that's the cost to change the circumstances, then why not?' I replied, hardening myself from within, for it was absolutely imperative to not let emotions stray me from the course.

'What if you never wake up? What if they were never able to resurrect you from the other side? What if the technology proves to be a failure?' Anne said, trying hard to dissuade her fiancé from taking this decision. She was sounding hysterical, and the stammering made it worse. 'Wouldn't it be regrettable that you lost so many precious years of life for nothing?'

Precious years? There were hardly any left. His recent MRI scans had indicated that the years of therapy had failed to treat cerebral palsy, which had surfaced in my body three years ago. It had been progressing slowly all these years, but the pace had quickened now. The debilitating symptoms—twitching of cheeks, the spasm in the diaphragm area, late night seizures and even drooling—had started to manifest. The doctor had made it clear that the onset of symptoms now meant that in five or six years, I might be half-parlysed, on a wheelchair, with almost zero life expectancy. And this was his most optimistic guess.

At that time, I knew that perhaps this program might send me to a future where there would be a cure for this horrible neural disorder. The NeoGen Life Extension Program was more than just a potential technology that could stagnate human aging, making them hibernate in ice, only to wake up in a desired future. This program was a chance for me to beat the fate that awaited me with the normal course of life. Apart from being the first human to go under ice, there was a bleak chance to beat death itself and meet the generation yet to take birth.

It was like becoming the next Neil Armstrong, taking a giant leap into another world for the good of all humankind. It was like a revelation when my enterprise, NeoGen, acquired this technology. The concept completely changed my perspective towards life. I had achieved everything I wanted to in my youth; my enterprise had been featured in the Fortune 500 list, my wealth had nearly tripled in the last two financial years and I was currently in a stable romantic relationship. However, God had other plans for my health.

If all those millions of people who were living through the smallpox epidemic of the eighteenth century could only wake up a hundred years later to get access to the vaccine, they would've been alive.

So, here it was, I had a chance to do exactly that.

Now, signing up for the craziest experiment of all time would not only give me access to a future where there is a cure to my ailment, I might just leave a stamp in the history books to come.

Was that enough to leave my present life, my loved ones, the wealth I've accumulated and the amazing life I've built here? I think it is. The programme would propel me towards an adventure – a risk, an uncertainty, something that induced an adrenaline rush in me. Cryonics gave me something that this hopeless life couldn't offer. An ambition.

'Are you just going to stand there, not even facing me, not say a thing?' Anne said, breaking my chain of thought. 'The least you could do is have a meaningful conversation in these final few minutes we have together.' I could feel her sobs getting louder than before now.

'I have seen it working, Anne,' I said, taking her hands in mine. 'There has been progress in cryopreservation and successful resurrection amongst animal subjects. They jumped their timelines and woke up in the future. It's not a pipe dream any more, Anne. It has the potential to realize humanity's wildest dreams.'

I remember her looking at my face in bewilderment. Perhaps she thought I was a freak, and was not able to process the sacrifices I'd be making, even if I did wake up in the future. I think it was at that exact moment that she had decided to move on and not be party to my mad obsession. But I was looking at the bigger picture. I was already the first human to subscribe to the NeoGen Life Extension Foundation. There was nothing that could change my mind now.

The awkward silence that ensued lasted until a knock sounded. Anne opened the door to reveal a half-bald man standing there in a lab coat. He cleared his throat before saying, 'We are ready for preliminary testing.'

And since then, I have been floating in stasis … unaware of the passage of time … devoid of any life … with my body in suspended animation … hoping to reach a moment in the future where resurrection from cryo-preservation is possible in humans without brain and tissue damage. Till that time, I would be considered 'legally dead' in state records, my friends as well as family members would have presumed me dead and hopefully, moved on with their lives.

***

Some would wonder, wouldn't the tissues and organs degenerate in ice? How can someone be frozen at -130 degrees and still be expected to stay alive? Wouldn't the cells rupture due at this extreme temperature? Wouldn't the blood freeze, pressurizing the blood vessels and organs, which may in turn burst due to excessive strain? Wouldn't there be irreversible brain damage, making future revival virtually impossible?

This leads me to another conversation that I have access to in the deepest corners of my brain. It was with another woman, by the name of Dr Weiss, who later became head of NeoGen's versatile team of cryo-preservationists. It was Dr Weiss who made me aware of the ambitious cryonics projects she had been leading for almost a decade now. This conversation happened months before my last memory with Anne.

10 March 2025

'Hello, Mr Sorokin. It's so nice to finally meet you,' Dr Weiss was a blonde woman, probably in her forties and looked like someone who had experience walking about in a lab coat. Her rimmed glasses looked extremely geeky as her ID swung down her neck like a pendulum as she walked abruptly towards me.

'Likewise, Dr Weiss. I won't keep you long,' I said, as I scanned the place around me. The lab looked dingy, dilapidated and the scientists working on the project seemed in dire need of funding from my tech enterprise, NeoGen Inc. 'I have to make up my mind today, Dr Weiss, on whether we should fund this project or not. I can't delay it any longer.'

She nodded calmly.

'I understand that you are a very busy man, Mr Sorokin,' she said, as gently as possible. 'So, I believe you already have your answer?'

'As a matter of fact, I do.' I sounded so sure of myself and borderline narcissistic.

'So you came all this way to tell us that you don't find potential in this technology, and NeoGen Inc. isn't interested in supporting this?' she asked.

I didn't reply to that, but I did catch a hint of sarcasm.

I looked at my watch. 'Well then, that sums it up. Since you already knew our decision, there's no point of stretching it any longer. It was nice—' I was cut off in the middle of the sentence even as I extended my hand towards her.

'A last tour of the facility then, Mr Sorokin, for old times' sake,' she asked politely, fixing her eyes on me.

I was confused with the request. *What was the point*, I thought. But I couldn't say no straightaway.

'Come on.' She prodded.

I looked at my watch again and realized that I was already late for my weekly meeting with Dr Kipling, my occupational therapist, who was working to improve my motor skill responses, which had become a little patchy lately as an effect of cerebral palsy. It was becoming increasingly annoying as I kept losing my control while doing basic tasks like opening jars or using a pair of scissors.

What harm could a half hour tour do? I asked myself. I did consider leaving right away but ultimately gave in.

'All right, Dr Weiss. Twenty minutes.' I said, finally.

'Perfect.' She nodded and gestured towards a brown door on the left of the room. 'Here, please.'

There was a dark and long narrow corridor. Our steps echoed as we walked. The surroundings were eerily silent. Even the noise of the traffic outside didn't penetrate the lab's walls. We both walked in silence for some time, and I finally started the conversation with a question that had often made me curious when I thought of cryonics and its impracticality as a scientific concept.

'Dr Weiss, why would you think icing a body would make it survive for decades and centuries? On the contrary, it's the worst thing that could happen to a living body,' I said.

'Yes. The freezing is a problem, Mr Sorokin. Ice is solid after all and has the potential to impair the cellular structures of the body,' she said.

'I hope you are going somewhere with this, Dr Weiss. For right now, you aren't being a good advocate of the technology you've been working on for a decade now,' I said, trying to be completely honest with my feelings towards cryonics.

'Patience, Mr Sorokin. I assure you we've managed to overcome all our problems. Cryonics is totally viable,' she said, as our footsteps started echoing. The faint outline of Dr Weiss was visible, as we passed through the dark corridoor. Her confidence in cryonics was surprising to me at the time.

I didn't reply. An awkward silence ensued between us again as we walked through the lifeless laboratory. I could see faint lights at the end of the corridor; there was hardly any source of light besides those. *Have they actually found a protocol to preserve a body in ice?* I asked myself. I always had immense faith in science and how it could transcend human experience, but my reservations with cryonics and its practicality remained intact.

In recent years, I had greenlit NeoGen Inc's own attempt at a particle accelerator, a self-driving car project and the world's first robotic mission to the exoplanet *Proxima Centauri b*. But stagnating the aging of a body in ice, for decades and centuries, looked next to impossible even to me.

'Cryoprotectants,' Dr Weiss said, suddenly, looking straight ahead.

'What?' I had asked.

'That's the liquid we use to prevent damage to biological tissues. It is called cryoprotectant. It's a mixture of formamide, dimethyl sulfoxide and glycerol.'

'So, you mean to say the body turns into ice safely using these … uh … cryoprotectants?'

'No, not ice. You can say it turns the body into glass,' she said and looked at me for a reaction. 'The cryoprotectants prevent actual freezing and put the body in a glass-like phase. It ensures that hydrogen bonding doesn't stop in cryo-state, which is essential for proper protein and DNA function.'

I was completely puzzled with this revelation. Before I could say anything, she started again. 'We pump out all the water from the body, replace it with a sizable quantity of cryoprotectant, which you can think of as a medical grade antifreeze. It leads to vitrification of the organs and blood vessels.'

I gave her a confused look.

She explained it in layman terms. 'I mean, instead of instant cooling, the liquid immensely slows down the rate at which temperature drops within it. It prevents body tissues from turning into ice crystals and keeps them stable. It is actually quite revolutionary.'

'Does it actually work?' I asked, as her reasoning removed some of my doubts.

Dr Weiss nodded. Her brown eyes glistened behind the frameless glasses. We both finally stopped talking, and I found us standing at a large area installed with huge cylindrical tanks, numbering around thirty; all of them were made of steel. On each one of them, 'LIFE EXTENSION PROGRAMME' was engraved in large letters. The blue neon bulbs installed on top, from which light reflected on the lustrous steel containers, gave the whole basement a very dystopian look.

'And these are the tanks, we believe, that could store human subjects in stasis, in the not-so-distant future.' Dr. Weiss pointed towards one of the steel containers on her right. A stream of white vapour was constantly erupting out from these containers. Sensing my confusion, she explained, 'This white vapour is liquified nitrogen, in which we would freeze the bodies in an inverted position.'

'Right,' I replied. 'Why inverted position?'

'Studies show that this is the best possible position to minimize damage to intracranial vessels in the brain,' she said. 'It would take six to twelve hours to cool the body and fill it with cryoprotectant. It would be ready then for long term storage.'

'And all this while, the body wouldn't age at all?'

'The cells would be in a dormant stage ... in suspended animation. The freezing at -190 degrees Celsius would halt all biological processes. Think of it as a pause button while watching a film at home. When you click pause, every character stops in mid-scene, and so does the plot.'

'All right. So far so good. What about the future? We still don't have the right tech to revive people in cryo-suspension state. This limitation alone makes the project aimless.'

'Yes. That is definitely a roadblock, I must admit,' she said with a sigh. 'But that doesn't make cryonics not worth looking into. At some point in science, we must take a leap of faith, Mr Sorokin.

I am certain that we are half a century away from thawing frozen bodies and restoring them like they were never frozen. We rely heavily on the future of nanotechnology that has shown some tremendous potential recently to reverse any cryo-injury especially the impairment of cytoskeleton or hampering the matrix qualities of tissues.'

'Matrix qualities?'

'A complex network of molecules in the tissue that were found to be collapsed as the body freezes at extreme temperatures, making regeneration impossible,' she explained, dumbing down the concept to help me understand. 'But cryonics has answers to all these questions.'

Dr Weiss's faith in cryonics was rubbing off on me. She had an explanation for every doubt I had. There was no question that Dr Weiss had spent years developing this revolutionary tech, but I couldn't let my emotions dictate my decision. There was funding worth billions of dollars involved, and most importantly, the confidence of investors in NeoGen, which may be in jeopardy if this futile project was greenlit.

I began. 'I am sorry, Dr Weiss. Your faith might be unshakable when it comes to cryonics, but you can't expect anyone to be on board with cryonics when there is a lack of any concrete result. No major tech enterprise would be convinced with the viability of cryonics. It is impossible to assure the shareholders to fund—' I was cut short. This was the second time in as many minutes that Dr Weiss had taken the liberty to do so.

'Who said we don't have results, Mr Sorokin?' she said as blue lights from the neon bulbs overhead shone on her glasses. 'Surely, you don't expect us to ask for funding without any proof of progress.' She paused briefly. 'Come this way.' She gestured with her outstretched arm at another room going south.

I followed her into the laboratory. Dr Weiss's retina was scanned by a machine that unlocked the door to reveal an inner lab, in which around fifty scientists were constantly working. But working on what?

Dr Weiss slid a microscope in front of him and asked him to look through the lens. I was slightly confused but did what she asked me to do. Through the lens, on the glass tray, I could see a barrel shaped organism with four pairs of chubby legs, constantly moving ever so slightly. One could clearly notice a protruded mouth, pointy toes at the end of legs and what seemed like an anus.

'This is one of the tardigrades, also known as water bears, that we revived from a piece of ice we retrieved from Antarctica,' Dr Weiss explained.

'Pretty small for bears,' I said, as I fixed my eye back on the lens.

'They are not actually bears but microscopic organisms, just 1.5 mm in length.'

'For how long was it frozen?' I asked, still scanning the being that was locomoting ever so slowly.

'It slept for three hundred years in ice, all cells frozen, and was successfully resurrected eighteen months ago.'

'Interesting,' I said, finally picking up my head from the ocular lens.

'Come this way, Mr Sorokin.' Dr Weiss directed me again. In the deeper parts of the lab, there were scientists in their lab coats, standing next to their respective glass cylinders, and holding a board and pencil in their hands.

'Welcome Mr Sorokin to the section in which we pursue advanced cryonics,' Dr Weiss said. 'And these are …'

I was already busy looking at what was enclosed within the glass cylinders. *Simply marvellous,* I thought as I had realized what they were even before Dr Weiss could explain.

'Organisms that survived cryonics experiments?' I asked without taking my eyes off the glass cylinder, which had a small white sticker pasted near its bottom. *Rattus norvegicus,* it said. 'What's this?' Inside the cylinder, there was some kind of organ, reddish-orange in colour and about 3 cm long.

'This is a mouse brain that has been kept alive using a mixture of chemical fixatives like glutaraldehyde and cryoprotectant. We managed to cryopreserve it for three years. This is the first vertebrate's organ that has been successfully stored and revived, giving us hope that we could advance to more complex species,' Dr Weiss explained.

By this time, I had been proletyzed to see the potential in cryogenic technology. If we could keep organisms alive, or at least some organs of their bodies, then it won't be long before we develop technology to keep humans alive. If only NeoGen could harness this technology and patent it as soon as possible, the company could generate trillions of dollars if we built our business around cryonics.

There was another glass cylinder with artificially regulated temperature, which was the subject of attention for most of the scientists. The cylinder had *Rana sylvatica* written on its base. 'Did you revive a complete organism?' I asked, looking at the animal that was frantically jumping inside the cylinder, full of zeal and energy.

'Yes, its species is called Wood Frog, and it's found in the southern Appalachian region of North America.' She took a pause, and then spoke again, 'We froze it for two months.'

'And?' I asked, as the frog jumped around the cylinder, looking at our faces with its wide black eyes.

'All its vitals are normal. There is zero tissue deterioration, no traces of ischaemia in blood vessels and even the neural stem cells are performing as expected. It hasn't aged a day during suspended animation,' she said, scanning the readings off a board hung underneath the glass cylinder.

'This is incredible,' I almost whispered, as though in a trance, without taking my eyes off the creature. Seeing it was almost like attaining enlightenment. I knew the possibilities were immense, if ever cryonics was applied on humans. I wondered why people believed in the afterlife. It is certainly wishful thinking … it's unattainable. Instead, one must accomplish eternal life. We must strive to stretch our existence as wide as possible.

After two minutes of observing the effervescent amphibian, I asked, 'Why didn't you put all of this in your pitch report to us, Dr Weiss? It could surely have provided you with funding that could last your lifetime.'

'I know, but this is too important a development to disclose in front of a dozen profit seeking businessmen, Mr Sorokin. We don't want to make public the progress in cryonics, and even if we end up getting funding from somewhere, we will still want our privacy,' she said with determination in her voice. 'This is a defining moment, Mr Sorokin. Just think of what is possible if we learnt to extend life beyond our time – long distance space travel, brain transplantation, cure for terminal patients and what not?'

Terminal patients? Yes, of course. Hibernating them in deep freeze and waking them up in a future where there is a cure available. This was my first thought when I heard of cryonics – a life-saving option for myself.

'Investors can help you immensely if you reveal these results in your pitch report, Dr Weiss. This technology needs big corporations to let cryonics achieve greatness,' I advised.

'Like nuclear power achieving greatness by becoming weapons of mass destruction?' she said bluntly, stumping me completely.

'Touché,' I replied, with an awkward smile on my face. 'So, why haven't you begun any work on human cryopreservation?' I asked, after a few moments of silence.

'It's simple. There are no human subjects to volunteer. I mean who would be crazy enough to sacrifice their present, only to be frozen at sub-zero temperature in a suspended animation and be resurrected in an unknown future – that is in a best-case scenario,' she said, looking at me. For a second, I thought she could decipher my true and crazy thoughts.

Yes, who would be crazy enough. I can think of only one.

'All right, Dr Weiss. I will personally fund this project because of the immense potential I can see in your team. The progress is tremendous in terms of experiments, and it makes me feel that cryopreservation could be the next big thing in future. Also, I will not interfere in your work in any way, I understand you must work at your own pace to develop this.'

Dr Weiss replied in her calmest ever tone. 'That is incredible news. We thank you immensely, Mr Sorokin.'

'However, financial support is not the only thing that I would offer you today. I have a human subject in my mind who could volunteer for cryo-preservation,' I said, as Dr Weiss raised her eyebrows. This was the closest that I could get to seeing her shocked to the core.

'Who?' she asked.

'Me,' I said, without looking directly at her.

***

After months of deliberation, Isla De Pascua in Chile was bought after paying an exorbitant price to the government in Santiago. It took almost four years for NeoGen to build a hybrid facility, away from civilization, in the middle of nowhere, in the quietest island. The region was carefully chosen, where calamities like earthquakes, tornadoes and nuclear holocaust could be avoided. A separate power-grid was constructed, in case a massive power failure ever hit this country. Legal strategies were deployed to ensure that NeoGen never becomes solvent, goes broke or ceases operations for decades and centuries.

The design that was finally given a go-ahead looked like a medieval fortress that could stand the test of time. Cryonics did become the most expensive investment of NeoGen as the years progressed.

The advanced manifestations of cerebral palsy were apparent in me by the time construction started at Isla De Pascua. The stiffness in muscles and spasticity were slowly increasing in frequency. I would wake up with intense muscular pains, either in my limbs or back. Tremors and jerking movements in the middle of meetings and conversation indicated that the stopwatch of my existence was ticking … and ticking fast. Mundane tasks like picking up books or buttoning a shirt looked impossible without Anne's help.

When I took on the wheelchair, the next round of funding of three billion dollars to the Life Extension Program was sanctioned. That was enough to build an advanced tomb-like chamber that could place thousands of cylindrical steel tanks under high surveillance.

My faith in going under the ice was getting stronger with each passing day. However, it proved more difficult to convince Anne, who was distraught at the idea of saying goodbye to me earlier than expected. I was transferred to the palatial accommodation at Isla De Pascua, when half of my body got paralysed.

The speech disability had kicked in already, along with epilepsy. Things turned darker for me when partial blindness exhibited itself. One by one, my brain had started losing control over its functions, and that was when doctors had predicted that it was just a matter of days. By the time the year 2031 ended, things went from bad to worse.

In the final hours, I felt like I was on a quest for prolonging my existence, almost like Gilgamesh, the hero of a 4000-year-old epic from Sumeria. Just like Gilgamesh, I was searching for the fountain of youth, or the Philosopher's Stone, that could give me a victory over death.

***

5 January 2032

As preparations for my deep freeze were underway, my life was hanging by a thread. A very high fever, which refused to cool down, along with an increasing risk of cardiac attack, a complete and what seemed like permanent lack of appetite – all while my body refused to take in the supplements.

I don't know what was more painful for Anne – to see me in pain or the fact that I wouldn't entirely be dead but be in a stasis for a long period of time. My endeavour made no sense to her, and I could see that she had already bid me goodbye in mind.

'It is simply not possible, George, to mess with the natural order,' she would debate when I was being moved to Isla De Pascua. 'You can't just refuse to make a journey from birth to death. It can have consequences.'

'You … underestimate … science, Anne,' I said, making an effort to speak. 'Death … doesn't … have … to be … inevitable.' As soon as I finished speaking, I knew she wasn't convinced. If it was up to her, she would ensure a ceremonial burial, with a funeral minister reading Bible verses.

In the final moments, my mind was calculating permutations and combinations on how future revivals could go wrong. What if I never woke up in the future? How would I feel if everyone I loved and cared for died centuries ago? What if I don't understand the language of the new world any more? The questions were erupting in my mind, one by one.

I was being held in some kind of mechanical stretcher, with a team of cryo-preservationists surrounding me. My ECG and blood pressure were being recorded for every second, with a bunch of medical analysts predicting when I might take my last breath. The pain was too unbearable for me to make sense of what was going on. But one thing was certain, all of them were waiting for my death, as the real process would begin then.

'Are the injectors ready?' I heard someone saying.

'Yes,' another replied.

'The temperatures have stabilized inside the chamber. We can begin as soon as we get the reading,' someone else said, amidst noise of running feet. Everything sounded cluttered, yet under control.

The cryo-preservationists were looking for a proper moment to freeze me. The brain would still be active for half an hour, even when a human is declared dead. It was in this half hour that my cryo-preservation was due.

'Any minute now,' someone said as everything slowed down for me.

The constrictions began in my body. I could feel my arms and legs cooling down. No movement was possible at this juncture. The vasculature and lungs were failing, I felt breathlessness. This is it,

I thought. Bradycardia emerged, followed by the blood pressure changing from normal to hypotension. The inevitable was here.

I could hear the cardiac activity going down in the ECG, and activity in the room going up as some other machines were starting up. That was my last memory.

On 5 January 2031, at 11.45 a.m., I was declared dead as my heart stopped beating.

And now, I can't hear them any more. Am I dead? Then why is my brain still active? Why do I then have access to my memories? Maybe the moment at which I am frozen, I am not fully dead or alive, somewhere between two worlds. I am between past and present too, as years, decades pass me by. I lay still in the steel chambers in one of the most isolated corners of the planet.

Do I think I will be resurrected? I can't be sure. Maybe this is how I stay alive. It's crazy how death still hadn't taken over me as the brain is still active, somehow. I lie quietly, counting every moment, every passing second … yearning to be awakened. Like the mummified Pharaoh Tutenkhamen of Egypt, I craved everlasting life.

As the clocks ticked, and the cycle of seasons passed over and over again, I could finally feel something moving around me. Faint voices that somehow reached my brain. The first sensation appeared in my body.

Am I being resurrected? Are we in the future already?

I hope so.

Cryosleep

Part II

It was very painful, as my veins filled with a gel-like substance, containing high frequency photons that constantly bombarded my cells. Life bloomed in my body once again, and one by one, all organs were revived from dormancy. It seemed as though time was going in reverse. It felt like my body was being extracted from a grave. Darkness soon began to fade. My eyelids reacted, twitching at the first rays of light that fell on my face.

A high-pitched noise was adding to the discomfort. My dry lips cracked open for the first time in many years, desperately asking for water. My throat ached as I tried to swallow air. As though in answer, moisture was injected within me. And my pale skin slowly turned pink. My bone marrow began the haematopoiesis, my heart relaxed between two heartbeats and my blood completed the first circulation.

'Take it easy.' I heard a voice for the first time in forever, it seemed like a man's. 'Rebirth is a complex process. The body takes a massive beating. Just be patient. You are almost there.'

I could say nothing, but I groaned in pain. I could feel the weakness within me, along with a headache that made me want to throw up. I still wasn't able to open my eyes, but I could sense that a high intensity bulb was pointed straight at my face.

There were loud celebrations going on somewhere close to the place where I was lying. *What were they cheering about? What was this world?*

But somehow, things were different now as compared to when I was frozen. I now had awareness of time and space. I could feel the passage of time, how days and nights were passing, the size and layout of the room as well as objects placed in it, based on noises. The screeching voice made by rotating doors of the chamber, the clanking of metal that meant that a steel tray was lying next to me and the muffled voices of those around me led me to the fact that I was enclosed in some kind of glass compartment.

Over time, I could also make out the familiar voices of people who were around me most of the day. There were many different voices, but one stood out the most; once in the morning and once in evening, a man came to visit. He was probably checking my health indicators on his visit and after discussing something with two other people, seemingly a man and a woman, he would leave.

'He is recovering well. A job well done, team,' he said on one of his evening visits.

It was on the sixth day of my new life that my eyes slowly opened up, and I could make out blurry images of heads hovering over me. I still felt weak, but I was much more in control of my body.

'Welcome to the year 2102, Mr Sorokin. Congrats on your new life,' the familiar voice said, my *bis in die* visitor. However, this time, I could make out who the person was. He was a completely bald man with well-defined ridges on his forehead.

There were five people in the room, and everyone was standing about, looking at me and probably smiling. I could only guess as they all were wearing masks.

'Thank ... you.' I could barely speak. I tried getting up but couldn't. I realized that I was no longer enclosed in a glass compartment.

'Your revivification is almost done. You are completely recovered from your neurological disorder now. And your body responded very well to reanimation fluid. In some hours, you will be able to walk and do things normally without the threat of cerebral palsy hanging over you,' said the bald man. His eyes sparkled from the jubilation of the experiment's success.

I nodded in reply as speaking took too much effort. I then noticed something tied to my left wrist. It was a kind of transparent gadget that had digital numbers flashing on it in green colour. I tried to rotate my wrist to see what it was, only to realize that a part of the gadget was injected within the veins of my wrist.

'This measures the health of your organs in real time. The green digits indicate that your health indicators are in normal range,' said the bald man as he noticed him looking at the gadget. He nodded at his two assistants, beckoning them forward.

They helped me to my feet, and I stood naked until they wrapped a hospital robe around me. My feet looked pale and the veins were protruding prominently. The reanimation fluid was slowly reaching every last corner of my body and it was just a matter of time before the pale would turn to pink.

I was assisted by the men, one on each side, as I tried to walk. The feeble quadriceps in my thighs slowly came into action, like a piston that's been out of work for many years. The cracking noises from my tibiofemoral joint came, as the bubbles burst in the synovial fluid. I could feel the cold floor against my soles, as I managed to take one step after another.

A wave of painful cramps resulted as I tried shifting my body weight on my legs. I found my thighs shaking and felt like an infant learning how to walk. As I made an effort to move, with shooting pain somewhere in my back, I realized I was getting out of breath very quickly.

'The pain is normal,' the bald man said. 'Your muscles will

adapt very quickly.'

'Where are … we … going?' I asked with much effort, accompanied by a cough.

'Think of it as a bath, Mr Sorokin,' one of the assistants replied. I could barely understand what he was saying under the surgical mask, as the fluid inside my ears muffled sounds. "We will spray you with a high intensity anti-toxin liquid. It will negate any possibility of you causing an epidemic, in case you are carrying any viruses or organisms."

I nodded in reply. My feet were still shaking, and the pain was rising and ebbing as I endeavored to take a step forward. There was a perpetual danger of going off balance. However, my muscles were able to carry my weight as the reanimation fluid miraculously revitalized the vascular tissues that were immobilized for decades. It seemed that assistance would be required for days, to regain full muscular strength. But the headache was gone, and so was the visual blurriness. I was really alive. I really had beaten death.

Inside a small room with glass walls, the bald man's assistants sprayed me with antitoxin spray for fifteen minutes. The tiny droplets, sprayed with high-speed, stung me like a swarm of bees. I was regaining strength every minute now, and by the time I came out, I was surprisingly feeling a lot better. Being one of the first human beings to jump from one century to another made me feel invincible.

'You have a visitor, Mr Sorokin,' said one of the assistants as he helped me into a fresh hospital gown. 'A very important one, I must say.'

'Who?'

'She owns this facility and the program you were enrolled in … Anne Hendricks.'

I wasn't prepared for this shock, it shook the earth under me. *How is this possible? This can't be true.*

Noticing my shocked face, the assistant spoke. 'You know her, don't you? She seemed to be from your time. Life expectancy has considerably risen since the last century. Technology, medicine, diet, environment … everything has improved human experience. It is common for people to survive beyond a hundred years. Ms Hendricks is—"

'One hundred and two years old,' I replied, unable to help myself. The last image I had of Anne flashed through my mind. 'Where is she?'

The blonde assistant pointed at one of the glass walls of the chamber, on the other side of which I could see an old person in a wheelchair. The faint outline of her frail body was clearly visible. Her sparse white hair formed a halo round her head. I couldn't stop my feet from moving towards her.

We were on different timelines now. I was the same age as I had been when she watched me die in that cryonics facility seventy-five years ago. The suspended animation of my cells inside the frozen chamber had kept me young while Anne had lived a full life, aged as her cells withered over time. As I moved forward, and her faint outline started to become more and more apparent, I realized the gravity of this surreal moment. Here, at this moment, both Anne and I had defied the laws of physics and biology.

The adrenaline rush made my heart beat faster. I could feel butterflies in my stomach come to life as I got closer. In this excited state, my eyes fell on the gadget that rested on my wrist. There was no green digitization on it anymore. The entire interface had turned hot red.

Is there something wrong? What is happening?

Ignoring the red signs on my wrist, I hurtled towards the glass window. I could now see Anne's face and her eyes, which were now clearly wet. She had been waiting for this moment for decades to see whether I had a chance of making it.

Everything went blurry now and I could no longer keep my balance as my feet gave way and I fell on the floor, mere feet away from the glass screen. I could see Anne, her beautiful face contorting in horror as she stared at me on display.

I began to crawl towards her, but one of the assistants caught hold of me. Then everything went dark.

***

My head had started aching again. My body felt weak. Something was wrong.

'Mr Sorokin, we were waiting for you to gain consciousness,' the bald man said. 'We have made arrangements for your final moments.'

Final moments? What were they saying? The confusion was too much to bear.

Underneath their masks, the muffled voice of the doctor sounded worrying. The hint of remorse was difficult to ignore.

'We regret to inform you, Mr Sorokin, that your body has rejected the reanimation fluid,' the bald man informed me. I couldn't believe what I was hearing.

For me, the world came crashing down as I processed what I heard. I suddenly felt helpless, my worst fears had come alive. At that moment, I didn't know how to react.

This didn't make sense. What was going on?

'But I woke up fine from the stasis. Didn't I? All my vitals were normal. you … you said so yourself.' It was difficult to speak. Even after almost a century, I was still familiar with this weakness. The ailment was coming back and I could feel it.

'Yes, I did say that,' the doctor replied. 'We resurrected you perfectly fine, but, you see, it is always unpredictable with the human body. You can't mess with the cycle of nature and not have consequences.'

Anne … She'd said it once in a time long lost to the ashes of the past. Even after all these years, she stood right. It was true then … you can't get past death. It is inevitable. It would come eventually.

'The technology is still nascent, Mr Sorokin. Perfecting it would take decades, perhaps centuries,' the doctor tried to explain.

'Then why did you wake me now, when you could've waited?' I said. The vexation in my tone was quite apparent. It was difficult to wrap my head around the fact that my time was extremely limited now.

'The united government has passed a law that made cryo-preservation unethical. We had to choose between shutting down the Life Extension Program or resurrecting the bodies using the current technology. We chose the latter, as it at least gives our clients a shot at life,' the doctor explained calmly. 'Experimentation on you helped us to learn more about cryonics than ever before. Your sacrifice won't go in vain.'

'Sacrifice? I paid a fortune to live forever,' I screamed in fury. The exasperation was uncontrollable.

At that moment, the gadget on my wrist started beeping.

'You should not waste your time in letting anger get the best of you, Mr Sorokin. Time is of the essence. You must make the most of what you have. Try to—'

'How much time do I have?' I asked, trying to rein in the rage that seemed to take over me. I couldn't believe that science wasn't able to save me. I was as helpless as the rest of the humans. The journey, from genesis to destruction couldn't be avoided.

'You have approximately five minutes to live before your brain stops functioning,' said the doctor immediately, as if he'd been waiting for the question.

'Five minutes?' I asked in disbelief.

'Actually, it's four and a half minutes now. Your heartbeat is already abnormal.'

'This is ridiculous. You people made zero progress in cryonics in all these years? I signed up for nothing!'

'Cool down, Mr Sorokin. Isn't this what you wanted? Most of your generation is dead and long gone, and only you came back from the dead. You've exceeded your own potential by stepping into the future. Even if it was for only half a day. You have reached a certain level of invincibility by opting for this program. You decided to sign up cryo-preservation, and you got a glimpse into the future. What more could you want?'

His statements did little to comfort me. Instead, they seemed to mock me.

'We have arranged a little tour for you to take in your final moments, Mr Sorokin. You should not focus on what is coming. Instead, you must see the things that you have missed in all these years.' As the doctor spoke, the dark room he was in came to life.

A video played, perhaps standard footage that they would show to those patients who failed the cryogenics test. It was a fleeting moment of triumph, reminding the clients that they have made this far, and how right they were in subscribing to the Life Extension Program. But as a client, I was too dazed. Nothing made sense any more.

A hologram appeared in the middle of the room, with lifelike images. It was a recorded video that included three dimensional visual effects containing history and politics. I tried hard to focus, but my brain was fixated on my impending end. Death could come any minute now.

It was the end. I could feel it. It was pointless to make any effort to escape your circumstances, jump timelines and hope to break the cycle of nature. Even with all the wealth in the world, one cannot buy another day of life. Everything seemed senseless, pointless, worthless. The images in front of me came to life.

The footage looked as authentic as seeing events unfold through my own eyes. Things moved so rapidly that I couldn't notice everything. As each second passed, information worth decades flashed before my eyes. It was hard to comprehend what was going on as my distracted mind counted the last moments of this life.

But some things I did glimpse: a barrage of news and paper headlines pieces of history and iconic images … but to me, they held no meaning. I could see an official, a human, meeting an extraterrestrial creature … the world coming together under one government … humans discovering space with near light speed …

Personal technology resulting in bionic chips installed in humans … the rise of cybernetic organisms …

And then images started to blur.

There was darkness now.

This time, it was forever.

About the Author

Ankush Sam Thorpe grew up in Punjab, a northern province in India in the 90s. A graduate in Anthropology and a postgraduate in Genetics, his fascination for science began early in life. In his early teens, he was obsessed with 90s Hollywood science fiction films, especially *The Terminator* and *Jurassic Park.*

His love affair with science fiction began with the Sidney Sheldon novel *The Doomsday Conspiracy* and solidified with Dan Brown's *The Lost Symbol* and George Orwell's *1984*. However, his passion for storytelling grew with Isaac Asimov's short story *Nightfall*, which inspired him to create his own tales. In 2011, at the age of twenty, Ankush wrote his first short story, 'A Stitch in Time', exhibiting his fascination with science and history.

During the Covid pandemic he found the time to create characters, dialogues, and storylines based on the scientific concepts that keep him enthralled to this date. Presently living in the city of Toronto, he continues to pen more stories with science as the central theme. In addition, he is an Instagram junkie as well as a die-hard Test Cricket fan.

Books by BluOne Ink

Kali Imprint

Sri Aurobindo & the Literary Renaissance of India
by Pariksith Singh
ISBN: 9788194954781 | ₹995

Sri Aurobindo and Philosophy
by Pariksith Singh
ISBN: 9789392209017 | ₹995

Somewhere Among the Stars
by Adi Varuni
ISBN: 9789392209215 | ₹395

The Eternal Feminine
by Dr. Alok Pandey
ISBN: 9788194954774 | ₹699

Integral Education
by Partho
ISBN: 9788194954705 | ₹499

BluPrint Imprint

Identity's Last Secret
by Makarand R Paranjape
ISBN: 9788194954798 | ₹1495

Swayam Se Parichay (in Hindi)
by Pariksith Singh
ISBN: 9789392209185 | ₹195

Chhutti Ke Din (bilingual in Hindi and Rajasthani)
by Pariksith Singh
ISBN: 9789392209024 | ₹699

Anjali Geetan Ri (in Rajasthani)
by Ikraam Rajasthani
ISBN: 9789392209277 | ₹250

Jana Awjanar Majhe (in Bengali)
by Bimal Chakravartty
ISBN: 9789392209277 | ₹250

Occam Imprint

Confidence Cures
by Lt Gen. S. B. Sehajpal and Mrs Kiran Sehajpal
ISBN: 9789392209260 | ₹395

War Despatches 1971
by Brigadier B. S. Mehta
ISBN: 9789392209123 | ₹899

March to Justice
by Navdeep Singh and Frank Rosenblatt
ISBN: 9788194954712 | ₹995

The Fighting Fourth
by Brigadier Jasbir Singh, SM,
ISBN: 9788194954750 | ₹699

Once Upon a Time in RIMC
by Brigadier Jasbir Singh, SM
ISBN: 9788194954729 | ₹250

Design: A Business Case
by Brigitte Borja de Mozota and Steinar Valade-Amland
ISBN: 9788194954743 | ₹795

MRA Made Simple: Seriously?
by Pariksith Singh, MD and Lynda Dilts-Benson
ISBN: 9781954261006 | $29.99

Compliance Made Simple: Seriously?
by Pariksith Singh, MD and Lynda Dilts-Benson
ISBN: 9781954261013 | $55.99

Forthcoming Titles by BluOne Ink

Snakes in the Ganga: Breaking India 2.0
by Rajiv Mlahotra and Vijaya Viswanathan
ISBN: 978-93-92209-09-3

Hindutva: Origin, Evolution and Future
by Aravindan Neelakandan
ISBN: 978-93-92209-06-2

All Stray Dogs Go to Heaven
by Krishna Candeth
ISBN: 978-93-92209-08-6